# A. A. HASKER
## Cows didn't graze in Brum

C000161273

# THE AUTHOR

A A Hasker was born in the poorer part of Birmingham in the early 'twenties. He spent his childhood in the dreary slums of Birmingham during the depression. Hasker attended Rea Street School, a tough place where survival of the fittest easily could have been the school motto. He left school at fourteen and worked in a factory, first on the machines and then as a blacksmith striker.

Also at this time, Hasker joined the Territorial Army - altering his birth certificate to show he was seventeen. A year later at fifteen he transferred to Man Service, Royal Army Medical Corps and trained at Royal Victoria Hospital on the shores of Southampton Water.

When war was declared two years later, Hasker saw service in northern Norway and was evacuated from the Narvik area; served in South Africa and Madagascar; posted to North Africa and joined the Desert Rats. For the invasion of Salerno, Hasker was attached to the American 5th Army. He returned to England in January 1944 to train for the Normandy landings. He was eventually invalided home and underwent major surgery.

In 1948 Hasker started his own business and after seven years went to Australia, where he had a variety of jobs including working on a sheep station. He returned to England three years later, settling once again in Portsmouth and restarting the family business with his wife and two sons.

His hobbies include writing and travelling. *Cows Don't Graze In Brum* is A A Hasker's second novel. His first novel, *Eternity Must Wait*, was published in 1992. Hasker has written many short stories and a new novel is under way.

Front cover by Brian Copping

# A. A. HASKER
## Cows didn't graze in Brum

Copyright © A A Hasker 1993 UK


Published by A A Hasker 1993


All rights reserved. No part of this publication may be reproduced, stored in a retrieval system, or transmitted in any form or by any means, electronic, mechanical, photocopying, recording or otherwise, without the prior permission of the publisher.

This book is sold subject to the conditions that it shall not by way of trade or otherwise, be lent, re-sold, hired out or otherwise circulated without the publisher's prior consent in any form of binding or cover other than that in which it is published and without a similar condition including this condition being imposed on the subsequent purchaser.


Printed in Great Britain

# Chapter One

There was little difference between the house and street from any other that filled the industrial centre of Birmingham. Built at the beginning of the industrial revolution to house the workers, by builders who were instructed to erect as many houses as possible per acre, the result was ribbons upon ribbons of monotonous, vermin riddled hovels erected with slide rule precision. Each house was of the same low standard, with only slight variations; twelve houses to a quadrangle, subdivided by a six foot wall, six houses aside. Each yard had its own entrance, better known to the dwellers as entries. There was no inside running water or sanitation. Water was supplied by one tap located on the dividing wall, right next to three dustbins without covers, which were usually overflowing with rubbish.

The wash-house was enclosed in one corner of the yard, together with three toilets which served six families, giving off a permanent stench of human excreta, as invariably one or other of the toilets was out of action and overflowing after someone had used a half page of the Birmingham Mail as toilet paper. The wash-house was an antiquated, brick built shed with no window or door, both having vanished long ago for firewood to stoke the copper solid fuel boiler where the tenants boiled their washing.

There was also an old iron mangle with wooden roller; where it came from nobody knew, or who it belonged to, but everyone without exception used it, including the children who had great fun squashing black beetles and spiders between the rollers, and occasionally squashing their fingers!

The story starts during the great depression between the two wars, when politicians and the Prime Minister himself had promised the men in the trenches homes fit for heroes to live in. Like all political dreams and promises, the homes never materialised and the men returned to that other hell they left behind four years previously; that is those who survived that mud ridden hell.

The working populace became immune to the smells, human excreta or otherwise, for the factories had been belching out chemical-impregnated soot for years, biting into the brickwork till it crumbled like sawdust. Transport in the city still relied on horse and carts, the roads (horse roads to the residents) littered with horse droppings. To some enterprising children, this was a source for making a few pennies. They would collect the manure in buckets and sell it to the few people who were lucky enough to have a small, handkerchief sized garden, but they were few and far between and the children would have to venture far away from the district to sell their valuable merchandise.

It was into these squalid surroundings that Alex entered the world and so far this was the only part he had seen. For him the world ended at the bottom of the street. Today was his big day, at nine o'clock the final umbilical cord would be severed. He had reached the golden age of five. This in itself was a minor miracle, for diphtheria, meningitis, scarlet fever and tuberculosis were all rife, and had taken their toll on many children. Many more were crippled with rickets, due to poor diet caused by poverty. Alex had been tied to his mother's apron strings since the day he was born, her constant companion. He had three sisters at home, but as usual with sisters, they all disliked him, not that it worried Alex, he lived in a dream world.

'Are you out of that bed, Alex? It's time for school!' his mother shouted up the narrow uncarpeted, wooden staircase.

A small muffled voice answered back, his mother straining her ears for any sound to indicate that he was moving from his bed.

'I don't want to go to tucking school.'

'Less of that language, Alex! If you use it at school the teachers will tan your arse!' Her voice echoed off the bare walls of the stairwell.

The threat of the teachers scared him. His three sisters had drummed school discipline into him, administering the cane for the smallest misdemeanour. He lay on a bulging feather mattress on his iron bedstead, curled up in terror under an old army blanket, not daring to set foot on the bare floorboards. For months he had been dreading this very day.

Anything he said or did wrong, one or other of his sisters would say, 'God help you if you say that or do that at school, the teachers will belt that arse of yours.'

That threat would keep him quiet for an hour or more. Now he was preparing to meet that ogre who ran the school.

He only moved when he heard his mother's foot on the first wooden step, which creaked and groaned in protest. He shot out of bed and was wrestling with his short trousers when his mother came into the room. He looked up at her as he balanced on one leg, whilst his other foot negotiated the trouser leg.

'I don't want to go to school, our mom, I want to stay here with you.'

She felt a twinge of pity for him but dare not show it, for even at this tender age he could twist anyone round his little finger and extract pity by just looking at a person. This included his sisters at times. They loved to torment him but in spite of their open dislike, inwardly they could tolerate him.

2

'Alex, if you don't go to school they will send me to prison. You have to go because if I go to prison there will be no one to cook your spotted dick pudding.'

She had reared her family entirely alone, her husband had died a year after Alex was born, finally succumbing to his illness brought on by the ravages of war. He was one of the unsung heroes. The Pensions Board had decided in their infinite wisdom that she wasn't entitled to a war widow's pension.

'You see, Mrs Edwards,' the Board explained, 'hundreds of thousands of men died in that conflict and all their widows must be kept by the State, they died in action.'

'Yes, and my husband died a slow death. It took him six years to die and I had to nurse him every day. He went away a fine upstanding man with a good job and three children, and came back a wreck, unable to work.'

The Board didn't look up at her directly, but each one scribbled something on their pads.

'Is that your final word then, no war pension?'

The president of the Board looked up and nodded his head.

'I am sorry, Mrs Edwards, yes.'

'Well then, you had better have these.'

She searched in her handbag and withdrew her husband's three war medals and threw them on the table. She regretted it bitterly a few days later because she could have got five shillings for them at the pawn shop; it would have kept them in food for a week. From that day on she was determined to beat the system, she would win through with the help of her children, and she instilled in them that they would never get something for nothing.

She straightened her son's iron bed, smoothed out the feather mattress and blanket, picked up the chamber pot and followed Alex downstairs. The downstairs room was about twelve foot square, as were the two bedrooms stacked one above the other. The room served as lounge, kitchen, dining room and clothes drying room when it was raining on washday. It was lit by a large brass kerosene lamp which hung from the centre of the ceiling with a circle of black greasy soot above it. An old solid fuel stove served for cooking and heating, cosy in the winter but hell in the summer. The iron stove was the family's pride and joy, polished till it shone like burnished steel. The room was furnished with a rickety deal table, and a three piece suite of early Edwardian vintage now the worse for wear, split in places with sharp needles of horse hair protruding through the worn imitation leather. Four dining chairs leant against the table, two with no backs, one with a rickety old back about to fall off at any moment, and one old Windsor chair of somewhat antique persuasion.

3

Alex sat at the table munching a doorstep of bread, thickly plastered with pork dripping, and sipping tea from a cracked cup. The only cup in the house with a handle. The tea was stewed and diluted with only the tiniest drop of milk. As soon as his mother left the room to empty the chamber pot, he tipped in some more milk and gulped it down, sniffing loudly.

Karen, his eldest sister, came down the stairs. Her dress, though old, was neatly pressed as she was fastidious about her clothes. Her hair, brushed and combed, hung loosely round her shoulders. Although she could never afford shampoo, she combed her hair regularly, for she was as proud of her natural blonde hair as she was of her appearance. She threw Alex a look of contempt.

'Look, Mom, he's got the cup with the handle again. I am not going to drink out of that bloody jam jar again. Just listen to him, Mom, he's shovelling snot again.' She turned her attention to Alex. 'Why don't you go and blow your nose, you dirty little sod?'

In reply, Alex lifted one side of his bottom and farted loudly.

'You bloody disgust me, you horror.' She held her nose as she passed and swiped him gently across his head with her free hand.

Karen was thirteen, eight years Alex's senior. This would be her last term at school. She was an intelligent girl, always top of her class in most subjects and had circumstances been different, she would probably have been head girl. She had never known what it was to have a new dress. Her clothes came from the rag market, her sisters fared worse for they in turn wore her cast offs. Dressed in this state she didn't find favour with some of the teachers, hence no promotion.

Karen did have hidden love for her young brother, although she despised his filthy habits. She spent the long dark nights of winter teaching him to read and write. He was quick and eager to learn. She would sit with him for hours in front of the fire with paper and pencil. Her greatest ambition was to become a teacher, but in their present financial circumstances it was just a pipe dream.

'Take him to school for me, Karen.'

Her mother was preparing the washing as she did every Monday morning, as Monday was her turn to use the wash-house. She looked through the window at the square patch of sky between the houses.

'I hope it doesn't rain today, I've got your Aunt Aggie's washing to do. She's paying me two bob and giving me the soap. If I'm careful with the soap I might manage my own washing too.'

'Aw, Mom,' Karen moaned - she hated refusing her mother anything - but sadly looked at Alex, 'I ain't taking him to school. Look at him. The arse of his trousers is all patched up and hanging out, and that patch of snot on the sleeve of his pullover. He's not a very pleasant sight; his socks round his ankles and the sleeves of his pullover darned in various shades of wool.' Karen's face bore a look of pain as she inspected her small brother, trying to spot some finer points but finding none. 'Why don't you use a hanky, Alex? Mom will find you a bit of rag.'

At the moment, wiping his nose on a makeshift handkerchief or his sleeve, wasn't one of Alex's top priorities. His brain was working overtime trying to figure out how he could avoid school. So far a headache and upset tummy had failed to move his mother, and only brought on fits of giggles from his sisters.

His mother returned from the wash-house. Always a laborious job it entailed several visits to the lone tap in the yard with two buckets to fill the old boiler. It wasn't so bad today as it wasn't raining, although there was a slight nip in the air to warn them of the forthcoming autumn and winter. She lit the fire with an old orange box, chopped into small pieces. Following this delicate job, she tipped Aunt Aggie's washing in and sent up a silent prayer. Wiping her hands on the old potato sack that served as her apron, she returned to the task of preparing Alex for the most emotional day of his short life.

His other sisters had finally dragged themselves from their beds. Helen, two years younger than Karen, and Polly, two years younger than Helen. Between Polly and Alex there was a gap. Perhaps this was the one blessing of the great war, or he may have had another four sisters or brothers. After the war there had been another two year pause whilst his father managed to regain his strength, as he was in poor health when he returned from the trenches.

Helen had reached the romantic age. What little money she earned, she spent on romantic penny novels or visits to the local flea pit to see handsome film stars who she mooned about for days. After school she would throw herself down on the old sofa with a novel she had either exchanged with a school friend or bought from a second-hand book shop for a halfpenny. She was always complaining about the sharp horse hair stuffing coming through the worn, so called leather cloth, but once absorbed in her latest romantic novel, the discomfort of the sofa was completely forgotten.

Polly, the youngest of Alex's three sisters, was something of a tomboy and always joined in a game of football with the local boys, her dress tucked down her knickers and her hair tied back with a piece of ribbon. At first there was some opposition from the boys, but after she had laid into a couple of them with her bare fist, they soon changed their minds. She often played goalie between two rolled up coats used as goal posts ten feet apart. They did try moving them another couple of feet wider but she soon altered that; like her mother, no one dared argue with her.

'Right, Alex, are you ready?' His mother's huge frame darkened the doorway, her arms bared to the elbows and the old sack apron already wet through.

'I don't want to go to tucking school.'

Tears rolled down his cheeks freely, as he backed into a corner of the room, crouching down as if trying to make himself invisible. His sisters burst out laughing.

Karen shaking her head in disgust said, 'Don't you dare let the teachers hear you swear like that they will tan your arse.'

This brought on a fresh flood of tears and his small body racked with sobs.

The school was just a couple of streets away. His mother pulled and dragged him every inch of the way, much to the amusement of onlookers, most of whom had seen the same thing happening over and over again. They turned into the street on which the school stood. The green doors leading into the playground loomed large in front of Alex. He made one final effort to avoid the inevitable.

He sat down in the middle of the road and screamed, 'I don't want to go to tucking school, our mom. I want to stop at home with you.'

Alex was a big lad for his age. A diet of bread and pork lard, stew and dumplings and suet pudding had helped his growth. But size meant nothing to his mother. She picked him up and tucked him under her arm, his legs and arms flaying around like windmill sails.

Several women were gathered around the small green door leading to the entrance. The school was at assembly and the soft hymn music wafted down the street. The women clung to their little darlings, inwardly grateful that a considerate education authority had taken them off their hands for a few hours a day. Several stared at the struggling figure. Some shook their heads in disgust, as if they had never heard bad language before.

One woman, braver than the rest said, 'That's nice, coming from a child like that.' She sniffed the air and tried to put on a bit of a superior accent. 'I wonder where he got it from.'

'Yes I know,' answered his mother, shaking her head. 'Poor little bugger has never been able to say F properly.'

'I didn't mean that, I meant his swearing. If my little ones showed me up like that, they would be in for a real hiding.'

His mother sniffed. She hardly ever lost her temper but when she did the recipient would know all about it. 'Showing you up, you say? Well you had better start tanning. Your little nipper has just shit himself with fright.'

The woman's attitude took a complete somersault. She looked down at her young son and sniffed.

'Why you filthy little bastard, why didn't you tell me you wanted a crap?'

She took his hand and fled along the street. It was a cue for another woman to start on Alex's mother.

'She is right, Martha, you shouldn't let the lad swear like that.'

Martha gave the woman a disdainful look. 'Now don't you start, Lizzie, I have got two lots of washing on and I ain't in a very good mood at the moment.' She looked at Lizzie's little girl clutching her mother's hand and smiled. 'Is she five already, Liz? Don't time fly.'

'Yes, she is five.' She tapped the girl's golden curls. 'Her father would be proud of her, he always wanted a girl.'

'Yes, I bet he would. Be a bloody miracle too. Wasn't your old man killed on the Somme, back in '17? You must have been carrying her for six years. Bloody long pregnancy!'

The other women tried to hide their smiles. Lizzie blushed a deep red. She was saved from any further embarrassment by the small door opening and a wizened old face poking through.

# Chapter Two

Alex had finally accepted the battle was over and school was inevitable. Occasionally his frame shook with a silent sob. The face at the door sported a hooked nose and a sharp, upward turning chin. The tip of the nose and chin were almost touching and a wart on the side of her nose sprouted long hairs. Her eyebrows met in the middle giving a long dark line across her wrinkled forehead. Alex's grip tightened on his mother's hand and a scream was silenced by a deep sob and shudder. He pointed at the apparition.

'Look, Mom, a witch!'

This started the remainder of the kids screaming and shouting. The teacher, an old hand at the game, smiled through her wizened old features. The smile altered the whole character of her face. As if by magic, the children stopped screaming, and Alex saw her in a new light. He didn't even cringe when she took his hand and led him into the school.

'Come along, children, let me take you to your classroom, and, mothers, you may go along to see the headmistress; she will interview you.'

Feeling secure in the teacher's grip, but alone in his life for the first time, the sobs getting fewer and fewer, Alex marvelled at the sights around him. Big white balls hung from the ceiling. It was the first time he had seen electric lights, and he stood outside the classroom, staring at them. The building was enormous.

The witch had been handling children for forty years. She stared up at the lights and then at Alex. She touched a switch on the wall and they burst into bright light. Alex's jaw dropped.

'Would you like to try it, Alex?'

He lifted himself to his full height and switched the lights on and off.

She stopped at a classroom and told the children to wait there, then vanished inside. A few minutes later, she led Alex and three other children into the room. It was almost full of children sitting at their desks. The four new children were lined up in front of the teacher's desk, which was raised on a platform a foot high. They faced the other children. There was a slight murmuring from the class but a stern look from the teacher put a stop to that.

'These are your new classmates, children.' She tapped Alex gently on his head with a ruler. 'Tell them your first name.'

After the formal introduction, as she tapped each pupil's head in turn they were allocated their desks. Alex was seated next to a pretty blonde girl with blue eyes and decently dressed in a nice floral frock.

She spotted the patch of dried snot on the sleeve of Alex's pullover and edged away.

'That makes me feel sick,' she whispered.

Alex tried to conceal it by folding his arms.

Midmorning, there was a murmur from the class as the door opened and two of the older boys struggled in with a crate of small bottles of milk. The teacher tapped her desk with the ruler. Silence fell on the class.

'Right, children, have your halfpennies ready.'

They stopped at Alex and put a bottle on the desk. He pushed it away.

'I don't want any milk.'

'But Alex, you must have your milk,' said the teacher. 'It will make you big and strong. Don't you have any money?'

Seeing all the other children pulling the required money from their pockets - his own mother could not afford to pay for milk every day - he tried to cover his embarrassment by shouting, 'I don't want your tucking milk! I don't drink tucking milk! That's for babies.'

There was a gasp from the other children, although the teacher had detected a touch of pride in his voice.

'All right, boys, carry on. Alex doesn't have to drink milk if he doesn't want to.'

The blonde next to him waited patiently for the teacher to turn her back and carry on reading her book and eating her apple. When all was clear, she bent down under the desk and started to pour the milk down a small hole where the central heating pipes vanished.

Alex gasped, 'What are you doing?'

'I hate milk. My mom said I have to have it and tells the teacher, so I always pour it down this little hole.'

Making sure the teacher was still absorbed in her book, he ducked under the desk.

'Gis it here. I love milk.'

'But you said you didn't want any milk.' She stared at him, still holding the now half filled bottle between her knees.

'Never mind what I said, my mom hasn't any money.'

A smile spread across her face and she gladly gave him the half finished bottle. At one stroke she had solved several problems. Getting rid of the milk, Alex loved milk and his problem was solved, as was the caretaker's and teachers'. Their rest-room was just below the classroom and for several weeks there had been a strong, obnoxious odour filling the rest-room. The school caretaker had been unable to solve the problem. The teachers were incessantly complaining, and most of them had decided to have lunch in their classrooms. Gallons of strong disinfectant were used to rid the room of the smell, but all to no avail. A call to the local authorities and a visit from the vermin catcher failed to get rid of the smell.

The rat catcher said with a shrug of his shoulders, 'No trace of a rat here, perhaps one has died somewhere. Without taking the building to pieces we're not likely to find out. Give it a couple of weeks and if it doesn't improve we may have to do that but I can't find any trace of rats at all. They usually leave their droppings around and urinate a lot, but that doesn't smell like rats' urine to me, more like sour milk.'

Little did he realise how near he was to the truth.

Dinner time came, a two hour break. Alex's first session was over and it was nothing like his sisters had suggested. He ran all the way home, sliding along the tram track that ran across the top of the street to the top of his own street.

'How was it, Alex?' his mother greeted him. She was still in the wash-house, but he could smell his favourite cooking, beef stew and dumplings, and spotted dick.

'It was all right, Mom.'

He took off his jumper and soaked the sleeve with the snotty patch in the hot water. His mother smiled to herself and took the pullover off him and started to scrub it, then ran the sleeve through the old wooden mangle. She held it before the open fire below the boiler and watched the last of the dampness turn into steam. Satisfied she couldn't get it any drier, she returned to the house. Alex was sitting at the table, his head in one hand and his elbow on the table, staring at the old kerosene lamp above him.

'Why don't we have electric, Mom?' was his simple question.

She laughed, not to ridicule him but to explain in her simple manner. 'Electric is not for the likes of us, Alex. That costs money.'

'So does paraffin for this lamp. Wouldn't it be better if we had electric?'

She knew if she carried on listening to his questions it would go on and on, and after all it was washday.

'It's not as easy as that, Alex. It's a long story, I think you had better ask that teacher.'

She unrolled the sleeve of his pullover. The patch of snot had vanished leaving a light patch of wool, as if the spot had been bleached.

'This is the best I can do, Alex.'

'That's all right, Mom.' He slipped the pullover on and examined the patch. It didn't look too bad. 'Can I have a piece of rag for a handkerchief, Mom?'

She looked curiously at her small son, he was learning fast. Only the first morning at school and he was already conscious of his appearance. She found an old torn pillowcase, which had seen better days, and cut off a square. He immediately blew his nose in it and stuffed it in his pocket.

Kathy was already in her place at school when he sat beside her. Both her parents worked and she always stayed for school dinners, although she hated them. Never more so than on Fridays when they had boiled fish. The whole school hated it, for the stench filled every nook and cranny of the huge building.

'We had stew here, it was greasy.' She curled up her tiny nose.

'My mom made stew too, it was lovely. After, we had spotted dick and custard. My mom lets me scrape the cloth she boils the pudding in afterwards.'

The teacher came into the room. Silence descended on the class as she took her seat. She called the register, a little surprised to notice none of the new pupils had failed to turn up as they usually did on the first day.

The two boys seated in front of Alex were playing around and giggling. One of them lifted his bottom and broke wind. The other boy laughed. Alex and Kathy held their noses. Alex put up his hand.

'Miss, he's farted.'

The rest of the class burst out laughing and the teacher rapped the ruler on her desk for silence.

A boy at the back said, 'Let your wind go free where ever you may be.'

Alex laughed, 'In church, in chapel, let it rattle.'

There were roars of laughter. The teacher knew how to handle it. She let it go for a few minutes then rapped the desk again with the ruler.

'All right, children, that's enough.'

Much to the surprise of his sisters, who for months had been tormenting him about what to expect, he liked school, and for the first time any of them could remember, he washed that evening. To him that had always been a hated ritual that was carried out in the mornings. He washed and combed his hair, and when he went to bed he folded his clothes.

He was never late for school and he made friends easily. He liked Kathy, but she was just a girl and a supplier of milk. His best friend was Arthur, who sat just behind him. Arthur was in much the same position as himself, except that he had four sisters and a brother - a brother he hated. Archie was four years older than Arthur and, as Arthur said, 'He knocks the shit out of me.'

'What are you three doing down there?'

Arthur's mother caught them smoking behind the sofa. Smoke was rising in clouds. At first she'd thought the sofa was on fire. They were puffing away merrily on Woodbines. She dragged Arthur and his brother from behind the sofa by their ears; Alex ran for his life.

'Where the bloody hell did you get these fags?'

She made them empty their pockets. Several full packets of Woodbines fell out. Astonished, she picked them up and gasped, 'Where did you get these from?'

'I found them, Mom,' Archie said.

'Don't you lie to me, you little sod! Where did you get them from?'

She lashed out hard across his ear. He burst out crying; several times he told her he found them and several times he received a bashing. Just at that moment his father limped into the room, saw the cigarettes on the table and help himself.

'What's the matter?' He coughed as he inhaled and his breath smelt of beer. 'What's going on?'

'It's this lying little sod, said he found the fags. Just look at him. You don't go round finding cartons of cigs, lying little shit!'

'Leave him alone, Nell, the kid could be telling the truth.' He put the packet of fags in his waistcoat pocket.

'That's just like you, isn't it? You don't give a shit what they do. Well, I do.' She took the packet from him and scooped the rest up, and caught her son by the ear. 'I am taking you to the police.'

Next day, Alex asked, 'What happened last night, Arth, when your mom caught us smoking? I didn't like mine much. I was ever so sick when I got home.'

'She took our Archie to the police station. They took the fags but said he couldn't be sent to prison as no one had reported the cigs pinched. But my mom found out that he had been nicking them from a commercial traveller's van. She said she will tan his arse if he does it again.'

During the second week, one of the children gave out some small, hard-backed books with large writing in them and pictures. Alex opened his book and laughed. He closed the book and placed it on his desk.

'That's silly, Miss, anyone can read this book, it's for babbies.'

The teacher put her book down and stared at Alex. Astonished to know there were people who took an interest in their children. School to most families was just a convenient place to put the kids for a break from their usual monotonous routine, and hope they would learn just enough to get a job in some sweat shop, working forty-eight hours a week for a pittance. But a pittance in these hard times would help the family survive.

'What do you read, Alex?'

'Anything, Miss. Our Karen taught me. Not this stuff, Miss.' He picked up the children's book with large letters and childish pictures. 'This is for babbies, Miss.'

'Babies, Alex, not babbies,' she corrected and beckoned to him to come to her desk.

She opened the book she had been reading and turned to the first page. It was Uncle Tom's Cabin. In a clear voice he started to read without stumbling over one word. The children were enthralled. Because Alex read so well, they became absorbed in the story. Amidst groans from the children, the teacher took the book and marked the page. Alex was a gift from heaven. No longer would she have to worry about leaving the children. She could nip off to the teachers' rest-room for a quiet smoke or a cup of tea, or both, safe in the knowledge that the story would keep the kids content and quiet.

'I can write too, Miss, and do joined up writing, not this babbies' stuff.'

She smiled to herself. What a pity a gifted child like this happened only once in a blue moon. Pity his grammar wasn't as good as his reading.

'Who taught you to read and write, Alex? It's very clever.'

'Our Karen, Miss, she taught me every night when it was dark. Sometimes she would clip me round the ear.'

She sent up a silent prayer of thanks, thinking she must have had a guardian angel on her side. To have a pupil of five who could read, and read well, she doubted if it had ever happened at the school before. She would discuss this with the headmistress at tea break without laying it on too thick, for a boy like this would be in great demand with the other teachers and the headmistress had her favourites amongst them.

Alex was looking at her book about Uncle Tom, eyeing it enviously. But she lifted her desk lid and slid it under. That book was to be her salvation. With a bit of luck, reading a chapter a week it may see the term out. Miss Harris was the most fortunate teacher in the school.

## Chapter Three

Miss Harris kept dark the secret of her latest windfall from her fellow teachers. An inveterate smoker, this was her golden opportunity to slip off to the teachers' room for a crafty smoke without interrupting her pupils' lessons. Even at this early stage, she realised she had a boy with ambition and possibly a brilliant future. Putting him in charge of the class at such a tender age would cultivate his ambitions, and also ease her conscience. As she sat in the rest-room for the second time that morning, she looked at her sallow complexion through her small makeup mirror and moistened her lips with the tip of her tongue. She popped a mint into her mouth to mask the smell of tobacco smoke on her breath should she happen to bump into the headmistress in the passage.

Alex was a good boy, she thought to herself as she brushed her hands down her skirt to remove any creases; pity he was dressed so badly. So she was quite content to keep her little secret till three days before they broke up for the holidays as she knew he would progress to a higher class when they returned. She laid it on thick, praising Alex for not only his reading but his maths as well. It seemed there was hardly a subject he didn't grasp immediately. One by one the teachers came to the classroom to watch this minor miracle and see what standard Miss Harris had forecast he would attain next term.

'He should definitely go up at least three classes and come into mine,' said the only male teacher. He was also the music teacher of sorts, though music wasn't his standard curriculum and he was forced to fit it in between official lessons.

But it was Miss Pimm who won the official lottery. Miss Pimm was the oldest teacher in the school. A robust woman in her late fifties whose life had been dedicated to teaching the poor. The cynics amongst her fellow teachers reckoned she was there when the school was built and that it was built around her. She loved the children and they in turn loved her. Two days after taking a new class she knew every one of her pupils' names off by heart, whilst retaining also in her memory the names of most of the children she had taught over the years. She was stern but just. Her spare time was spent visiting friends and acquaintances collecting any cast-off items of clothing, and passing them on to her poorest pupils.

The third week into the term, she called Alex to her rostrum and quietly said, 'Wait behind, Alex, till after class, I wish to speak to you.'

Alex's reaction was immediately one of suspicion. He looked up at her, his eyes widened in surprise.

'I ain't done nothing, Miss.'

She gave him a benign smile and softly said, 'I know that, Alex, I just wish to have a private word with you.'

From the first day, and like the previous teacher, she too had forecast a brilliant future ahead for Alex. He was a boy with ambition and the brains to go with it. She couldn't see him with a dead end job in some foul smelling Dickensian factory, or spending the rest of his life in the Birmingham slums. While he read flawlessly to the class, she didn't vanish to the teachers' rest-room. She stopped and listened to him, and took the time to correct him if he made a mistake, which wasn't very often.

She told him, 'Study maths, Alex. Remember the man that masters maths can master the world.'

While the remainder of the class were taking reading and writing, subjects that Alex was well ahead on, she would issue him with maths lessons.

Alex sat alone at his desk fascinated as to why she had asked him to stay behind. It was some five minutes after the last pupil had left before she called him to her rostrum. She fiddled around under her desk and brought out a parcel wrapped neatly in brown paper and tied up with string.

'Alex, I want you to take this parcel to your mother. You are not to open it in the street.' She smiled and tapped the top of his head and frowned. Alex was in the habit of using a dab of cooking lard to keep his hair neat and tidy. 'All right, Alex, you may go.' She wiped her greasy hand on a page of her daily newspaper and smiled to herself.

Arthur, his best friend, and Kathy, his supplier of milk, were waiting outside for him, wondering why he was kept behind.

'Miss Pimm gave me this parcel. I have to give it to our mom and not open it in the street.'

They squeezed and shook the parcel in turn, trying to guess what the contents were.

Kathy was shaking it by her ear when Arthur said, 'It could be a dead cat or even a dead rat, Alex.'

Kathy screamed and dropped the parcel. 'Don't say such stupid things, Arthur,' she shouted.

Arthur laughed. At the end of the street Kathy went one way, Alex and his friend went the other, using the tram lines, pretending to be a tram, skating along on the shiny steel tracks.

Arthur, always the inquisitive one, followed Alex into his house and looked over Alex's shoulder as his mother unwrapped the parcel and spread the contents on the table. There was a pair of

15

short trousers and two woollen jumpers without any patches in the sleeves. Both Alex and his friend whistled through their teeth.

'Are they new, Mom?' Alex asked, as he held them up to the window.

'Not really, Alex, but they have hardly been worn. Try the shorts on, they look your size.'

'If they don't fit him, I will have them, Mrs Edwards,' said Arthur as he held up the second jumper. 'Alex don't want two of these, Mrs Edwards.'

Alex slipped off his old pullover and tried on the first grey pullover. It was a perfect fit, as were the shorts.

'They are great, Mom.'

It was the first time he could remember any clothes coming into the house, new or second-hand. He couldn't remember when he first got the ones he was wearing now. He faintly remembered the patches, and eventually patches on top of patches. Unlike Arthur, he hadn't an older brother to get hand-me-downs from, only three sisters. Mind you, Arthur's older brother was a bit of a tearaway and he hated Arthur, so by the time they reached Arthur they were just about worn out.

Alex's mother picked up the letter in the parcel. 'Dear Mrs Edwards, I hope you won't mind accepting these few clothes. They belonged to my sister's grandson; he's about the same height and build as Alex so I thought Alex could wear them for school.'

This last sentence was meant for her, for knowing the circumstances most of the women, such clothes would soon find their way to the pawn shop where they would fetch at least two shillings. However, Miss Pimm had no need to worry on that score. Alex's mother would sooner starve than deprive any of her children of the chance of looking decent. It gave Miss Pimm great satisfaction to see Alex, her favourite pupil, turn up at school the following Monday decently dressed for the first time in his short life.

Decked out in his finery, too scared to play the usual rough games with Arthur for fear of spoiling his new clothes, Alex rushed home to change. But not before he had paraded up and down in front of his old friend.

'Do you like my new clothes, Mr Fisher?'

But Mr Fisher could neither walk not talk. A victim of the war, badly gassed and shrapnel in both legs, he sat in his old Windsor armchair all day long, an army blanket wrapped round his legs and shoulders. Still, Alex knew he was listening as his eyes would light up whenever Alex stopped to talk to him.

He was a pathetic sight, a broken down hero of the war. Alex was the only child who bothered to stop and talk. A kindly neighbour, a carpenter by trade, had put a hole in the seat of the chair. Mrs Fisher had placed a chamber pot beneath it and several times a day she would come out with a bowl of warm water and sponge him down. A labour of love she called it, for the thought of having him institutionalised in some hospital appalled her.

She still had a deep and sincere love for him, although being a healthy fit woman, this didn't stop her from taking a lover to satisfy her biological needs and help keep her family together. Her boyfriend was the local fishmonger. He was due round every Thursday with his horse and cart. The neighbours and locals from a good many houses round about knew when he called, for the next day being Friday, was also Mrs Fisher's washing day and Roger always kept her supplied with plenty of fish boxes to use as firewood for the wash boiler. When burnt, these reeked of stinking, burning fish. He also kept her supplied with fresh fish. No one objected for in the eyes of her neighbours she was an angel.

Alex loved old Mr Fisher. Although he was just forty years old, to Alex he was a very old man. He would always stop and have a chat.

'Alex, you should have known him before the war. He was so handsome in his blue uniform with his tight trousers with broad yellow stripes down the sides and a small busby hat on his head. He loved the army. We travelled all over India with his regiment. He was a sergeant when he was gassed. Look at him now, a human wreck.'

As she said it, tears came into her eyes as she recalled the past. 'The British Legion has bought him one of those wireless things, Alex. He loves music. You can come any evening if you'd like to listen to it. He enjoys your company.'

A few months later a tragedy occurred. Mrs Fisher ran into the house wiping the tears from her eyes with the corner of her apron. She sobbed on Martha's shoulder.

'What can I do, Martha? I'm in the family way.'

It wasn't anything new for the neighbours to rush in and burden her with their troubles. Whenever anyone was in trouble, they invariably looked to Mrs Edwards to sort things out. She was the local agony aunt. Likewise, if anyone was sick they would ask her opinion before spending a valuable two shillings at the doctor's. The only medical experience she had was during the war when she volunteered to help out with the wounded soldiers at the local hospital, but that was sufficient for her neighbours to treat her like a fully qualified doctor.

Alone, she made Mrs Fisher sit down by the fire. She made a cup of tea for them both, and sat down opposite. Mrs Fisher was given the only cup with a handle.

'Come on, Flo, tell me all about it and let me see what I can do, and stop snivelling, that won't sort the problem out.'

'It's not me old man's, Martha,' she sobbed, another fresh outburst of tears streamed down her cheeks, the cup and saucer rattling in her hand.

'Good heavens, Flo, everyone would know that! It's Roger's, the fish man. Bloody hell, Flo, that man's very good to you and it's not a crime to want a bit of loving. Certainly no one can say you've neglected your old man. There are not many women do what you have done. They would have had him put away in some dreary hospital and left to rot.'

'But what can I do, Martha? I still love my old man. I know that might sound strange, but Roger is also very good to me, with that fish and firewood it just keeps me going. His wife is dead and I think he enjoys looking after me. Some weeks he brings me groceries.' She repeated the question over and over, 'What will the neighbours say?'

'Don't be a prat, Flo. Most of them know what's going on and them that don't can go and sod themselves. But they don't have to know. How much money you got?'

She took her purse from the large pocket in her apron and sorted through it.

'About ten bob, Martha, but half of that is for my rent and I must get some food. That eldest boy of mine eats like a bloody horse.'

'You must get Roger to raise a few pounds.' She looked questionably at Mrs Fisher, who had resorted to more sobbing. 'You have told Roger, haven't you?'

Mrs Fisher shook her head.

'Then you must tell him. Get a few pounds off him and I will take you round to see Mrs Baker. She'll get rid of it for you. She will need you at her place for the day so you can leave your old man to me, I'll look after him. Make some excuse, tell him you have to go to the Parish for more money. Go and get your coat, we'll nip round and see Mrs Baker now and make the arrangements. Good woman, Mrs Baker. She was a SRN at the local hospital till she met that no good for nothing husband of hers. He is just a lazy drunken layabout, or she could have made something of herself. Lovely home too, spotless. You'll be safe with her.'

18

Mrs Baker took her to the top room of the house. It was set out like an operating theatre, everything white and sterile. She examined Florrie and confirmed she was two months pregnant. Arrangements were made to carry out an abortion the following week. 'I have a couple more before you, Flo. Does that boyfriend of yours know about it?'

A very subdued Mrs Fisher now had confirmed what she had hoped was a mistake on her part. She shook her head solemnly and in a hushed voice said, 'No, I haven't told him yet, but he comes to the house tomorrow. I will have to tell him all about it then. I was hoping I was wrong, but it was just a slim chance, so now I must tell him.'

Mrs Fisher's nerves were on edge all morning till she heard the familiar call of Roger shouting his wares, 'Fresh fish, fresh fish o.'

She didn't wait for him to come to the entry. She rushed out and adjusted the blanket round her husband's shoulders, kissed him on the forehead and prepared to meet Roger halfway down the entry. It was far better than at her house, more private. They could talk there without being overheard.

She put her head on Roger's shoulder and sobbed, 'I am pregnant, Roger.'

He put a comforting arm around her shoulders. 'Are you certain?'

'There's no doubt. I have been to see Mrs Baker. Roger, I want an abortion. It would kill my husband if he found out. She will do the abortion next week, but I have to get five pounds.'

He patted her shoulder gently. 'Don't worry, try and get out tonight. I'll meet you outside the Dolphin pub at seven, you will have the money. I am very sorry, Flo, I took all the precautions possible. Now wipe your eyes, I'll go and fetch your boxes and some fish, and bring it to you as if nothing has happened.'

She scuttled off back to her house and was waiting for Roger when he returned.

'What's the matter with Mrs Fisher, Mom. She keeps crying? Is Mr Fisher going to die?' Alex asked his mother the following day.

'No, Alex, she isn't very well herself. She will be all right in a day or two, so don't you start worrying her, she has enough to put up with, with her sick husband, poor woman. Now go out and play with Arthur.'

It was a fortnight before Mrs Fisher was back to her old self again, cheerfully cleaning her husband a few times a day, and making sure he was warm. Perhaps her conscience was worrying her, for she seemed to be over protective towards him. She never allowed Roger, her lover, into the house for several weeks although he remained loyal to her, bringing her fish and fish

19

boxes for firewood as usual. Though he too seemed troubled by his conscience, for as well as fish he loaded her down with bags of groceries and was constantly asking after her health. He never came right into the house. As soon as she heard his familiar shout, she ran down the entry and met him halfway, brushing his cheek with a slight kiss.

'Be patient, Roger, leave it a few weeks. It was very hard losing the baby, and me a Catholic too.' She smiled and dashed back into the house.

# Chapter Four

Karen was settled in her job. No disgusting factory work for her, she worked in an office as a junior typist, but she was already considering attending night school to learn shorthand. She had filled in the necessary forms for a place at evening classes, but was told she must wait till the following year. It made no difference - she was so determined that on the first night of term she sat at a desk. But it wasn't long before the tutor realised she didn't belong in the class and ordered her to leave. She begged him to allow her to stay or at least loan her some shorthand books so she could study at home. The tutor relented, allowing her to stay for the evening, and also loaned her several shorthand books.

'Karen, you say your name is?' the tutor smiled at her. 'Well, Karen, make sure that next year you sign up in time. Study these books thoroughly, then come back and see me again in a month's time.'

Helen wasn't so lucky. Two days after leaving school she found herself a job in a factory that would have been condemned in a Dickensian novel. The building was still lit by gas lamps and a gigantic steam engine supplied the power for all the machinery. Helen had to operate a drilling machine and from her measly wage of eight shillings a week, she had to buy her own drilling bits at a cost of tuppence each. Also, should she happen to break the gas mantle over the machine she was responsible for replacing it; another tuppence. The workforce was also obliged to devote two hours of every Saturday morning to cleaning down the machines and sweeping the shop floor, tasks for which there was no pay.

From the remainder of her wages, Helen gave half to her mother and with the other half she was supposed to clothe herself. She always returned home at night smelling of industrial suds. Alex used to be sent out to play with his friends, while she bathed in a small galvanised bath in front of the fire, having first drawn water from the outside tap and warmed it over the ancient stove. Once a month, she visited the local corporation baths. For threepence she could wallow up to her neck in hot water, day dreaming of the day when she would have a nice home with a real bath and constant hot water, for like her sister she was fastidious when it came to personal hygiene. She hated the factory for even after bathing, when she dressed, the stench of suds still clung to her clothing.

'I wish I was like our Karen, Mom, a nice clean job and always dressed nice with her hair done smartly.'

'Never mind, Helen.' Her mother would console her, saying, 'keep looking in the newspaper every night, you may stumble on the right job.'

But Helen knew it was an impossible task, she was lucky she had a job at all. She would be stuck in that factory till she either married or died. Even if she got married there was no guarantee she could leave work. The depression was still biting hard.

Alex came rushing down the entry one day making his usual hooting sound trying to imitate a train. He was about to break some item of news to his friend, old Mr Fisher; he was seven and going up into the juniors. As he swung into the yard, holding the brickwork in one hand and the other arm outstretched, he stopped dead. Old Mr Fisher wasn't in his chair. Strange, Alex could never ever remember a day when he wasn't there. Even when it rained, he was always seated in the doorway of his home with the door wide open. Mrs Fisher had strict orders from his doctor that he must be kept in the fresh air at all times. It helped his battle against the gas which still filled his lungs.

The door of the house was wide open. Alex stuck his head inside, but there was no chair there. He went into the wash-house where Mrs Fisher was stoking the copper boiler with Mr Fisher's old windsor chair, burning it bit by bit, for come what may, Friday was her wash day. Be there sunshine, rain, hail or snow, she couldn't miss her turn. Every few minutes she would stop and wipe away the tears with the back of her hand. But everyone knew his death was a blessing in disguise. For the last ten years Flo had done everything for him. Fed him like a baby, lifted him from his chair to the horse hair stuffed, leather cloth sofa. She mashed his food like that of a small child and spoon fed him.

'What's happened to old Mr Fisher, Mom? He's not there and Mrs Fisher is smashing up his chair,' Alex asked his mother as he stuffed his mouth with great bites of bread spread with plum and apple jam, his cheeks bulging out like those of a hamster.

'He died, Alex.'

Alex saw his mother was terribly upset. Although she agreed with the general opinion of the neighbours, the man had suffered enough, for years his life had been that yard where people spoke to him, a fixed stare on his face at the overflowing bins and the coming and goings of the neighbours to the one and only tap. It was difficult to know if he understood a word they said. It seemed as if Alex was the only one who could make any form of contact.

'Mrs Fisher came out to feed him a bowl of thin broth but he was already dead. His worries and Mrs Fisher's are all over now.'

There were two things the neighbours revelled in, weddings and funerals, and the send off for Mr Fisher was the topic of conversation for months. The hearse was pulled by two magnificent black horses. He was well represented by his old regiment; they sent six bearers with a sergeant in charge, and a boy bugler. The entry wasn't wide enough to take the six bearers and the flag draped coffin, so it was wheeled to the street on a trolley and then carried to the hearse by the bearers all dressed in blue walking out uniforms with wide yellow stripes down their tight fitting trousers and small busbies on their heads - just as Mrs Fisher had described his pre-war uniform to Alex. The sergeant, a silver mounted cane under his arm, headed the cortege, while three bearers walked either side of the hearse, each man picked for his size; the boy bugler walked behind the hearse. Several neighbours and a contingent of ex-servicemen representing the British Legion attended the funeral. Alex was allowed the afternoon off school and Mrs Fisher let him place his small bunch of flowers on the coffin.

It was a splendid funeral and no one intended missing it. Neighbours came from all around to line the streets and pay their respects, although it was doubtful if any of them would have bothered to pass the time of day with him when he was alive. Bobby Jones, the local bobby, was at the corner standing smartly to attention, resplendent with his chest full of medals, as he held up the traffic to allow the cortege to pass uninterrupted. Those at the graveside, including Mrs Fisher, didn't shed a tear till the coffin was lowered and the boy bugler sounded the last post. The funeral was the talk of the street and a talking point in the pub for many weeks.

After what was considered a respectable interlude, twelve months to the day after the funeral, Roger moved in with Mrs Fisher. This caused tongues to wag from envy as well as spite. Her eldest son had enlisted in his father's old regiment. Her daughter, now fourteen, was still at home and got on well with Roger. She could talk to him and he would answer, unlike her own father who had been a burden during her short life. She never understood her father's illness; she was just a baby when he returned from the war and could never remember him as a tall, smart man in uniform. All her memories consisted of her mother cleaning him down several times a day and the intolerable smell, and the spoon feeding with mashed up food. His sickness was something that happened in the war, a war she knew nothing about and didn't want to know. So when Roger joined the family it was like a breath of sunshine, even if he did continually smell of fish. She grew to love him, a father she never had.

A few weeks later Mrs Fisher was sitting having a cup of tea with Martha, her best friend.

'You know, Martha, life has changed for the better. Roger gives me two pounds a week and is always buying me groceries. I have my widow's pension, and my lad in the army allows me three bob a week, but I never spend it. I have put it in the Post Office Savings Bank, I don't need it now. You just don't know what it feels like to have money in your purse at the end of the week.'

'No, but I would love to have the chance. Still with Karen and Helen working it's not so bad, mind you, what they pay my Helen it's hardly worth her going. That bloody factory want reporting to someone. It's a bloody fire hazard there and them girls have to work hard. Some nights my Helen comes home knackered and falls asleep at the table. Now they're talking of doing an extra hour each day and no extra pay. These factory bosses can do exactly what they like with the workers.'

'Roger is talking about opening his own shop. He has always wanted a fish and chip shop. I hope he does, my Sally won't have to get a job in one of those factories then.' She sipped her tea slowly. 'I suppose you know some of my neighbours are talking about me behind my back, what with my old man dead just twelve months and then Roger moving in.'

'Bugger the neighbours, Flo. You nursed that husband of yours day and night for over ten years, when you could have had him shut away in some institution. No man could have had a better or more caring wife. I bet if your old man is watching over you he is as happy as you are. Good luck to you, Flo.' As an afterthought she added, 'If Roger ever gets a bit of finny haddy to spare, be a good girl and don't forget me.'

'I'll never forget you, Martha. You stood by me during that trouble and your shoulder was always there for me to cry on, though heaven knows you had enough troubles of your own.'

The depression was biting deeper and deeper. Those in work were the lucky ones, but wages were being cut more and more till a man was fortunate if he brought home enough to keep his family from starvation's door. The Means Test was brought in. No man or woman could get Parish Relief if they had anything of the slightest value to sell. This meant that furnishings were reduced to basics, the beds they slept on plus a table and chairs, anything else had to go. Married couples were forced to help out their elderly parents. Professional men sang for pennies in the streets. Ex-service men paraded up and down the streets with barrel organs, while small girls danced pathetically to the music. Out in all weathers, some days the buskers would be lucky to collect a shilling. Helen's wage was cut once more.

She arrived home with her wage packet crying, 'I haven't picked up five shillings this week, Mom.'

She emptied her packet with disgust onto the table. There was just a half crown, a two shilling piece and three pennies.

'And I broke my drilling bit again today, that means I have to spend another tuppence on a new one. Soon I will have to pay them to go to work!' She put her arm on the table and rested her head, sobbing loudly, 'It's not as if they have no work, Mom, there's plenty. The metal polishers are working overtime till ten at night and they are only paying them flat rates, no time and a half like it should be. We must be one of the few factories with work.'

Her mother picked up the two shillings.

'You keep that, dear.'

She left the rest of the wage packet on the table and patted her daughter's head. That extra sixpence made a lot of difference to her budget, but there was no way she could watch her daughter spend the rest of her life in that sweat shop and reap no reward.

'I wish I could give up that job, Mom, I hate it. One more pay cut or if they make me work more hours with no extra pay, I shall have to walk out, Mom. Another two shillings in each wage packet wouldn't be missed. The bosses treat us like dirt. They come round once a month and heaven help any girl who isn't at her machine, and those swine dressed in nice suits and shirts with silk ties. A little fat one there always hesitates at the top of the steep wooden staircase. One of these days someone will put a foot up his bum and send him flying. The steps are very steep, everyone hopes and prays that one of these days he is going to tumble down them. He is always the last down, so he would take the rest of them with him.'

Karen was luckier, she worked in an office. As the senior members were dismissed, she was given more responsibilities and her hours lengthened. However, she had one of the few decent bosses and he increased her wages slightly. With the aid of an old typewriter her boss had lent her to take home, she became very proficient. The news got round the neighbours that she owned a typewriter and soon she was typing letters for them at tuppence a time. It served a dual purpose, for not only was she learning to type faster but she was also earning a few more coppers. This paid for her fortnightly appointment at the hairdresser's. She must keep up her appearance. Those that didn't know her called her snooty, but her temperament was far from that.

Alex was maturing fast. He would do anything to earn a penny: run errands, fill the copper in the wash-house with water from the tap in the yard. On a couple of occasions he was even seen cleaning windows. It was at the coal yard that he got his most brilliant idea. Each saturday he would fetch coal for his neighbours at a penny a time; usually a quarter hundred weight to last over the weekend. The coalman charged him an extra penny to borrow a small wooden barrow which had tiny steel wheels that usually squeaked as he pushed it along. When he returned with the barrow, the coalman wanted to charge him again for the second loan. He went home to tea disgusted.

'That coal bloke is on to a good thing, our mom. A penny to borrow that stupid barrow, then he wanted to charge me again when I fetched Mrs Ling's. Sod that, he can get stuffed. I'll make my own.'

'That's enough of that language, Alex. I thought you would stop swearing once you went to school.' She tried to hide a smile as she changed the subject. 'I wish Polly could get a job, she's been after six this week and each time there was a queue outside the factory. Some of the girls are earning less than tuppence an hour, bloody slave drivers.'

It was always Alex's job to go to Lipton's grocery shop and fetch half a dozen cracked eggs in a basin and six pennyworth of bacon bits left over by the bacon slicer. With cracked eggs you always knew they were fresh. Alex noticed some empty egg boxes in the back room.

'Can I have an empty egg box, sir?' he asked the manager.

The manager nodded towards the back. 'I sell them for tuppence, Alex.'

It had been a bad day and tuppence was his sole earnings. He handed over the money and dragged the box home along the pavement. Karen loaned him another tuppence to buy a pair of old pram wheels from the local junkyard. He made himself a barrow and stood back to admire it. It was a bit shaky but suited the purpose.

# Chapter Five

With his own transport, Alex didn't get on so good with the coalman. He marched into the yard proudly with his barrow and held it under the dealer's metal scoop as he weighed out the twenty-eight pounds. The coalman looked at the barrow.

'You should be using my barrow, son, I ain't weighing this out for the good of my health.'

But the coalman's hostile attitude didn't scare Alex.

'Sorry, Mr Saunders, but giving you a penny each time I use it isn't fair.'

A lengthy argument ensued, but nothing would deter Alex from the stand he'd made. 'If you don't want to serve me, Mr Saunders, I can always go and see Mr Pearce. I know it's a bit further away, but with my own barrow it really doesn't matter.'

At the thought of losing customers Mr Saunders backed down.

'All right, son, but you are taking the bread out of my kids' mouths.'

'My heart bleeds for you, Mr Saunders,' chipped in Arthur who had been waiting behind Alex with one of Mr Saunders' barrows. It was a saying he had heard his mother (who could be described as a philosopher of poverty) use on several occasions, but it's doubtful if he knew the full meaning of it.

'Why you cheeky little sod,' shouted Mr Saunders as he lashed out at Arthur.

But Arthur had seen it coming, and was too quick for him. He ducked and Mr Saunders' hand came in contact with the metal scoop instead. It hurt. Instantly he put his coal ingrained fingers into his mouth and sucked hard.

Saturday afternoons they would wander down to the rag market to watch the hawkers selling their wares from stalls or the backs of their carts. The man with the chinaware was their favourite. Like a juggler in a circus he would lift a basket from his stall, shouting to the punters everything they should know about the goods on offer - greatly exaggerated and laced with suggested humour, a nudge and a wink. This usually consisted of a twenty-one piece tea set or a larger dinner service, all of which would be spread out in the basket. Whilst the crowd held their breaths, he would throw it in the air then catch it without breaking a single item. Another of his favourite tricks was to line up half a dozen large dinner plates along his arm, do a ten minute spiel, then lifting his forearm let the plates slide together like a magician with a pack of playing cards. Again, there would be a long sigh as the punters released their breath.

Tired of watching the traders, they collected a couple of specked apples and wandered down to the local park. Arthur was the first to see the crowd of boys heading towards them and nudged Alex.

'Trouble, Alex.'

They were within spitting distance of the roundabouts when the eldest boy in the crowd broke away and started the roundabout revolving with one of his feet whilst keeping the other foot on the ground using the ride like a kid's scooter.

'Wot are you doing down here?' the boy shouted at them, a snarl on his face.

The other six lads were shouting around them. The lad jumped from the roundabout and confronted Arthur and Alex. He stood in front of them, legs apart and a defiant look on his face that spelled trouble.

'We don't have kids from your street in this park. Me and my mates here use this park, see.' He poked his fingers in Arthur's chest.

Arthur knocked the boy's hand away and retorted, 'So bleeding what? It's not your fucking park, we can come here any time we like, so there!'

They were outnumbered, it was foolish to take on half a dozen at a time, specially when the leader was head and shoulders taller than either of them, and probably two or three years older. Lead by the taller boy, the rest of the lads became braver, but Arthur and Alex stood their ground. One or two of the smaller boys hesitated when they saw that neither of them showed any sign of fear. They waited for their ringleader's next move. He put his fists up in a gentleman Jim Corbett stance. Arthur didn't wait. He ran forward and brought his foot up sharply between the tall boy's legs. A look of anguish and surprise crossed the lads face as he slowly sank to his knees, his hands cupped round his crotch. The look on his face changed to that of sheer agony, his mouth screwed up like a letter O as he sucked in his breath. Arthur gave him a slight push and he fell on to his back still clutching his crotch.

'You shouldn't have done that,' said one of the boys in the crowd, as he slowly backed away. 'That's not fair.'

Alex and Arthur charged headlong into them, fists flaying. But the other lads had lost all interest in fighting having seen their leader collapse in a heap, writhing on the floor. Arthur put his foot on the lad on the ground.

'Listen, shithead, we will come to this park whenever we like and you or anyone else won't stop us. Understand?'

The boy, now openly crying, shook his head.

Arthur came from a tough school, he had to be tough to survive the hidings he got from his older brother, not to mention the occasional punch delivered from any one of his four sisters, all of whom were older than him. Unfortunately he suffered from one great weakness. A punch on the nose, no matter how slight, and he bled profusely, blood pouring from his nose like a red fountain.

Tragedy struck again in the community, it was never far away. Poor old Emily Smith in the yard opposite was evicted. Her husband, a carter for the L.M.S. Railway, met with a freak accident. His horse, heavily laden with large bundles of hay, bolted. He tried to control it, but the reins jerked from his hands pulling him from the cart down under the steel rimmed wheels, crushing his head. Witnesses said a boy had thrown a thunder flash under the horse's legs. Being an old war veteran, the horse had reared up, then bolted. It happened just before bonfire night.

Everyone advised her to approach the railway people for compensation, but her answer was always, 'Well they did pay for a decent funeral and his boss sent me a five pound note, and the men collected another five pounds between them.'

But the money was soon spent on gin, for after her husband's death she felt she could no longer face life alone and took to drink, leaving nothing with which to pay her rent.

'Only another two days to bonfire night, Arthur.'

There was no need for Alex to tell him. Bonfire night was one of the highlights of the year, and both of them had been preparing for weeks, counting down the days. The wash-house roof was weighed down with wood and baskets the boys had collected from the fruit market. It was also a chance for any family to get rid of any bug ridden mattresses without the neighbours knowing where they came from. Pride still played a certain part in the poorest of the poor.

A couple of nights before the great day, the baskets and wood, plus any other rubbish, would be stacked in the middle of the yard. It would start with a reasonable sized pile, but gradually throughout the night, people would furtively bring out their soiled and vermin ridden rubbish to add to it. Two days later, what started out as a moderate sized bonfire would reach some ten to fifteen feet high. No one asked questions as by the time the fire took hold, anything combustible would burn. As the fire deepened, lines of bugs tried to escape, the kids picked them up and threw them back laughing as the vermin crackled in the flames.

Within days, another family had taken over Mrs Smith's former home. He was a giant of a man, six-foot two in his stocking feet with a chest like a beer barrel. Both his arms and chest were covered in brilliant tattoos. Come hail, snow, rain or sunshine, Mr Kingsley would stand in front of the solitary cold water tap, stripped to the waist for a wash. He was very thorough, washing under his arms and using a small nail brush to scrub the back of his neck and up over his close cropped hair. The kids gathered round to watch with admiration in their eyes. After washing, he would drop to the floor, do twenty-one press ups, then run on the spot for five minutes. It wasn't long before the boys were imitating him, but leaving out the cold water wash.

Mr Kingsley was ex-army with a long record of overseas service which had taken him to Egypt, China and finally on to the north west frontier of India. Rumour had it that he was a sergeant major, which wasn't hard to believe when his voice was heard booming across the yard like a clap of thunder. On hot summer nights he sat on his doorstep and soon collected a crowd of admiring children (and some grown men), enthralling them with stories of his experiences abroad. Within a couple of months he'd inspired two youths to enlist; others could hardly wait till they came of age. When he talked about his experience in foreign parts, he would stare dead ahead with a dreamy look in his eyes. Alex and Arthur realised that there was another world beyond the boundaries of Birmingham, well illustrated by Mr Kingsley.

He was often invited to the corner pub by the men, but his answer was always the same, booming out in his strong parade ground voice, 'Beer makes you piss, I only drink brandy, whisky or gin, in that order of preference. I can't afford that luxury now, so I don't drink at all.'

His square jaw would clamp together and that was the end of the conversation. One man tried to persuade him, but Mr Kingsley looked him straight in the eyes and glared. Since then, no one had dared to try again.

The kids loved him. He answered their questions truthfully and treated them like grown-ups. The women loved him, constantly throwing him admiring glances. Unfortunately it didn't last for long. They had lived there for two years, when one spring morning as dawn was breaking, a terrible rumpus erupted in the yard. The sound of heavy footsteps echoed off the walls. Neighbours rushed to their windows to see what was happening.

Alex was just in time to see two burly Redcaps banging on Mr Kingsley's door, trying to push it in with their shoulders. Two more Redcaps were crouched behind the wall opposite his house, and two civilian policemen stood guard at either exit entries in case he scaled the walls and made a run for it.

'Come on, Kingsley, you bastard, we've been chasing you round the country for two years. You won't get away this time, you're completely surrounded.'

He started kicking the door with his heavy hobnailed boots. One violent push and the door collapsed inwards with a loud bang. There was a crash of glass as Mr Kingsley came flying through the window without opening it. Broken glass and rotted wood flew everywhere. Picking himself up from the floor, one of the Redcaps rushed to grab his prisoner who was now laying amongst the smashed window. He rolled over and the Redcap fell flat on his face.

'You bastard, Kingsley, I've cut my fucking hands. You will pay for this.'

The second Redcap tried to tackle him but there was no contest, more like a mouse tackling an elephant. Mr Kingsley broke free and vaulted over the six foot brick wall landing on the two Redcaps crouched behind it. They fell as if they'd been pole-axed. He dashed for the entry but the civilian police barred him. In a flash they had him on the ground and handcuffed before he'd realised what hit him. By now a large crowd had gathered to see what was happening.

His immediate neighbours who liked and respected him, were shouting, 'Let him go, you rotten bastards!'

Immaterial of his crime, he could have been a mass murderer for all they knew, it wouldn't have stopped them from expanding their lungs and putting the Redcaps' birthright in dispute.

The two Redcaps who fell inside the house, rejoined the fray, punching and kicking their helpless victim. The Redcap who was still on the ground, slowly rose to his feet. He stared blankly around, then spotted Mr Kingsley standing helpless surrounded by two Redcaps and two civilian policemen. The Redcap walked over to him and with all his force slammed his fist into the defenceless man's stomach. Mr Kingsley sank slowly to the ground, and as he did so the Redcap kicked him hard in the chest.

Bobby Jones, the local policeman who knew all about enforcing the law on his own beat, put himself in front of the prisoner to prevent any further violence and shouted, 'Come on you Redcaps, there's no reason for this heavy stuff! He's your prisoner and can't hurt anyone now.'

'We want this bastard and we want him now. Keep your fucking nose out of this, it's military business.' With his military cap back on and the peak laying flat against his nose, causing him to raise his head back and peer down his nose, he said, 'We don't want any of your civilian namby pamby.'

He caught hold of the handcuffs holding the prisoner and tugged hard. Mr Kingsley winced with pain. Bobby Jones was no mean man himself weighing in at sixteen stone of solid bone and muscle, with twenty years service behind him, broken only by his time in the Welsh Guards. He caught the Redcap by his well polished brash buttons on his tunic and lifted him clear off the ground.

'Listen, you sadistic bastard, this is my beat, these are my people. I saw you bastards in the last war, you were bloody sadists then and it seems four years of war hasn't altered your attitudes. You have your prisoner, he's safe and can't hurt you. Touch him once more and I won't be responsible for my actions.' He lowered his voice. 'Since he has lived here, this man is most respected in the community both by the kids and adults alike. If any of his neighbours get at you they will lynch you, and they look very angry to me. You can rest assured I intend to put in my own report about this disgusting behaviour.'

The Redcap was a little subdued by this outburst, but he couldn't let this civilian get the better of him.

'You can do what the hell you like mate, the army wants this man and our instructions are to bring him in by whatever means we choose.'

He turned his attention to the prisoner. 'This should mean at least another two years for you, Kingsley. With the five years you have left they'll put you where the birds won't shit on you. You should be out in time for the next war.'

He and his mates burst out laughing at the stupid joke and tried to brush Bobby Jones aside.

'Laugh, you ignorant bastards. I shall be writing a long report about this incident and I'll see my superior officer to make sure it reaches the right quarters. When I'm finished with you, who knows, you may be in prison alongside him, then I hope he knocks ten bales of shit out of you.'

It was a talking point for the area with everyone wanting to know what it was all about. It was rare to see a military policeman in peace time, although they had been frequent visitors during the war. No one could ever remember such a rumpus so early in the morning, and on a Sunday too. It was a week before Mrs Kingsley calmed down enough to talk about it, and then she only spoke in confidence to Martha. She often popped over for a cup of tea. As she sat at the table she was unable at first to control her emotions and burst into tears as she related the story.

'He was out in India, long before we met. He was having an affair with this officer's wife. Her husband was the son of a lord and a right bastard, not only to his wife, but to his N.C.O.s and

32

men of the regiment alike, treating them all like shit. His wife hated him, but no worse than the men did. Reggie was a sergeant major at the time. One night, when her husband was supposedly on duty, he slipped back to his quarters and caught them in bed together. The husband paid one of his native servants to spy on them. I doubt if any of his own men would. Of course there was a hell of a rumpus. He bashed his wife and of course Reggie couldn't stand there watching so he invited him to the gym to fight it out, man to man. The officer refused and went to hit his wife again. Reggie hit him and knocked him out.

Normally, for the sake of the regiment, it would have been kept quiet, and she would have been sent home and Reggie transferred to another battalion. But at that moment two officers, the Colonel and the Orderly Sergeant, walked in to see what was going on. The officer lay unconscious on the floor and there was Reggie and the officer's wife half naked. You didn't have to be Sherlock Holmes to work out what was going on.

Reggie was arrested on the spot, court martialled and sentenced to six years in prison. At that time, on the frontier was considered active service and striking an officer carried the death sentence so Reggie was lucky. The officer wasn't very popular with his brother officers or the Colonel but Reggie was well liked. He reckons the C.O. put in a good word for him. There was a hell of a scandal, she tried to do herself in. Reggie was sent back home to finish his time and dismissed from the army. When the troopship docked in Southampton, there was utter confusion while they disembarked so he managed to escape. A couple of dockers saw him handcuffed and felt pity then hid him inside a crate and later smashed his handcuffs off.'

'What finally happened to the lady?'

'Well, her husband was asked to resign. He'd been warned several times about the way he treated her. The lady returned to England on another ship. Her family completely disowned her. I believe she is working up north somewhere as a nurse.'

To Alex and Arthur, the scuffle was far from over. They related it over and over again to anyone who would listen, embellishing the story so that every time Mr Kingsley came out looking like the real hero, and finishing up with at least half a dozen Redcaps screaming on the ground for mercy. It was only Bobby Jones that prevented them being murdered. Mr Kingsley was still the kids' hero and as far as Alex was concerned, it was going to stay that way.

# Chapter Six

It was about the time of Mr Kingsley's affair that another member of the team joined them. Horace, an only child, was a quiet unassuming lad, very shy but always clean and tidy. It was no surprise to the neighbourhood when they learnt that his father had worked all through the war on munitions as, when the factory returned to its peacetime role, he had still kept his job throughout the great depression, thereby enabling him to keep up his decent standard of living. His father had been a conscientious objector, which didn't go down to well in an area where so many had lost sons and fathers. Like all his previous homes, the family was ostracised. The war was still fresh in people's memories so when the news got round Horace's life was hell, more so when he came to school well dressed and always with a penny pocket money. His father was accused of not only being a conchie, but also of doing a returning soldier out of a job. Unlike their neighbours, they had a nice home with good furniture.

Alex first came into contact with Horace at school when he came upon him cowering in a corner of the playground with all the kids berating him, calling his father a coward, and occasionally putting the boot in.

'Your old man was a conchie and a coward.'

The more they shouted the larger the crowd grew till there were at least fifty kids shouting and screaming abuse. Alex, who was now a monitor, pushed his way through the crowd to see what was going on. He shielded Horace from any further brutality with his body and turned on the crowd.

'Sod off the lot of you!'

The crowd hesitated, this had been good fun and here was that monitor showing off, trying to stop them. Horace was like a tightly tied bundle of clothing, cowering in the corner with his hands and arms shielding his head. Some of the crowd started to disperse whilst others were telling Alex to mind his own bleeding business. Alex clenched and unclenched his hands, his face turning a deep shade of purple.

'Go on, get off, you lot. Leave him alone.'

Horace, a shivering heap, looked out of the corner of one eye, his face still shielded by his arm. Seeing it was safe, he struggled to his feet with Alex's help. He searched through his pockets and offered Alex a penny.

Alex shook his head. 'When you come out to the playground again, stay by me.'

Arthur hadn't forgotten his best friend spoiling the fun. On the way home he asked Alex, 'What did you stop the scrapping for? It was great fun. His old man was a conchie, Alex. He's no good.'

'Well, Horace ain't a bleeding conchie, is he? You haven't got a lot to shout about, your old man got his mate to put a German bullet in his foot so he could get away from the trenches.'

Arthur's love for his father bordered on hatred. He was always coming home drunk, knocking his wife and kids about. When he wasn't drunk he was spending his last few pennies at the bookies. It was common knowledge throughout the neighbourhood that his father had a self inflicted wound, and he was fortunate that a kind hearted medical officer had turned a blind eye. The wound hadn't been too serious. It made him limp at first, but that gradually improved as the years went by. However, there were times when the limp was quite convenient and became more pronounced, particularly when he was looking for a job or a bit of sympathy. Still, Arthur couldn't stand there and have his father insulted even if the accusations were true.

Besides, Kathy and Elizabeth were walking beside them. He pushed Alex away then put up his fists. But Alex was too quick for him and rushed in punching Arthur on his most vulnerable spot, his nose. Blood gushed out like a fountain turning the front of his shirt red. Elizabeth screamed and soon a small crowd gathered, only to be broken up by a passing teacher who ordered them to report to the headmaster the following morning.

Arthur and Alex didn't speak to each other for over a week, each one waiting for the other to make the first move, but it was Horace who finally healed their wounded pride.

Arthur was standing alone by the bike shed, when Horace walked up to him and said, 'I'm sorry, Arthur, I can't help it if my dad was a conchie, I'm not. When I'm fifteen I want to join the Navy.'

From inside his jacket pocket he took out a roll of papers he'd got from the Navy Recruiting Office. He couldn't remember when he first went to the office. He had passed there when his mother took him to town and he'd become attracted to the bright posters.

'My mom and dad don't know I go to the recruiting office regularly, and I read all about the Navy in the library. I go there two or three times a week.' He laughed. 'My dad thinks I go there to study. He wouldn't let me take any Navy books home. The last place we lived, the man next door had been in the Navy for years. My dad didn't like me talking to him because he told me all about the foreign places he'd visited. I have to be fifteen before I can join. My dad wants me to go in the factory where he works, but I don't want to go into any stinking factory. I want to see the world.'

They became so engrossed in his ambition that they could almost smell the sea breezes; alas it was only the local fish and chip shop.

Alex watched as Arthur walked across the playground with his arm round Horace's shoulder. He went to meet them but didn't say a word. Arthur remained silent. Horace was officially a friend and under their combined protection so whilst he attended this school and enjoyed Alex and Arthur's friendship his misery was finally over.

The three of them became inseparable. At first Horace's mother was reluctant to encourage their friendship, they weren't quite their type, but it wasn't long before she realised Horace wasn't coming home bruised and battered with his clothes torn. He no longer sat at home staring into space silently brooding. His whole attitude had taken a change for the better.

The school wasn't given to the pupils doing homework, but Horace studied hard at the subjects that would be of use to him when he joined the Navy. He had only mentioned the idea of joining the Navy once to his father, bringing the wrath of God descending on his shoulders. After that he never dared bring up the subject again. Not that he cared any longer as Arthur and Alex would always lend a sympathetic ear to his driving ambition, and this gave him all the encouragement he needed. His father was under the impression that he was studying to get an apprenticeship in the tool room of his factory.

'Your future will be made, Horace. Toolmakers have the cream of the factory jobs, always in demand, and the money is good.'

'Yes, Dad,' Horace would answer without looking up from his book.

His father nodded towards his mother. Taking his pipe from his mouth, he pointed the stem at Horace bent over his books at the dining room table, under the light of the brass oil lamp suspended from the ceiling. 'Good lad, our Horace, mother, studying like that he will go a long way.'

Horace, with his brain riding the rolling waves of the Indian Ocean or ashore in foreign parts thought, yes, a bloody long way, all the way round the world if I get the bloody chance, no stinking factory job for me. The wide world beckoned and should another war start he had no intentions of following in his father's footsteps as a conscientious objector. His father may be thick skinned enough to stand the insults, but he himself had suffered too much.

With his home-made barrow, Alex had stumbled on a way to make money. It was in greater demand than he had ever imagined possible. He made a deal with the manager of Lipton's to take all the egg boxes off him for tuppence a time. When they were chopped into firewood they realised four pence profit. On occasions, the neighbours would borrow the barrow to do a moonlight flit. He charged them four pence for the loan of the barrow, and if he or his friends helped it would be a shilling for each boy and barrow, and a promise to keep his mouth shut if the landlord's agent made any enquiries as to the flitters' whereabouts.

The depression became deeper and deeper, having a profound effect on Alex that was to stay with him for life. More and more men were reduced to singing in the streets for a few odd coppers. Those lucky enough to work, clung to their jobs and the bosses cut their wages again and again, reducing them to just above starvation level, using the excuse that the depression was also hitting them. But they still kept their large houses on the edge of town. They still managed to ride around in their large cars, in some cases chauffeur driven. The Salvation Army organised soup kitchens and farthing breakfasts for the children. Tuberculosis, meningitis, diphtheria, rickets and scarlet fever were accepted as a matter of course. Rickets became so bad that a reluctant government was forced to subsidise a ration of a third of a pint of milk daily for each child. The newspapers organised boots and shoes for the poor children. A few children were issued with woollen pullovers with blue short trousers for the boys and skirts for the girls, all clearly stamped with the donors' names so they didn't finish up in Uncle's.

'Coming down the canal for a swim, Alex?' shouted Arthur through the open door.

Martha called him in. Horace had a snow white towel rolled under his arm, Arthur had a piece of torn up sheet. She hated the idea of them swimming in that filthy canal. It wasn't unusual to see a dead rat or dog floating on the water, which itself was permanently covered in a green slime patterned with a film of oil. She opened her purse and sorted out two pennies she could ill afford.

'I've got my own money.' Alex left the two pennies on the table and shouted, 'Trar, Mom. Be back at teatime.'

They ran all the way to the canal. His mother picked up the two pennies. It was no good talking to them, she knew they were heading for the canal, but she wouldn't rest till they were back home safe and sound. Her only consolation was that both Arthur and Alex were very good swimmers.

'Last one in the water is a sissy,' shouted Alex as he hopped along the towpath, first on one foot then the other, skilfully removing his shorts.

He took a flying header into the water. The thick scum parted, rippling along the canal bank. Horace stood on the towpath, his hands cupped round his private parts. Arthur rushed up totally nude and as he passed Horace quivering, he slapped his bottom. Horace lost his balance and toppled into the water. The three of them raced towards the basin where the barges unloaded and turned for their return passage. It was a dozen times larger than the swimming baths.

'Sod off, you little buggers,' shouted a bargee from the stern cabin of his barge.

'That water is filthy, you silly little sods,' another bargee shouted. 'You will go down with the fever.'

Treading water, Arthur turned and shouted, 'Bollocks.'

Putting his thumb to his nose he started to wiggle his fingers. The bargees threw shingle they were carrying as cargo. Taking a deep breath, they rose from the water and turning over, plunged under the water. Unfortunately, some shingle caught Arthur on his bottom before he vanished under water.

Ashore, and out of range of their missiles, he examined his bottom, rubbing it.

'Is it red, Alex?' He turned towards the water and bent down.

It was a chance too good to be missed. A boot was put against Arthur's buttock and pushed hard. Arthur was catapulted head first into the green slime.

He rose shouting, 'You stupid prat, Alex.'

'It wasn't me,' Alex answered and burst out laughing. 'It was Horace. Serves you right, you dunked him earlier.'

They both lent a hand to get him out of the canal.

It was a short cut, but a dangerous one, across the railway shunting yard. Goods trains were being shunted all over the cobweb of railway tracks. Men with long wooden staves were running in all directions, as small engines shunted goods wagons from one line to another.

'Piss off, you silly little idiots,' shouted a man with a long stave.

Then a small engine rolled past and the driver shouted, 'Sod off!'

Seeing the train was starting to speed up, Arthur gave the man a two fingered salute. The man retaliated by throwing a lump of coal. It missed and fell clear of the lines onto a tuft of grass forcing its way between the lines. Arthur picked up the lump of coal and was just about to throw it back when Alex caught his arm. A money making idea sprang to mind as he searched around and found several more lumps of coal.

'Bloody hell Arthur, there's a fortune lying around these tracks.' He wrapped the bits of coal in his towel. 'Our mom can use these when she does her washing or cooking.'

His mother soon discovered the coal by itself didn't burn well, but mixed with one or two knobs of better coal it burned quite well, although not of much use on the open fire as it exploded like miniature hand grenades, spitting angry hot embers across the room.

It was a long hot summer. The locals loved it. Most of the kids ran about shirtless and the girls just in their skirts and knickers, not only saving on the washing but also helping to prolong the life of their clothes. It wasn't so good for Alex and his friends. Less money fetching coal for the neighbours and that year there was less flitting. Like lost souls, they wandered around the streets occasionally going to the local cinema known as the bug hutch.

Alex ran errands for the usherettes and the cinema manager. This entitled him to free entry and almost a free run of the place. Once the lights went out, plunging the cinema into darkness, Alex sneaked into the men's toilets and opened the side window. It was ten feet from the ground, but this didn't stop them. Using an old clothes line he had secreted in one of the dark cupboards, Alex dangled it out of the window. Horace would be the first up, followed quickly behind by Arthur, his hand finally reaching over the window ledge, huffing and puffing as he was pulled through by his two mates. Alex slapped him on his head.

'I told you before, don't both of you get on the rope at the same time, you are pulling the karzy pipe away from the wall. Old Mrs Finney will twig us and know something is going on.'

'All right, Alex,' said Arthur in a hushed whisper. 'What's on tonight?'

'Tarzan. The only trouble is there's some girl in it, spoils the picture.'

They crept out one by one, a decent interval in between, and sat in the first available seat.

After the second sitting they went into the street shouting and warbling like Tarzan himself. In the yard where they lived, the clothes lines were stretched right along the length of them. They used these to swing along like the ape man. Two more lads joined in.

'Can I play, Alex?'

A young girl stood there sucking her finger.

'No, piss off,' Arthur shouted, 'we don't want any girls in our games.'

Arthur returned to his acrobatics on the wash line. He stopped suddenly.

'Wait a minute, Elizabeth, you can play, but you will have to be a Zulu.'

'Ooh, can I, Arthur?' She grew excited, 'I will be a Zulu, Arthur.'

'All right, Lizzie, wait here,'

He vanished, running down the entry. A few minutes later he reappeared with a tin of Zebra grate polish, a thick black gooey substance. He also had with him a piece of cloth, already blackened from his mother's vigorous polishing of her grate, for like most of the women thereabouts, her grate was her pride and joy which she polished till it looked as if it had been burnished.

'All right, take your frock off.'

She obediently obeyed. Beneath she wore only the tiniest of vest and knickers, both badly torn. When he put the first dabs on her arms, she started to protest.

'Will it come off, Alex?'

Alex assured her it would. They painted her face, chest, arms and legs. There was hardly a square inch they missed. Several neighbours who were passing, burst out laughing as she ran away with the rest of the crowd. She joined in, swinging along the clothes lines.

Alex had just sat down to his tea next day, when there was a hefty banging on the door.

'Right, don't knock the door down,' shouted his mother as she opened it.

She could hardly believe the apparition that was pushed before her. A small girl, all black.

'What happened to her, Molly?'

'You need ask, Martha? It's that bloody lad of yours, him and his two mates painted my girl with blacklead last night. I can't get the blessed stuff off so I've had to keep her home from school today. I took her round to the chemists and the stupid bastards couldn't stop laughing. Just look at her, Martha, ever seen anything like it? You needn't laugh, Martha, it's not bleeding funny. I've washed the poor little sod a dozen times today.' She lifted her dress and turned her round. 'Just look, Martha.'

'I'm trying not to laugh, Molly, but you have to admit it's funny.'

'It's not so funny when you can't get the bloody stuff off. I've used buckets and buckets of hot water. I've scrubbed and scrubbed, but the more effort I put into it, the harder it becomes.'

Still trying to control the laughter building up inside her, Martha gave the woman a shilling she could ill afford, just to get rid of her as quickly as possible. Then she went back into the house and collapsed on the sofa, convulsed with laughter.

'You will be the death of me, Alex. Whatever did you paint her like that for?'

'She wanted to be a Zulu. What did you give her, Mom?'

'A shilling.'

'Never mind, Mom, I will give it back to you.'

'Don't worry, Alex, It's the best laugh I've had in years.'

Poor little Elizabeth and her mother minded. She was kept home from school for a week. When she did return, there were still traces of the offending polish around her eyes, ears, finger nails, and below her nose like she had a moustache. Some days her mother had scrubbed her so hard with such hot water that her skin had wrinkled, giving her the appearance of someone suffering from advanced tuberculosis.

# Chapter Seven

The three were getting well known around the rag market as cheeky buggers, but willing to do anything for a few coppers. Mr Hawkins, the chinaware man, took a liking to Alex and would let him help set up his stall, although this didn't go down too well with the chinaware man's regular helper. Alex tried to avoid him as much as possible. His breath stank of stale beer and cigarettes. Mr Hawkins would have sacked him months ago, had he not been such a kind hearted man who knew it would mean more hardship for the man's wife and children. Instead, he gave the man half a crown for the afternoon's work, not a princely sum, but enough to lessen the hardship a bit.

One week the man had more drink than usual. He shouted at Alex, catching him round the neck and squeezing at the same time, whilst spraying him with spittle as he coughed out the words, 'You trying to do me out of my job, you little bastard? I've got eight kids and I need that half a crown the miserly old bastard gives me.'

Alex was brought up in a neighbourhood where only the fittest survive. Being without a father or brother he had learnt the art of self defence at an early age. Without a second thought he brought his knee up sharply between the man's legs. This had the desired effect. He let go of Alex's throat and sank to his knees groaning, clutching his private parts.

'Why you little bastard,' he groaned, his face screwed up in pain.

Alex surveyed the situation. The man was head and shoulders taller than himself but in spite of his drunken stupor, a blow from him delivered in the right place could still put Alex in hospital. He turned to run and bumped into Mr Hawkins.

'Stay here, Alex.'

Mr Hawkins caught the man by the lapels of his coat and brought his face to within a foot of his own.

'Now listen to me, you drunken bastard. I know you call me a miserly old bastard and you think I'm a soft touch. I've seen you pocket a few coppers from the punters, and I've watched you giving your so called mates extra cups and saucers and just charging for half. I suppose they stand you a pint in your local. Believe me, from now on it's got to stop. I've been at this game too long to be taken for a prat. As for those eight kids of yours, they have my sympathy being saddled with a dad like you. If you spent your dole money and the few bob you earn on food and decent clothes, I wouldn't mind, but the poor little sods look half starved. I know most of the half a crown I give you goes on booze and that poor wife of yours is lucky if she gets a bloody shilling.'

The man looked downcast, staring at the ground. Mr Hawkins shook him.

'Are you listening?'

He shook his head.

'Well listen good, this is your very last chance. Come here smelling of booze just once more and you'll be out, and very lucky if you don't get the toe of my boot up your arse as a parting gift. If you lay your hands on Alex once more, I will get some of the barrow boys to frog march you through those gates.' He pushed the man away.

He stared vacantly at Mr Hawkins. It wasn't the first time he'd been warned, but he knew the boss wasn't kidding. This time he was speaking with conviction and plainly meant exactly what he said.

He tried to apologise in a slurred voice, 'I am sorry, Mr Hawkins.'

'What's more, I want you waiting at the gates at exactly twelve noon to help me and Alex set up the stall, instead of loafing in that pub till the last minute with those cronies of yours.'

He agreed with Mr Hawkins. With a baleful look of resignation on his face, he nodded his head. That afternoon, he hardly glanced at Alex. He realised Alex was no fool, he was both intelligent and a hard worker.

The following Saturday the three boys were on their way to work at the market. Horace, the cleanest of them and the most respectable, helped out on a sweet stall. The stall owner had a reputation for his home-made peppermints and throat lozenges, so he couldn't have Arthur hanging round with his snotty nose, hence the job went to Horace. Arthur helped out at various stalls, running errands.

Around the market hall, which sold wholesale fruit and vegetables, were several old stores used by the wholesalers. A rather fat man was sitting on a crate outside his store. He looked the three of them up and down, and made an instant decision that he could trust them. He was smoking an evil looking pipe, occasionally expelling a stream of brown spittle into the gutter several yards away. He removed the pipe as they approached.

'You look like strong lads.'

They stopped dead in their tracks, this sounded good.

'My man hasn't turned up for work and I want a few spuds moving.'

He pointed to a great pile of sacks of spuds, each weighing a hundredweight, that looked as if they had just been tipped off the back of a lorry. The truth was, he never did have any man working for him. Labour was cheap and he could always catch a passing man willing to earn himself a few coppers for a bit of casual work.

'We can't now, mister.' Alex looked up at the fascia board. Like the whole of the building, it was long overdue for a lick of paint. He could just make out the name, 'Mr Perkins'. 'But we will help you when we finish our jobs in the market.'

Mr Perkins looked downcast. The fruit and vegetable market closed at twelve. Then the other market men came in with their barrows, horses and carts, selling most other goods both new and second-hand.

'What time do you finish?'

'When the market closes, Mr Perkins. But we are strong lads. If it is quiet we might pack in a bit early.'

Mr Perkins had a reputation not only for being a skinflint, but also for the amount of beer he could consume, as the size of his belly bore testament. From a sitting position it almost covered his knees. It was also reputed that he never smiled, but on this occasion he bestowed Alex with a rare smile. Alex's forthright answers had impressed him.

'Well, I'm sorry son, I must get them shifted this morning. But I tell you what. If you three lads come here next Saturday morning, I'm expecting some more sacks then. You can have a shilling each. How's that?'

They nodded in agreement; Perkins had won again. He usually managed to get a couple of men at half a crown each. That was five shillings, this meant he would be saving two shillings.

'How old are you, son?' he asked Alex. 'Them sacks weigh a hundredweight each. Think you can manage them?'

'I'm ten, sir, and Horace is twelve, but don't worry, we can handle them.'

Arthur agreed with him. Like Alex, he would do anything for a few coppers, and Horace would agree with anything either of them said or did.

The following Saturday they arrived at Mr Perkins' at seven. Mr Perkins liked punctuality.

When Alex had told Mr Hawkins, he laughed and said, 'Watch the old sod, Alex, he would skin a flea for tuppence.'

But in spite of his reputation, at the end of their shift around eleven-thirty, Mr Perkins gave each of them an empty potato sack and told them they could pick up any of the vegetables scattered about the warehouse floor to take home. He threw down a couple of cauliflowers from a broken crate. He was pretty liberal with his advice too.

'Lift the sacks high on your backs, across your shoulders if you can. The higher they go, the lighter they feel.'

This was a tip for which Alex was to be grateful many years later.

'In a few weeks time, you will have muscles like old Samson himself. Night time you'll sleep like the proverbial log, a good body and a healthy mind.'

After that piece of useful advice, he would slap his outsize beer belly with both hands and vanish into the pub across the road.

'If I'm wanted, you can come across and get me. I'll be in the saloon bar.'

What he had omitted to tell them was that for the first few weeks after handling the heavy sacks of spuds, they would find they had aching muscles they didn't even know existed.

Alex arrived home that night, hoping to surprise his mother with the sack of vegetables and chinaware. He had made an agreement with Mr Hawkins that instead of paying him a shilling, he would give him some china. Mr Hawkins was very generous and let him have all the china which had slight chips. Alex soon discovered he could sell this for two and sometimes three times as much as his boss would have paid him.

Unfortunately, Alex's mother wasn't so happily surprised by the sack as he had hoped. He could see she had been crying. So had Polly, who was laying outstretched on the sofa. She was dabbing her eyes with her handkerchief, instead of reading her usual romantic novel. She must have been crying very badly as the handkerchief was as wet as a sponge. The air was thick; it was obvious there had been a bad argument.

'Go out and play, Alex.'

He protested, 'I have been working hard all day, Mom. I'm starving, any tea?'

She cut him several thick slices of bread, spread them with margarine and pushed the jam pot across the table towards him. With hands shaking, she poured him a cup of tea from an old brown teapot. Suddenly she shot up from her chair, sending it flying backwards, as if she'd just remembered something. She grabbed Polly's arm and dragged her from the sofa.

'Come on, my girl, get to your feet! It's no good snivelling, I'm taking you round to see Mrs Baker.'

This brought on another flood of tears and deep sobs from Polly. She had a good idea of Mrs Baker's reputation. Polly, a romantic, was also a coward when it came to any kind of pain, and the thought filled her with terror.

'Wipe those bloody tears! Let's see what Mrs Baker can do for you.'

Alex was halfway through his tea, his head resting in his hand and his elbow on the table, he stared into the dying fire. It had been a very hot day, but the fire was the only means of cooking. There would be no more cooking now till the morning. Arthur came in. He didn't knock as the front door was wide open.

'What's up, Alex? On your own?'

'Yes, our mom has taken Polly to see Mrs Baker.'

Arthur's jaw sagged. Unlike Alex, he was well acquainted with the facts of life, learned from his elder brother, as well as two very knowledgeable cousins living next door, who filled him with valuable information, all be it mostly figments of their imagination.

'Is she up the spud, Alex?' He always came directly to the point, and this was something he learned just recently. 'When our Rose came home up the spud, my old man asked her who had given her one. Then he went round the bloke's house with my brother and two cousins; bleeding old coward wouldn't go round on his own. They made him marry our Rose, now she hates his bloody guts. He's always pissed like my old man, he knocks our Rose about too. Then my two cousins and my brother go round and knock the shit out of him. Don't do much good, he does the same thing again the following week.'

'So it was that dirty bastard, Wally Hunter,' said Mrs Baker as she carried out the examination and confirmed that Polly was pregnant.

'Heaven's sake, Polly, what made you do it with him? He's a filthy pig. He works amongst those dirty rags and rusty metal all day long and I doubt if he washes more than once a week. His old man is just as bad. Talk about like father like son.'

'He said he wanted to marry me,' she answered in between sobs. 'They have a good rag and bone business.'

'Yes, and I suppose he ran you out to the Lickey Hills in that car of his and promised you everything. Well, Polly, if it's any consolation, you are not the first. To my knowledge, he has had another three young girls in the family way.' She lowered her voice. 'Old man Hunter is just as bad, he's had two young kids in the family way. They both take them up the Lickey Hills in their cars. I tell you, Martha, there are more babies made in the Lickey Hills than in all the beds in Birmingham!'

'Up the spout, you mean, our mom? Wally Hunter gave her one and now she's up the spout.'

Alex was sitting with Helen when they returned from Mrs Baker's. She looked at Alex hardly daring to believe her ears.

'Where the hell did you get that from?' His mother raised her voice.

'Arthur told me. Some bloke gave their Rose one and she had a baby.'

He turned towards Polly, who had taken her usual place, stretched out on the old sofa.

'You ain't going to marry that fat pig, Wally Hunter, are you, Polly?'

This brought on a fresh outburst of tears from his sister. She sobbed as she shouted back, 'Mind your own business, you silly little sod, and tell that Arthur to keep his mouth shut.' She sobbed into her handkerchief.

'It's a bloody good job that Arthur isn't here,' said his mother. 'Dirty little bugger, I'd box his ears for him. No, Polly isn't going to marry that Wally Hunter.'

It was almost nine o'clock, but still very light, it had been a very hot day, tempers flared. His mother ordered Polly to stay where she was. With a determined look on her face and the sleeves of her blouse rolled up to the elbows she meant business as she marched into Hunter's scrap yard.

He had no customers at this late hour but he kept open. When he saw Polly's mother, old man Hunter retreated to the hut situated between two mountains of scrap metal at the bottom of the scrap yard. A sliding window looked onto the two wide gates, thus enabling Hunter to see the comings and goings of his customers. It wasn't unknown for the kids to slip into the yard unseen, steal a lump of scrap metal and sell it back to him later in the week.

It had been the younger Wally Hunter who'd first seen the determined 'Amazon' stride into the yard. Wally was well aware of her fiery temper just as he was well aware what it was all about. Polly had been to see him earlier in the day, sobbing her heart out, and told him he had to marry her. He had answered her bluntly, telling her to 'Piss off!' Well aware of what her mother's reactions would be, he ran down to the far end of the yard to a cubby hole he'd made in the piles of scrap, for he was no stranger to trouble. It wasn't the first time he'd had a girl in trouble and experienced the wrath of his own father, along with that of the girl's angry parents. Old man Hunter knew nothing of his son's hideaway fortress.

Looking out of the dirty window, old man Hunter sensed trouble ahead. With his steel rimmed spectacles perched on the end of his nose, he picked up his newspaper, pretending to read, and looked up rather surprised as Polly's mother burst into the hut. He was seated behind a table littered with pieces of paper, bills and a metal cash box in front of him.

'What are you going to do with that fat slob of a son of yours, Hunter? He has got my Polly in the family way and this time he isn't going to get off scot free.'

'Hold on, Martha.' He pointed to an old wooden chair with no back. 'Sit down and let's talk things over sensibly. Let me call Wally in.'

'Don't bother, Hunter. As soon as he saw me he scampered amongst the piles of rags and metal. It's all right him putting these young kids up the spout but he never wants to face up to his responsibilities.'

'Come on, Martha, it takes two to tango. You should tell that girl of yours to keep her legs closed.'

A sickly grin spread across his face as he tried to treat the whole affair like a great joke. However, the look on her face told him she wouldn't accept that. He had known her for years, a determined woman who'd brought up her kids alone since her husband died. With her threatening finger a few inches from his face, she made a slight movement towards him. He slid back his chair.

'Don't you talk about my Polly like that, you fat grease ball. Your son took her up the Lickeys in that new car of his and you above all should know how susceptible a young girl is to that kind of treatment. She is only just sixteen, not much older than that young kid you put in the family way.'

The sickly grin vanished from his face, and was replaced by a look of fear. His own house was just a few feet away, and his wife could be seen working in the kitchen. He slid the glass panel of his hut closed.

'Sshh, Martha.' He nodded towards the house. 'The wife.' He lowered his voice. 'What do you want me to do, Martha? Make him marry your girl?' He brightened up. 'That wouldn't be such a bad thing, it may quieten him down. Polly you say, that's your youngest girl. Not a bad looker, make a nice little wife for him.'

She was speechless for a few minutes, staring at him in disbelief.

'Marry him? I'd sooner see her in her grave. Since your wedding day you've had more spare women than hot dinners, and that son of yours is a chip off the old block.'

It looked like he had used the same technique before. His face brightened.

'That about settles it, Martha. He would marry the girl but it seems all she was after was a bloody good time.' He picked up his newspaper and pretended to read. 'On your way, Martha.'

With that, she jumped up from her chair, knocking the newspaper from his hand.

'Don't you think either you or that fat slob of yours are going to get off that easy. If he kept himself as clean as that car of his, he might find someone stupid enough to marry him. You don't frighten me, Hunter. I've taken Polly to see Mrs Baker and she wants five quid to carry out the termination.'

'Five quid! You must be mad, Martha. She could get it done down Harley Street for that.'

The thought of parting with decent money made beads of sweat erupt from every pore on his forehead. He mopped his brow with a piece of oily rag.

'If I thought I could squeeze that amount of money out of you I would take her to Harley Street, but that's for those rich debutantes, not for the likes of us. It's not five quid I want, Hunter. After the op I intend to keep her off work for a few weeks, so I want another five quid on top of that.'

'Ten quid!' He almost screamed, but quickly lowered his voice remembering he was so near his own house, and repeated in a hoarse whisper, 'Ten quid? You must have gone stark raving mad, Martha. You'll get no bloody ten quid from me.'

'Oh won't I?' She leaned over the table and pushed the glass sliding window open. 'I bet your missus would like to know about that young bird you keep in that house in Leopold Street. You pay the rent, Hunter? And all that nice furniture in there, did you buy all that? Nice little house, Hunter, I bet your missus wouldn't mind it instead of living in this filthy yard. Now, you listen to me. Ten quid or your missus will hear about it, and if she doesn't I'll take her round and show it to her.'

'Ten quid, Martha. This borders on blackmail. You can get seven years for blackmail, it's a very serious offence.'

'Maybe so, Hunter, but I know what a violent temper you old lady's got. If she finds out about your little bit on the side, you will be minus a couple of balls! Fetch the police if you like but I'm not moving from this place without ten quid in my hand.'

He returned to his old routine, repeating, 'It takes two to tango, Martha. Polly is partly to blame.'

'I realize that, Hunter, but I see no reason why she should do all the twisting and turning for the next nine months. You know, if we take you to court it'll mean five bob a week till the kid's sixteen.'

Reluctantly he opened his tin cash box and counted out ten pounds in dirty pound and ten shilling notes. He should have known not to cross words with Martha.

'Give this message to that son of yours. Next time he wants a bunk up give him five bob to find some floozy in town because if he comes anywhere near my Polly again, I will personally castrate him! I know my other girls are safe, they wouldn't touch him with a barge pole.'

As she left the scrap yard she heard him bellowing at the top of his voice for Wally. She could still hear him when she was halfway down the street. She laughed to herself, seeing the funny side of the situation.

# Chapter Eight

Mrs Baker, an ex SRN with several years' practise as a midwife, had an attic which she used to carry out abortions, it was as clean and sterile as any hospital theatre. The operating table was specially made for the job. Her instruments were sterilised by boiling over a methylated spirit stove. A bed with clean sheets stood in one corner and everything was tailored to be pushed into a recess of the room, should the police become too inquisitive. Nothing was left to chance as being caught would mean at least two years in prison - and a big rise in the birth rate for the district.

Polly had been ordered to go to the local baths before she arrived. She was then given a clean white night-gown straight from the steriliser.

'Remove everything, Polly, we don't want any infection.'

While Polly was preparing for the operation, trembling and crying, Mrs Baker was talking to her mother.

'It's a bloody shame, Martha, these poor kids, Polly is the fourth this week. I had one last week, poor little sod was frightened to death, she couldn't have been more than fourteen at most. I told her mother she could get a legal abortion, but she looked as frightened as the kid when I said that. Something fishy about that, Martha. The mother is living with this bloke, so I'll leave the rest to your imagination.'

Martha shook her head in disgust.

'It's a good job you're here, Mrs Baker, there would be more misery around than there is now if you didn't help these people out. I wouldn't trust my Polly with anyone except you.'

As she prepared to leave, Polly became more frightened and sat down on the edge of the bed weeping.

'You ain't going, are you, Mom?'

Her small frame shook with sobs, but her mother knew it was no time to get sentimental. Otherwise she would end up grabbing her hand and running down the stairs, letting her go the whole way with the pregnancy. This was a good lesson for Polly in facing up to reality. Her mother realised it was a hard thing to do, but to give in to her now would lead to disaster all round. Allowing her to go through with the pregnancy would only create a bigger burden on their meagre resources. Another mouth to feed, another body to clothe, and heaven knows she was finding it hard enough now to make ends meet on her frugal income.

With a lump in her throat and a comforting arm round her daughters shoulders, she said, 'Pull yourself together, Polly, I will be back here in a couple of hours time and it will be all over by then.' As she kissed her forehead, fighting back the tears, she could feel her daughter's frail body trembling beneath the thin gown. 'Be a good girl and do exactly as Mrs Baker tells you.'

Between bouts of sobbing, Polly remained in bed for a few days, on her mother's insistence. It wasn't long enough for Alex though, because when she eventually came downstairs she once again commandeered the old sofa. Every time Alex looked at her, she burst into tears. He hadn't the slightest idea what the real reason for this was, and put it down to her usual bad moods. She refused to work, although her mother and sisters tried every method of persuasion they could think of. She was well aware that the news was already round the factory, that she had paid a visit to Mrs Baker, and from the youngest girl to the top management, all knew of Mrs Baker's profession. Polly would be the target for every innuendo and insult floating round the factory, although she wouldn't be the first. There were many girls and married women who had paid a secret visit to the illegal operating theatre. Then there were the men, thinking she was an easy touch, who would make improper suggestions. So every time work was mentioned there would be another bout of hysteria.

Apart from her moods, this had no effect on Alex. Life went on as normal, whilst he continually searched for ways of making money, no loopholes remained unexplored. He now had three home-made barrows. Each one had 'A. Edwards, Haulage Contractor' painted on the side in boyish scrawl. He ran errands, collected bundles of clothing, often including husbands' suits and anything that was pawnable, and queued outside Uncle's every Monday morning for the women to collect their possessions from him. It didn't net a lot of money, but what else could he do on a Monday morning before he went to school, and it saved the women wasting their time queuing.

His neighbours were well aware that one day he would make something of himself, although his work didn't stop him from playing childish pranks and games. Every day, whilst going to and from school with Arthur and Horace, they would all run and slide along the tramlines pretending to be some famous train.

Once day, it was a Monday morning, when they came along the tram track at speed, then stopped dead before they turned into their own street. For the few hours they were at school, the whole street had been transformed into a ready made battleground. Dozens of navvies dug a trench the whole length of the street. A mountain of earth topped the trench and half way down the street, two arched canvas tents had been erected. There was a six foot space between them, and slap bang in the middle was a large forty gallon oil drum which had been perforated with dozens of

52

pickaxe blows, and now held a white hot coke fire. It had hardly any flames, but a shimmering heat haze danced above the oil drum.

The weather was still very hot, four long wooden benches surrounded the fire, this being the marshalling point for the navvies. The elderly man attending the fire, blew a whistle and dozens of men clambered to the top of the trench, shovels in their hands, like a regiment of troops going over the top, each scrambling for a better place around the fire. Alex and his two friends were awe-struck when they saw the men place their shovels on the fire, each shovel well worn and gleaming like burnished steel. They put several strips of bacon or sausages on the shiny shovels, and then with the dexterity of a hotel chef, cracked a couple of eggs on the shovel. In seconds, the bacon, sausages and eggs crackled and spat.

Arthur exclaimed, 'Bloody hell, mate, my old lady would like that shovel!'

The man grinned. 'I bet she would like my sausages and eggs too. What you having for dinner, son?'

'Bleeding stew, that's what we have every Monday. Don't fancy swapping do you mate?'

The man laughed, but a big Irishman standing beside the fire wasn't amused. Standing at least six feet tall, he was almost the same around the chest. He wore a hat two sizes too small for his head, no shirt, and corduroy trousers tied up with a leather thong just below the knee.

In a loud voice he said, 'Well, it's time you were away, son. Go on, sod off and have your stew.'

'What you doing, mate? Putting gas in our house?' asked Alex, trying to balance himself on a large iron pipe. 'We heard some time ago that we would be having gas, but my mom said that will be when the pigs fly. Are we really going to have gas in, mate?'

The big Irishman had his back to them and didn't bother turning when he said, 'And what do you think those pipes are here for? Are you stupid, boy?'

'Steady on, Paddy, the lad only asked you. God, man, you fly off the handle at the least little thing,' said the old man tending the fire. He turned to Alex. 'Yes, son, we are fitting gas pipes.' He threw a look of contempt at the big Irishman.

They examined one of the men's large shovels. Arthur could hardly pick it up. He felt the smooth metal.

'My mom would love one of these.'

'That's no good to you, son, you haven't got any gardens, and it's too big for the new gas stoves you will get.'

'No, mister, I don't mean that for cooking, she would like it to crack over my old man's head when he comes home pissed. We don't have cooked breakfast in our house.'

It was a ready-made battlefield. They had seen pictures of the old battlefields and heard stories from some of the old soldiers, so it was immediately christened the Somme. Kids from miles around came to play in the trenches, but Alex and his mates held the section running in front of their entry as if it were some strategic position. The digging and laying of pipes lasted several weeks, and all the kids were universal in their disappointment at seeing the trench filled in a section at a time, although they were overjoyed with the finished results. The light was several times brighter than the old kerosene lamps, the only drawback being that it showed just how dingy the old houses really were.

'Wish we could find the money for a few rolls of wallpaper for this room,' said his mother, as they sat down for their first meal under the new light, which highlighted every nook and cranny. Even the dirty patches on the walls were now plainly visible.

Alex's business kept expanding. His three barrows were always kept busy as the depression was biting really hard and more neighbours were unable to keep up with their rents and resorted to moonlight flits. The three of them left their homes at seven every Saturday morning, first helping Mr Perkins to unload and re-stack his sacks of potatoes. At midday they would vanish to their respective jobs in the old rag market. Alex helped with the china stall, absorbing every detail about chinaware, collecting labels with the suppliers' names and addresses from the tea chests that the china arrived in.

Nothing appeared to go wrong. Old man Jenkins gave them potatoes and swedes or any other vegetables from broken crates. The fruit man gave them the bruised apples and occasionally, if they were lucky, he would give them bunches of overripe bananas. Alex always asked to be paid in chinaware.

There were weeks when Alex earned more money than his sisters in full time employment, and he often gave his mother five shillings a week; more than his sisters. He learned to save, he was convinced that one day they would get away from this vermin ridden hole and he would start his own business. His mother gave him an old square Oxo tin which he kept under the floorboards in his mother's bedroom. It was hard work prizing the loose board up every time he wanted some money, so he hit on the novel idea of placing the tin under a wide crack in the floorboards. So life went on, with Alex even more determined that he would have his own business one day.

The family had just sat down to Sunday dinner, when there was a loud banging on the door. It wouldn't have been a close neighbour as they would just tap the door and walk straight in. The banging grew louder, and whoever was outside was now knocking the door with a vengeance, becoming more and more impatient. His sisters looked at Alex, wondering what he and his mates had been up to.

'All right, don't knock the bloody door down,' shouted his mother, as she got up from the table. 'I'm coming.'

She angrily put down her knife and fork and went to the door. A woman stood there, her hands on her hips and a defiant look on her face. Angry would hardly be sufficient to describe her.

Red faced, she glared at his mother. 'That kid of yours, Marth! He's gone and pinched the wheels off my baby's pram.'

Alex gently slid off his chair, down under the table, unseen by the outraged lady. He wormed his way across the room, till he was hidden behind the door listening to every word.

'Right in the middle of the street, outside Tommy Lipton's. Him and his two cronies. I was inside Lipton's getting my bit of stuff for the weekend, when that bleeding Arthur and that quiet kid, Horace, lifted my baby onto the pavement. Then they took off the metal parts, the wheels and lifted the baby back into the pram without its wheels. I could have killed the little perishers!'

His sisters sat at the table, poker faced, not daring to look at each other for fear of laughing, each one imagining that tiny baby sitting outside the shop in a pram without wheels, and passers by wondering how she got there. It was too humorous to contemplate, and Helen couldn't contain herself any longer. Putting her hand over her mouth and holding her breath, she rushed upstairs into the bedroom, pressing her face into the depths of a feather pillow.

'Now come on, Molly. You don't know it's our Alex. I know he gets up to all sorts of tricks, but I don't think he would do that.' Inwardly, she knew that when the three of them were together he was quite capable of doing anything if it meant a few coppers in it for himself. 'How do you know it was him and his mates?'

'How do I know?' Molly raged, her face turning redder by the minute.

'How do I know?' she repeated. 'Bleeding hell, Martha, them are my wheels on that cart over there. My old man pinched the paint from a job he was doing and spent a good hour painting that pram. What are you or young Alex going to do about it? I ain't got no pram for the baby.'

She knew that Alex had arrived home a couple of days previously with the undercarriage of a pram, which he had made up into two pushcarts, because she had remarked at the time on the ghastly colour. The argument gathered momentum. Polly didn't have the restraint of Karen, and although she would have loved to stay to hear the outcome, like Helen she had to make a swift exit. She rose from the table smartly, knocking her chair backwards in the process, and covering her mouth, rushed upstairs and flung herself across the bed, her eyes red and watery.

Helen looked up from her pillow and with a voice that sounded more like crying, she whispered, 'Has she gone get?'

But Polly couldn't take her face from the pillow, and shook her head.

'Bloody hell, Molly, you can't say you haven't had your money's worth out of that pram. You must have reared at least six kids in it and it was second-hand when you bought it. I don't suppose it cost you more than two bob in the first place.'

'Well, that doesn't give your Alex the right to pinch it, Martha. I ain't got money to replace it.'

Alex stepped from behind the door to confront the irate woman.

'I didn't nick your bloody pram, missus. Your Samantha was there and said I could have the pram for sixpence. She took the baby out of the pram and held her while I removed the metal parts. At first she said she wanted a shilling, but we settled for a tanner. She wanted me to take the whole pram, but it was too filthy. She said it was no good, but I only wanted the wheels. I gave her the tanner and she told me to take them quickly.'

'What, my Sammy! She wouldn't do a thing like that.' She hesitated, knowing full well that Sammy would do anything for a penny. Her attitude changed. 'I will kill the little bleeder when I get home. Just wait, I will tan her arse till it's black and blue.'

This touched a soft spot with Alex. It was him that did all the bargaining with Samantha, and it was him who had convinced her that the pram was on its last legs so to speak, so in part he felt some kind of responsibility. He fished out a two shilling piece from his pocket and gave it to the lady. A smile spread across her face as she kissed the coin and put it into her black apron pocket, whilst conjuring up in her mind how she would spend it. A couple of packets of chips to keep the kids quiet, and a packet of Woodbines for the old man.

'You're a good kid, Alex. Thanks a lot, son.'

'One of these days, Alex, you will meet your match.' Karen told him after the woman had left, still counting her blessings, her hand clasped round the coin in her apron pocket. They sat at the table finishing their meal. His two sisters came down from the bedroom, their eyes red and wet with tears of laughter. It was then that Karen and his mother burst out laughing.

Alex enjoyed his job on the china stall on Saturday afternoons. The boss treated him as a son. His own son had vanished from home some thirty years earlier, after having a good education at Oxford University, paid for by his father. It appeared he was ashamed of his father's trade, in spite of the fact that his father was a self-made man, who owned a large house in the better part of the city's outskirts. He lived alone in the big rambling house.

'It broke the wife's heart, Alex, when he vanished. They said she had a heart attack, but I knew what it was. She idolised that boy. Someone told us he went to Australia after he graduated. I made no end of enquiries.' He shook his head. 'I visit the wife's grave every Sunday, Alex.'

Alex had very little memories of his own father. He died when he was quite young, but he knew at the time what a hole it had left in his young life, although over the years he often heard his mother say that it had been a blessed relief. And that was how it was with his old friend, Mr Fisher. He never spoke to Alex, although Alex always spoke to him. Old Mr Fisher's face always lit up when Alex stood in front of him talking. The people would say that it would be a blessed relief when he goes. He never understood this. Neither did he understand when the fish man moved in with Mrs Fisher, but after he did, Mrs Fisher always had a smile on her lips.

'Why don't you have a new wife, Mr Fleming? Mrs Fisher had a new husband and she is always smiling now.'

The old man put his hand on Alex's head.

'No one could ever replace my dear wife, Alex. I visit her grave every Sunday and I know she is there.'

They finished loading the horse and cart.

'Goodnight, Alex.'

Alex was brimming over with excitement when he arrived home one Saturday. His mother was preparing a meal on her newly installed gas stove. She was just about getting used to it after spending her life using the old coal fired stove, which also served as the only source of heating for the dreary house. He pushed his home-made barrow into the room. His sisters sighed as he emptied the chinaware from the barrow into a tea chest, yet another box to clutter up their bedroom. As it was now, they could barely squeeze their way into bed past all his boxes, and he was using his mother's bedroom for storage as well.

Alex sat down at the table, his elbows resting on the table and his head in his hands. 'The boss has got a new van, Mom, brand new. You should see it, all black. I sat in the cab with its real shiny steering wheel, it was great. He told the chaps in the market it could do up to fifty miles an hour.' He fell silent, his mind miles away seeing himself at seventeen driving along the country lanes. He started to hum like a motor car, in a complete daze. 'One day I'll have a brand new van.'

He was soon brought out of his daydream when Polly burst out laughing and said, 'Yes, and pigs will fly!'

But Karen, who always took sides with her mother, gave her younger sister a stern, disapproving look.

'Don't worry, Polly, one day Alex may shock us all. He has more ambition in his little finger than the three of us put together. He is already adamant there will be no factory job for him.'

'Well, I wish he would start now. Our bedroom is full of those tea chests crammed with chinaware,' Polly and Helen said in unison.

'So what? Since our Alex started working down the market we haven't had to drink out of jam jars or cracked cups. We don't make tea in a teapot all cracked without a lid, and we don't have to eat off cracked or chipped places or take turns using them. We can all sit down together now.'

The memory of those times, which hadn't been so long back, made Polly hold her tongue. It made her realise too that the abundance of food they now enjoyed was also what Alex brought home every Saturday night along with the china. Pity that Alex stuck to some of his childish pranks.

The whole family would be more than surprised to learn he held just over five pounds in the school bank; more than any other child in the whole school. The only person who wouldn't be surprised was his first school teacher, Miss Pimm. She had followed his progress with joy, from a snotty nosed urchin with his backside hanging out of his trousers to a lad who took pride in himself. She had approached the new headmaster.

'Mark my words, Headmaster, that boy Edwards will make something of himself.' She smiled to herself when she heard about the balance of his school bank account.

'Do you think he came by the money honestly, Miss Pimm?' She laughed openly.

'Believe me, Headmaster, there isn't a dishonest bone in that boy's body, and apart from that his mother would have half killed him had he ever done anything dishonest. He comes from a very poor, but honest and hardworking family. Karen, the eldest, used to go to this school. She's working in an office now. You must remember her. She should have been head girl, but most of the staff here could see no further than the ragged clothes she wore. She had the most beautiful blonde hair and blue eyes.'

Miss Pimm could remember most of her pupils from several generations of pupils.

'Ah yes, I think I do remember that girl, but that was a few years back.'

He dare not look Miss Pimm directly in the eye, for he had been the main instigator in denying her the promotion she has so richly deserved. So quietly, but guiltily in a lowered voice he said, 'Ahem, yes, Miss Pimm, I am pleased to see she is making something of herself.'

Alex could think of nothing but the new van his boss had bought. He waited impatiently for Saturday to come round when he could sit alone in the cab and let his fingers play round the shiny steering wheel. He was racing along a racetrack in one of those funny little motors he had seen on the cinema, with the wheels well away from the body of the car itself. They said the cars could do a hundred miles an hour. He whistled through his teeth at the thought of any car going that fast. His daydreams were brought to an abrupt end when the boss shouted through the side window.

'Come on, Alex. It's time to set up shop.' By the shop, he meant prepare the stall for the punters.

They were well into the summer and their summer holidays. Although it was still daylight till ten, as far as the three friends were concerned there were never enough hours in the day. Business really centred around Saturdays, and sometimes stretched into Sunday morning if they had a flitting job on. During the week they would spend some days swimming in the filthy canal or sun bathing on the towpath. Or they would search the corporation tip for metal, jam jars and rags. Sometimes they would vanish into the railway shunting yard to search for lumps of coal that might be laying around. The coal itself was a bad burner, but mixed with the best coal it was useful for fuelling the old copper washing boiler, and at tuppence a quarter hundredweight, they always had a ready market.

Alex had been storing his chinaware in the tea chests in his mother's and sisters' bedrooms and it was now becoming a problem, but he had a good clientele who helped him make a few shillings a week.

Helen, like Karen, had blossomed into an attractive young woman who turned men's heads when she passed. She had a regular boyfriend and talk of marriage was in the air. He was ten years her senior. Harry had a steady job with good, regular wages. 'Last week he had earned over three pounds.' She was telling her family all this as they sat around the table enjoying their tea.

'He deserves every penny of it. I don't know how you could let him touch you, never mind kiss him, after handling dead bodies all day long.' Polly shuddered. 'He's a nice enough fellow but bloody hell, Helen, an undertaker.'

Helen's eyes widened as she looked at her sister, the words tumbling from her mouth she spat out, 'How dare you!' Repeating it again, 'How dare you talk to me about allowing anyone to touch me! After what you did with that fat slob Wally Hunter on the Lickey Hills, you've no room to talk. At least my Harry takes a bath twice a week and always wears a clean shirt, collar and tie. Not like that filthy lump, fat Wally, with his dirty clothes and piece of grubby rag tied round his neck. Harry is a gentleman, always clean and smart, and I'm proud to be seen walking out with him.'

Polly burst into a volley of hysterical crying, and dashed from the room to her bedroom, her feet pounding hard on the uncarpeted wooden stairs, slamming the bedroom door behind her. It was always the mother who intervened to keep the peace. She hated family rows.

'You had no right to bring up that Wally Hunter affair. That's all over now and I don't ever want to hear you or anyone else bring it up again. Is that understood?'

It wasn't often they heard their mother in a fit of temper, but when she was they knew she meant it. Helen bowed her head like a dutiful daughter. The last thing she wanted to do was to upset her mother.

She shook her head and said softly, 'She does get up my nose, Mom. When I get married, I want to walk down the aisle in white, it means something to me. On my wedding night I want Harry to know that he is the first man I have ever been with. None of the neighbours round here will be able to make any snide remarks behind my back, and count the months before the first baby arrives!'

Her mother patted her hand. 'Helen, don't say it again, and try and pull yourself together and say you are sorry to Polly.'

'All right, Mom, you are right. I really am sorry. I shouldn't have said it.'

A few days later, the argument was completely forgotten and the three sisters enthusiastically discussed the arrangements for the forthcoming marriage. It meant a few shillings less coming into the family budget but a marriage in the house was cause for celebration, and their mother was soon caught up in all the excitement. But life still had to go on and Alex was constantly thinking up new ideas to make some extra money, much to the amusement of all the family.

The school summer holidays were over and the neighbourhood was back into its old routine. An early chill September mist had settled over the city. A stray leaf, which had lost its way from the small park half a mile away, fluttered along the street, a slight rustle as it bobbed across the irregular paving stones. Alex pushed along his barrow on the Monday morning. It was the cleanest barrow, not the one he collected the coal in. He knocked on the first door.

'Anything for Uncle's, Mrs Wilson?'

The door opened slightly, revealing a small child wearing only a shirt, a snotty candle curling round his top lip.

'Mom is just ironing Dad's suit,' squeaked the boy.

It was always the old man's suit for Mrs Wilson. It went to Uncle's on Monday morning after his wife had sponged off the stale beer and pressed it. Then out it came again on Friday.

There was a tap on the window as he passed the house. A new customer, or so he thought, but the face was drawn and grey. A lady beckoned him inside. Although it was a chilly September morning, the room was as icy as a butcher's cold store. She sat on the old worn out sofa, with a threadbare shawl wrapped round her shoulders, her straggly grey hair hanging down loose to frame her wax like face.

'Are you all right, Mrs Tanner?'

There was hardly any need to ask the question, she looked far from alright. She was comparatively new to the area, and with two school age daughters, they kept themselves to themselves. When she did speak it was apparent that she came from a better class of people; obviously she had seen better times. She didn't allow her children to play in the street with other kids. She wasn't a snob, her two girls only owned the clothes they wore daily.

As she touched Alex's hand, he shuddered involuntarily for her fingers were like match sticks and cold as ice.

'See if the pawnbroker will let you have sixpence on this, Alex.' She handed him a pathetic bundle.

'I will follow you up, son.' she said, her voice just a mite above a whisper.

Two boys with loaded barrows were already at their stations.

'Bleeding cold, ain't it, Alex?' said the smaller boy as he snuffled up the candle which was about to vanish in the cavity below the boy's nose. 'My dad reckons it's going to be a bad winter.' There was a note of conviction in his squeaky voice.

'How does your old man know? Your old man knows sweet fuck all. The only thing he knows is the way to the pub. He can never find his way back. The coppers have to drag him home after he's spent a night in the cells.' He turned to Alex. 'Ever seen his old man, Alex?'

Alex shook his head.

Candles didn't argue. The other boy had a reputation as a bully boy, more so if the other boy was smaller. One by one, the customers came to collect their pawnable goods, till Alex was left with just one.

It was almost nine and the other two boys had already left. Alex was looking anxiously at the large clock in the pawnbroker's window. He hated being late for school, Mrs Tanner still hadn't turned up. The small finger was already on the nine and the large hand was jerking upwards toward the twelve. He kept glancing down the hill. A look of relief came over him as he spotted the frail figure turn the corner, the pathetically thin and worn shawl wrapped round her shoulders. She made her way slowly up the hill, using the walls and window sills of the houses and shops to support herself. She stopped at the house next to the pawnshop, leaning against the wall her chest heaving as she fought to get her breath.

'Are you all right, Mrs Tanner?' he asked, as he grabbed her arm and slowly helped her the last few feet.

She sat down on the pawnbroker's step. It was a minute or two before she regained enough breath and strength to answer him. When she did, her voice was fainter than ever, and Alex was forced to put his head as close as possible to her lips to hear what she said.

'Take it in for me, Alex.'

Alex slapped the bundle down on the pawnbroker's counter. The old man didn't bother to unwrap it.

'Sorry, Alex, they're too old and dirty.'

'But the old lady is very sick, Mr Wiseman, she's too ill to come into the shop. Please, Mr Wiseman, she is very poor and very sick.'

The pleading eyes softened the old man's heart. Every day he heard sob stories that would tear a man's heart out and he should have been hardened to them by now. He pulled back the shutters and looked at the frail, pathetic bundle sitting on the step, her head resting against the wall. He shook his head slowly and put sixpence down on the counter. He didn't give Alex a ticket. Instead, he picked up the bundle from under the counter and gave it back to Alex.

'These people will have me in the poorhouse one of these days, Alex.' He looked at the sick woman again. 'Take her home, Alex.' He tossed another silver three penny piece on the counter. 'Buy some milk and give her a hot drink, and make sure she is warm. Then call the doctor. The lady is very sick.'

Alex helped Mrs Tanner to her feet. She looked so small and delicate, just skin stretched taught over bones, she couldn't have weighed more than four or five stones, at most half the weight of one of those sacks of spuds he stacked every Saturday. She broke into a fit of coughing, curling up into a small ball. He supported her as a trickle of blood dribbled from the corner of her mouth. The old pawnbroker rushed from the shop and helped Alex ease her onto his home-made barrow, using the bundle for a pillow. Alex took off his jacket and covered her. The streets were completely deserted. Those who had work were at their factories or offices and the unemployed were still abed, the warmest place in the house, and the children were all at school.

Alex lifted Mrs Tanner into the house. He rushed upstairs to fetch blankets, stood in the bedroom and gasped. His family had seen bitter hard times, but it was nothing compared to this. A solitary iron bed stood in the centre of the room. No blankets or sheets, just two mattresses which the family slept between. There was an empty wardrobe minus its doors; they'd been burnt months ago. He rushed downstairs. There was no sign of any fuel, just a mountain of burnt paper in the grate. As he tucked his coat around her, Mrs Tanner coughed and splattered his face and jumper with specks of blood.

He rushed from the house and jumped over the wall to his own house. His mother was in the brew house.

'You had better come quick, Mom. Mrs Tanner is spitting blood.'

'Why aren't you at school?' she asked, before the message sank in.

She wiped her hands on her apron, an old potato sack tied round her ample waist, and followed Alex. She guessed it would be serious, Alex never missed school. As she couldn't scale the six foot wall, she had to walk round. First down the entry into the street, and then into the other yard. She took one look at Mrs Tanner.

'My God, Alex, she's dying.'

Death was already etching its permanent mark on Mrs Tanner's face. His mother had nursed badly wounded soldiers during the war and death was no stranger to her.

'Fetch some wood and coal, Alex, and let's get some warmth back into this icebox.'

She searched for Mrs Tanner's pulse. Faint spasms slid up her wrist. She massaged her hands and arms to restore some warmth into her body, but she knew it was too late. All they could do was make her as comfortable as possible so she could die with a little dignity, if that was possible in such a hovel.

In minutes, Alex had the grate cleared out and a decent fire roaring up the chimney. No doubt it was the first real fire it had seen since Mrs Tanner and her two daughters had moved in. Mrs Fisher followed Alex in. Like his mother, she was no stranger to sickness and death.

'Bloody hell, Martha, she is on her last legs. I'll fetch the doctor.'

'Before you go, Flo, have you got a couple of old blankets to spare?'

Mrs Tanner's eyes flickered open and the sick lady went into a spasm of uncontrolled coughing. She gripped Martha's wrist, her long nails digging deep till they almost broke the skin.

'I am dying, Martha, see my girls are all right.'

Her skeletal fingers clutched at the blankets.

Alex lit the gas stove oven to give more heat in the room. His mother took the saucepan of milk from him and said gently, 'It's too late, Alex.'

He looked at the still form on the sofa, a blanket covered her head. It took some time for it to sink in, the fact that he'd just witnessed a woman dying. He stared open mouthed at the still form, the blood draining from his face. His mother put a comforting arm around his shoulders. He sobbed, 'But I only ...' The words faded away.

They waited for the doctor before preparing the body for its final journey.

'Just look at her, Martha, not a lot over thirty years old and she looks sixty. Those two lovely girls, I wonder what will happen to them? I bet she hasn't eaten a proper meal in months. She was much too proud to ask for help. If those two girls didn't have school dinners they too would starve. It's that bloody husband of hers. As soon as she fell for that second girl, he scampered. A few months after the girl was born they discovered she had consumption. I would love to catch hold of that husband of hers. I'd cut his balls off! Mind you, I doubt if she would have been any better off if he'd stayed with her. She told me once that he drank heavily. She came from a good family. You could tell that the way she talked, but after she married him her family disowned her. I never realised she was in such a bad way. She never asked anyone for anything. Let's face it, Martha, wherever she is now, she can't be any worse off. I have never heard of anyone coming back to complain!'

Bobby Jones, the local policeman, was called in by one of the neighbours. The doctor had left the death certificate. He looked at it, then the body. He searched round the room and found an old biscuit tin with all her personal papers in. Going through them, he came across photographs taken when she was a bride.

'Beautiful girl Martha!' He sucked in his breath with disgust as he read a letter. 'All the Parish gave her was twelve shillings a week and out of that she had to pay five shillings for this hovel. You would never imagine a thing like this could happen in a civilised country. Really makes me laugh when I hear all about the Irish troubles and absent landlords. They should come over here and seem how we treat people this side of the Irish Sea.'

Alex's mother made tea for the two girls and then waited in the street for them to arrive home. She told them not to go into the house but made them go to her own home. They were very shy and stood by the table, guessing that something had happened. She didn't have the heart to come out directly and tell them their mother had died. When she finally told them, she had to choke back a sob as they cried a little.

The eldest girl, Victoria, pulled out a round thick slice of brown bread from inside her blouse.

'I brought this from school dinners for her. She was very sick, Mrs Edwards.'

'I know that, darling.' She put her arms round the two girls. 'Her suffering is over now.'

The screaming started when a small, black Austin car pulled up at the bottom of the entry, and a sour faced woman and a very tall, thin man came into the yard to enquire the whereabouts of the two girls.

'Come on, girls, we have to take you away to a nice home where you will be warm, and have decent clothes and good nourishing food.'

The youngest girl screamed and kicked the tall man. He slapped her face and as he grabbed her again, she screamed once more.

'I want my mother! I want my mother!'

'Now come on, none of this nonsense. It's getting dark and we have a long way to go.'

The vinegar faced woman took hold of Veronica and the stern man grabbed Victoria, lifting her under his arm. A crowd had gathered outside the house, some of the women crying. Both girls were now screaming for all they were worth. The screams echoed inside the square of buildings. It was a sound that was to haunt Alex for many years to come. There was little doubt that the poker faced woman had done the same job time after time for she showed no compassion.

Helen's fiance had heard the news when they related the story. He rarely spoke about his work but Martha wanted news about any funeral arrangements.

'Yes, I brought her body from the hospital morgue. There is very little room to keep them there very long. Sorry, Ma, it's a pauper's grave. We've had four today. My boss does his nut. The Parish funerals hardly cover the cost.'

Within days Mrs Tanner's death was part of the street's history. Another month or two and it would be completely forgotten by most people but to Alex it was printed indelibly on his mind, and often he asked his mother what had happened to the two girls.

# Chapter Ten

Alex and his two friends were working in Mr Perkins' potato warehouse when a large black car pulled up outside, blasting its horn a couple of times. Mr Perkins was sitting, half awake, his hands resting on his extended stomach. At first he took no notice of the interruption, till a head appeared through the passenger window and a voice bellowed, 'Morning, Syd!'

The warehouse vibrated and the windows in the partition of the office rattled. He recognised the voice and immediately jumped to his feet, pushing on his well worn bowler hat at the same time. Exercising his thick, podgy legs for once, he ran to the front, and touching the brim of his bowler in a half hearted salute he answered, 'Morning, Mr Goldstein.'

The man at the steering wheel was almost as fat as Mr Perkins. He sat there sucking on a huge Havana cigar, an inch of white ash clinging to it as he rolled it from side to side in his mouth.

Mr Goldstein wore a loud, check suit and sported an enormous bow tie. A nervous twitch caused his left eye to wink every few seconds.

He looked round the street and quietly said, 'I want fifty bags of your best, Perkins. What you asking?'

'Seven and sixpence, Mr Goldstein.'

'Seven and six!'

The nervous twitch accelerated, and as he fidgeted in his seat the inch of cigar ash finally dropped off landing in a heap on the bright check suit. For the first time, he removed the cigar from his mouth and flicked the remaining ash through the side window.

'You are joking, ain't you, Perkins?'

'No, Mr Goldstein.'

He removed his bowler and wiped the sweat from the inside leather band and his forehead. He was well aware that Mr Goldstein only used this as a convenience for tax evasion. He owned several catering establishments throughout the county and every few weeks he would visit Mr Perkins or some other wholesaler to buy fifty bags of spuds not using his own name which he purposely omitted to enter in his books.

Alex was hypnotised by the beautiful, black vehicle. In a trance, he walked from the warehouse and stood by the car, his fingers lightly passing over the coach work, admiring every inch from the chrome angel on the bonnet, which looked more like solid silver, to the glistening back bumper.

'Like it, son?' Mr Goldstein's voice boomed out.

With a voice barely a whisper he answered, 'It's beautiful, sir, the most beautiful car I have ever seen!'

The fat man with his treble chin was proud of his car. His small eyes penetrated Alex's brain.

'Work hard and one day you might own one of these, son.' His hand caressed the steering wheel. 'Best car in the world, son.'

Alex sneezed, creating a horrendous act of sacrilege in the process, for a globule of snot hit the car's pristine paint work and was sliding down the door. Luckily Mr Goldstein hadn't noticed as he was still bargaining with Mr Perkins on the other side of the car. Alex tried using his bare knee to clean it off, rubbing it from side to side, but only succeeded in spreading the slime more. He bent down and wiped off the offending snot with the sleeve of his pullover.

Mr Perkins and Mr Goldstein finished their bargaining, settling for twenty-five whites and the same number of King Edwards at seven shillings and threepence a hundredweight.

Mr Goldstein took out a massive roll of white five pound notes from his glove box. Peeling off just the right amount, he slid a rubber band round them, and carelessly tossed the notes to Mr Perkins. Alex's mouth dropped wide open at the sight of the five pound notes for he'd never seen even one before and there must have been at least a hundred in that wad.

'I will be sending my chap round in an hour's time, Perkins. Get them loaded as fast as possible, he's got to get them round to some of my places today.' He bent forward and pulled a load of change from his trouser pocket. Sorting out two half crowns, he handed them to Alex. 'Here you are, son. You and your mates load them up, and make sure old man Perkins doesn't see me off!' he said, with a grin spread across his face.

Alex watched as the Rolls drove off, soon disappearing from view. Mr Perkins put his hand on Alex's shoulder.

'He's not a bad chap, Alex, his bark is worse than his bite.'

'I thought you were selling your whites at six shillings and ninepence, Mr Perkins?'

Mr Perkins burst out laughing. 'So I was, Alex, so I was, but let me teach you the first lesson in business. You see, Mr Goldstein is a very rich man and has to pay a lot of tax each year. So every month or so, he goes to buy stock which he doesn't put through his books. He knows I sell them for less, but he also knows that I won't let on about his fiddle, and that little bit extra I get enables me to sell the last few sacks at a reduced price. I'm happy, Mr Goldstein's happy, and my customers are happy. What's more, you and your two mates will be happy with an extra five shillings between you, so we're all bloody happy!' He patted Alex's back. 'Now I'm off to the pub, Alex. I'm leaving you in charge, you know where to find me.'

With that he wobbled across the road to the pub leaving Alex to think over his simple philosophy, and ponder on his first lesson in business.

The three of them sat drinking tea on a pile of sacks of potatoes. Mr Perkins had had a good day so he sent the barman over with three cheese and onion sandwiches.

'What, no beer?' said Arthur as the barman handed the unwrapped sandwiches over.

'Cheeky little sod!' he exclaimed, wiping his hands on his once white, but now beer stained, apron.

The conversation turned to the fat man in his car. Alex had talked of little else since.

'I will have one of those when I get my own business.'

Arthur burst out laughing. 'Yes, and one day pigs will fly!'

But this didn't deter Alex from his dreams. He spoke of nothing else all day, battering his mother's and sisters' ears with the same subject when he arrived home.

It was a long, hot summer, but Alex and his friends never became bored like most children of their age. They played hard and worked hard. Horace's mother had marvelled at the change in her son. At first, like her husband, she had objected to their friendship, but the difference now was nothing short of a miracle. Horace was no longer shy and withdrawn, in fact he was fast becoming something of an extrovert. She had been forced to take him away from his other schools. This had gone on from one school after another, where he had to put up with insults over his father being registered as a conscientious objector to the war. On many occasions she had cried herself to sleep, when Horace had come home from school all battered and bruised, his clothes all ripped. Complaining to the headmasters had only made things worse, so each time she was left with no alternative but to remove her son from school after school. One time when she had complained, the teacher was down right rude to her. But now, after six schools in as many years, Horace was finally settled, and the thanks could only be attributed to Alex and Arthur, although it had to be admitted that some of their actions did give cause for concern. Like the times when she gave him money to attend the local swimming baths, only to find the snow white towel he had taken came back filthy with scum from the canal.

It was almost the end of their summer holidays and as a midweek treat, Alex's mother was taking them into town, she had some business there to attend to. Once there, they would vanish into the town's museum and art gallery. Whilst waiting at the tram stop, the three of them as usual trying to climb the steel standard post which supported the overhead tram cables, a neighbour came staggering along with two white, but badly chipped, enamel buckets. As she set down the buckets beside the steel post they were climbing, the stench hit them like a body blow to a boxer's stomach.

Alex pinched his nose and shouted, 'What a bleeding stink!'

His mother, her face screwed up beyond recognition, looked at the woman, then at the two buckets. Both buckets were covered with a piece of cloth which had sagged in the middle, revealing a thick green scum which had filtered through.

'Bloody hell, Molly, what you got there for heaven's sake?'

'It's me piss, Martha. It's for the 'orspital. Since I had my last kid, my back has been giving me hell. The doctor thinks it's me kidleys. I always have trouble with me kidleys and me waterworks so the doctor sent me to see the specialist at the 'orspital. I'm in agony, Martha, they want me piss to test it.'

To emphasise her suffering, she clenched her fist and pressed it hard into the middle of her back, around the kidney region, distorting her face to display her martyrdom to pain.

'You silly sod, Molly! When they said they wanted a sample, all they want is a small bottle, an old medicine bottle would be more than enough. You don't need all that lot!'

'Look, Martha, it's me piss they wanted and it's me piss they're going to get. I have saved it all up for the last ten days. There should have been a lot more but I ran out of buckets. I was going to bring a couple of piss pots as well but I couldn't carry them, so I'm dumping these at the 'orspital and going back for the piss pots. I can't stop pissing, Martha!'

'Ten days!' gasped Martha. 'Smells like it's been stewing for a month! They'll never let you on the tram with those two buckets.'

'Won't they?' her Irish temper flared. Her red hair, now greying at the sides, glowed like the redness of her face, and although she had left her native Ireland some thirty years previous, the brogue in her voice became more pronounced when she was aroused. 'Won't let me on the tram, eh? Well, we'll see about that!'

The smell was getting worse, as the sun beat down on the buckets, penetrating the air up to twenty yards away. Several intending passengers took one look at the buckets, sniffed, then quickly walked away, thinking it better to walk further up the hill to catch the next tram.

They heard the tram approaching, around the bend a hundred yards up the hill, long before they saw it. The trams were old, but still continued to run despite the numerous complaints from passengers. The tram was late. It rounded the bend in the lines like a racing car, screeching to a halt at the stop. Alex and his friends rushed up to the top deck. It was almost full, but they were lucky, the front seats above the driver were still empty so they could sit there and make-believe they were driving it.

The conductor was standing on the platform, resplendent in his well pressed uniform with polished buttons, his three war medal ribbons proudly displayed on his chest. He blocked Molly's passage.

'What you got there, missus?'

'It's me piss. I have to take it to the 'orspital, they want it.'

She attempted to struggle up the two high steps, but he held up his hand to prevent her from boarding.

Then in a strong sergeant major's voice, he bellowed, 'You are not getting on this vehicle with those two disgusting buckets of piss!'

However, he failed to take into account her Irish temperament.

'I am coming on this tram whether you like it or not, and not you or bloody King George, or the Holy Pope himself, will stop me.' She made the sign of the cross as she mentioned the Pope's name. 'The 'orspital wants me piss and the 'orspital is going to get them, whether you like it or not. I will put them under the stairs.'

'Over my dead body, my lunch is under there. Get off those steps and take the bloody buckets with you. Four years in the trenches and I have never smelt anything like that. Your bloody kidneys must be gangrenous, it smells like a damn sewer!'

'Don't you insult me, you dirty bastard.'

She rolled up her sleeves, but the conductor still insisted she wasn't going to get on the tram. As the argument grew, so did Molly's Irish brogue, laced with the foulest language he had ever heard.

The driver left his platform and walked through the crowded tram.

'What's going on, Jim? All that time I made up has been lost, now we won't get a cup of tea at the terminus.'

'It's this stupid Irish bitch. She wants to bring these two buckets of piss on the tram.'

There must have been something radically wrong with the driver's sense of smell as he sniffed the air and said, 'For Christ's sake, Jim, let her on and let's make up for lost time. We're way behind schedule.'

Reluctantly, at the thought of being denied his cup of tea, he allowed the Irish woman on. She glared at him as she struggled on to the platform. She was about to put the buckets under the winding steel stairs, which lead to the top of the tram, when the conductor made his fatal mistake.

'I don't want the stinking things under there. Take them upstairs.'

She was just half-way up the stairs, when the conductor rang his bell. The driver, already behind time, let go of the brakes and the tram jerked forward, tearing one of the buckets from Molly's hand. The contents were now well and truly stirred. The green phosphates which had sunk to the bottom came to the top and the urine cascaded down the steps like a green waterfall. If the smell had been bad when it was trapped in the bucket, it was nothing compared to the smell now. Passengers rushed from the lower seats holding their noses as the conductor panicked, jabbing at the stop bell.

The passengers crowding onto the platform waiting to get off the minute it stopped were overwhelmed as the tram jerked to a stop. Molly stumbled, which sent the contents of the second bucket tumbling down the stairs as well, most of it covering the passengers and the conductor for a second time.

A young girl in a bright yellow frock, slipped on the contents and landed flat on her back, screaming, 'My God, my frock! It's my sister's and she doesn't know I borrowed it. She'll kill me!' Then she fainted.

Other passengers struggled over the top of her. The conductor, covered from head to foot in the foul smelling urine, kicked the two empty buckets into the gutter.

'Me piss,' she screamed, and kept repeating, 'me piss,' over and over again, as if it was some kind of precious liquid. 'You spilled me fucking piss. I'll kill you, you English bastard!'

She slid halfway down the metal stairs, screaming in agony as the lumbar regions of her spine bounced off the steps. She lashed out at the conductor as she landed on the platform. He grabbed her arms and threw her from the tram, where upon the drenched passengers stood around threatening to lynch her. She tried to scramble back on the tram, but the conductor pushed her off.

'If my missus smelt like you, I would shoot her and put her out of her misery.'

The tram moved away minus its passengers, with the exception of Alex and his friends who sat upstairs right at the front with the windows wide open totally indifferent to the awful smell that permeated every inch of the tram.

The conductor walked down the aisle to the driver.

'It will take gallons of thick disinfectant to get rid of this smell. We can't turn round till we get to the terminus. Buggered if I know what the inspector will say when he sees this lot!'

In all the confusion, Alex's mother didn't realise the three boys were missing till they waved from the top of the tram, wide grins on their faces.

## Chapter Eleven

Christmas was in the air and people were doing their damndest to forget all about the depression for a couple of days, as even the stingiest bosses were forced to give their employees at least two days off - without pay of course. Sitting rooms were decorated with tissue paper cut into strips and glued together with a flour and water paste to make coloured paper chains. This paste was continually drying out, causing the chains to keep breaking, but the occupants took it all in their stride, laughing and cursing at the same time while they made running repairs. In most households presents for the children were out of the question as was the traditional poultry dinner. Some families if they were lucky would get a leg of lamb or a piece of pork.

Christmas to Alex was yet another source of income. He would go carol singing with his friends. This meant singing round the posh houses near the great parks of the city. Posh was the term used for people with small businesses - shops or a small factory that employed two or three people. The houses were usually three up and three down with inside toilets and running water. They would have a pocket handkerchief garden back and front. Those just a cut above the rest might have a small car, such as a baby Austin or the like, parked on a garden path which had been specially widened for the purpose.

'What you doing here, mate?'

Four boys approached them in a threatening manner as Alex and his friends were just about to enter a potential victim's garden.

'This is our pitch. We don't want you kids singing on our pitch.'

'Who says so? We always sing here every year.'

'Well you ain't singing here now. It's our bleeding pitch, so sod off!'

'And what are you going to do about it if we don't sod off?'

When it came to self preservation, Arthur never lacked the guts to stand up for himself and his friends, in spite of his weak nose. He stood face to face with the tallest of the four boys, and could feel the boy's hot breath on his own face. The boy stepped back and with all his strength, punched Arthur smack bang on the nose. Blood came pouring out in a red stream. The boy looked startled to see so much blood.

'Bleeding hell! He's bleeding to death!'

The four of them turned and ran as fast as their feet could carry them, not daring to look back once as they faded into the darkness.

74

The lady of the house came to the door to see what the commotion was all about. She was a very small lady with a bright torch in her hand. She shone it on Arthur's blood covered face and almost fainted. He looked like he had been run over by a bus, not only his face but his shirt and the front of his jersey was saturated with blood.

'You had better come into the house and let me clean you up,' she said, after she had regained her composure. 'How did this happen?'

Arthur had learned to live with this disability and took it all in his stride, but this was the first time anyone had shown any sympathy. He managed to force out some tears as the lady took him into her bathroom and attempted to stem the flow of blood.

'I stumbled, lady, and hit my face on your gatepost. I think I may have damaged the post!'

'Ssh, ssh, never mind the post, it's your nose. The bleeding has stopped now but it's very red. I think you may have broken it. I thought I heard you arguing with some boys. That's why I came out to see what was going on.' She held the damp cloth to his face and cleaned round it. 'Now go straight home to your mother.'

'I can't go yet, lady. I must carry on carol singing, my mom needs the money 'cause my dad's out of work. He came back from the war wounded and he hasn't done a day's work since,' he told her, thinking at the same time that the lazy bugger was unlikely to work while he still had his crowd of scroungers round him.

Arthur's two friends dare not look at the innocent face he put on whilst explaining his predicament in case they burst out laughing. Arthur would have made his mark on the stage.

'What's that lovely smell, lady?'

'It's my turkey, son. I always cook it on Christmas Eve, then in the morning I can get on with my usual housework and preparations for the dinner.'

'It smells lovely, lady. What does it taste like? We have never had turkey. I think my mom has got a little leg of lamb.'

His heart rending story touched the lady's heart. She searched through her purse and gave him a pound note and his two friends a shilling each.

'I don't suppose you will get a turkey with that, but you are sure to get a decent size chicken. How many in your family?'

'I have ten brothers and five sisters.'

He thought he may have overdone it a bit, so he hurriedly stuffed the pound note into his trouser pocket.

Her eyes widened in surprise or perhaps disbelief, but after the initial shock she said, 'My God, where do you all sleep?'

75

She knew the street where he lived and was well aware that they were only two bedroom houses.

'Mom and Dad sleep in the big room with my twin sisters and my other two sisters who have just started school. My other sister sleeps on the landing in a small bed that Dad made. Me and my three brothers sleep in a big bed. Four more sleep in another big bed and my two eldest brothers sleep downstairs, after we have gone to bed.'

The poor lady was speechless, slowly shaking her head as she made mental calculations about the sleeping arrangements. She could hardly believe what she was hearing which was quite understandable as Arthur had almost slipped up as he conjured up his story, tossing the mathematical problem around in his head.

'Your poor mother must have her work cut out.' She made each of them a cup of hot cocoa. 'Now you boys go straight home and get yourselves warm.'

Arthur hesitated at the door and was about to say they didn't have any coal but Alex pushed him forward and whispered, 'Don't you dare.'

The lady stood at the gate and watched them fade into the darkness. When they were out of earshot of the poor woman, Alex said, 'Where the hell did you get that story from? The bloody lies were tripping off your tongue!'

'Well, we got twenty two shillings, didn't we? I knew when she saw my nose, it would be a soft touch.' He probed the tender end of his nose with his fingers and winced. 'Bloody painful, but worth it.'

'I was almost believing you myself,' said Horace. 'I felt like crying. You should start studying for politics. Me dad said all politicians are liars. In your case you should be Prime Minister!'

They sang carols in the next street and by the time they'd finished they were richer by twelve shillings and sixpence each. It would be their last night for carol singing and their best ever. Christmas spirits were running high and those who could afford a penny or two didn't hesitate to hand it over.

The streets were thronged with shoppers, leaving everything to the last minute in the hope that shopkeepers would lower their prices to get rid of their stock. The three of them strolled along the main street looking into windows. They came to a large corner shop with no glass in its windows, leaving the frontage full exposed to the elements, as were the two wide openings that swept round into the next street. Pyramids of shiny apples, oranges, pears and a variety of citrus fruits were displayed inside the shop. In front were rows of sacks full of nuts of every shape and size, the top of the sacking rolled down to display the goods. There were fruit and vegetables of every description. Two young girl assistants and three men were serving, all wearing heavy overcoats over their brown overalls, and fingerless mittens on their hands to keep out the cold. A chill wind was blowing straight through the shop. A sallow faced man with a pinched, bright red nose and eyes that squinted into narrow slits, looked as though he'd been crying, but it was just the effects of the cold wind biting into his face.

'What do you kids want?' He scowled, weighing each one up in turn, and wondering if they were potential customers, or shop lifters. He wasn't too sure, they may have already nicked something.

Arthur pushed himself forward and said, 'A pound of mixed nuts, mister, and my dad said don't put too many coconuts in the bag.'

'Piss off, you smart arsed little bleeder!'

His voice and general attitude told them he was in no mood for their sense of humour. For safety's sake, Arthur took a couple of steps back. It had been a hard day for the man, starting with his usual trip to the wholesale market at six in the morning. It was now nine p.m. and he still had two more hours to go, and in that time his boss was hoping he'd get rid of his entire stock. Alex's eyes fell on a white metal ticket, boldly printed with a sign - one shilling and fourpence - its metal prong stuck up the backside of a plucked and dressed chicken. There were just two left on the marble slab, both looking as cold as the assistants.

'I'll have that chicken, mister.'

'I told you three before, you little perishers, you haven't got that kind of money. I'm in no mood to sod about with you kids. Come on, piss off, there are people waiting to be served!'

Alex dug into this trouser pocket and pulled out a handful of coins, mainly copper with one or two silver ones. The squinting slits of eyes lit up. This would mean he had only one more chicken to worry about, and if the boss saw there was just one left when he arrived for the day's takings, he might let him have it very cheap. He threw the bird on the metal scales, juggling about with the round steel weights, a smile on his face.

'That will be three and fourpence son.' His attitude had changed for the better, but not for long. It soon turned to a scowl when Alex pointed to the discarded metal price tag.

'What do you mean, three and fourpence? It says one shilling and fourpence on the ticket.' He picked it up, and to emphasise his point, held it in front of the man's face. 'Here you are, it says one and fourpence.'

The man now at the end of his tether grabbed the metal ticket and threw it on the marble slab. The queue had grown longer by now.

'You stupid prat.' With his lips curled up, he snarled, 'Haven't you got the brains you were born with? That sign means one shilling and fourpence a pound. Are you bloody well taking the piss or something?'

Alex had the brains all right. Like his two friends, it had been a profitable night and they were in a jovial mood. Not so the crowd, now the cold was biting into their shabby clothes. Some were stamping their feet in a effort to keep out the cold while others were getting very impatient. Alex was laying down the law, with some of the crowd urging him on, whilst a few tried to curry favour with the assistant by siding with him, thinking that with a bit of luck they might get a few coppers knocked off their fruit and vegetables. It was starting to turn into a minor riot, which was only curtailed when a large, black shiny car pulled up outside the shop.

A silence descended on the crowd, as they all turned towards the car. A man wearing a heavy brown camel coat with a fur collar got out. The sweet smell from his expensive cigar filled the air, while the Fedora hat, set at a jaunty angle on his head, pulled down at the front, gave him the look of a Chicago gangster.

The assistant pushed Alex and his two friends aside and ignored the queue.

'Evening, Mr Ferris. Your fruit and veg are all ready.' He signalled to another assistant and shouted, 'Bring Mr Ferris's stuff out, Ernie.'

The man stopped serving his customer and rushed into the storeroom, returning with two small wooden boxes, followed by another young boy carrying a sack of vegetables.

The man looked round at the silent crowd, who were still gaping open-mouthed at him.

'What's going on, Ted?'

'These lads, Mr Ferris, giving me a bloody hard time.' He pointed at Alex, giving him a look of contempt. 'He thinks he's entitled to a chicken for one and fourpence.' He picked up the white enamel metal ticket.

'Ever had a chicken, son?' Mr Ferris ruffled Alex's hair in a kindly fashion.

It was Alex's turn to try out the same acting he'd just witnessed from Arthur. Making a sound like a piece of stale dry bread struggling down his throat, he did an Oliver Twist on Mr Ferris, bowing his head and looking helpless, he shook his head and murmured in a voice just above a whisper, 'No sir.'

The man, with a gesture of generosity, pulled out a well filled wallet and selected a couple of notes. The crowd craned their necks to see what was going on, gasping at the sight of the bulging wallet.

'How much do I owe you, Ted?'

'Four pounds and fifteen shillings.'

The crowd gasped. This man was just buying fruit and veg, but spending as much as most of them would spend feeding their families for a month.

'I put in that box of tangerines, Mr Ferris, and don't worry, I went right through the whole box, everyone was sound.' He gave Mr Ferris a sickly smile.

Mr Ferris gave Ted two white five pound notes. 'Give the lads a chicken each, Ted, and a pound's worth of fruit. Keep the rest for yourself and your staff. Cheerio, Ted, have a nice Christmas.'

Ted ran to the car, held the door open, and touched his forelock.

'Well, lads, I only have two chickens left. One of you will have to make do with some more fruit.' The assistant's attitude had done a complete somersault.

Horace said he would have the extra fruit as his dad had already bought a goose.

'You are lucky perishers. That was Mr Ferris. He was born round here. Started a small factory just before the war and never looked back. One thing about Mr Ferris, he never forgot his roots. Comes here every week for his greens and fruit. I dunno why, he lives out at Bournville in one of those big houses. He has plenty of servants and if he chose to he wouldn't need to lift a finger. From here he goes to the butcher's. My boss, Mr Ferris, and the butcher, all went to school together. After doing his shopping, he takes a drive down his old street. No airs and graces with Mr Ferris; never too proud to tell people where he was born.'

Alex couldn't take his eyes off the red rear lights of the car as it disappeared down the road giving fuel to his ambition. 'So there is a way out of here,' he thought to himself and said out loud, 'One day, I will have a big car like that, and a big house with electric lights, and a real bathroom. No pissing factory for me!' That night he went home determined more than ever that he would get away from the filthy, bug ridden slums.

The night was far from over. Everyone seemed in the jolliest of moods, the noise from the pubs was overwhelming with still another half an hour before closing time. That's when the fun really started, as the drunks beat a crooked path to their respective homes, sometimes to be met by their wife poised behind the door with some hard object in her hand. This would be the only time she was able to get her own back, when he was drunk out of his mind. After all, it was two days off work for which they wouldn't be paid. This meant a short week so most of them would rather have been at work. Still no good worrying, instead they just drown their sorrows in drink.

The butcher's window was all lit up. Rows of pigs' heads were neatly arranged along the front of the window, each picked for its size and displaying a polished red apple in its mouth. The three boys stood there, admiring the window.

'Why the red apple, Alex? They're dead, they can't eat them!' A wide grin spread over Arthur's face. 'Let's go inside and have a bit of fun.'

He selected a silver three pence piece from his pocket and went inside, followed by his two friends. Arthur's humour could be very dry at times. He sounded as polite as he possibly could, a solemn expression on his face, though this couldn't cover up the half-starved look that was always present.

'Excuse me, mister, could I have a pig's head for me mom?'

The butcher was a large, rotund man with a bloated red face. He wore a straw boater on his head set at a jaunty angle, with a blue and white striped apron tied around his ample girth. A smile spread across his red bulbous face as he looked at Arthur. Arthur stepped back. He didn't like the look of the razor sharp cleaver the butcher held in his hand, and shuddered as he thought twice about cheeking the butcher, but the man looked jovial enough.

'What's it for, son? Your mom want to make some brawn?'

'No, sir.' He shook his head innocently and with a straight face said, 'It's for our Christmas dinner. There are ten kids in our family and my dad is out of work.'

The fat butcher turned to his young assistant, a boy of sixteen with a bad case of acne and one finger that was constantly prodding his nose. He ordered him into the cold room at the back of the shop.

'Go and find the lad a pig's head, Charlie. The biggest one we've got, and for heaven's sake take your bloody finger out of your nose. If you had any brains you would poke them out.' He turned to Arthur again. 'How many brothers and sisters did you say you had, son?'

'No sisters, sir, all brothers; ten of them. I heard my dad tell my mom she was going to get it again. He said he wants his own football team.'

'Bleeding hell!' The fat butcher almost exploded and his assistant, thinking it was a huge joke, burst out laughing as he threw the large pig's head on the thick wooden table. When he had said find the biggest head in stock, he wasn't kidding. It was almost as big as a cow's head.

The butcher stroked it with pride and wondered why he hadn't selected it for his window display. He slapped the head with pride again and said, 'There you are, son, give me sixpence and I'll put it in a carrier bag.'

Arthur shook his head, almost crying by now, 'It's no good, sir, my mom won't have that one.'

Looking astounded the butcher asked, 'Why not, son? It's the biggest head in the shop.' He slapped it on the scales. The needle spun round and round. 'That should be at least three shillings, I was doing you a favour.'

Arthur had edged closer to the door with his two friends.

'My mom told me to get a pig's head and told me to tell you to leave its bleeding tail on!'

He grabbed the bag containing the chicken and fruit, and the three of them ran from the shop.

The butcher shouting after them, 'You saucy little buggers. I'll chop your bleeding heads off.'

He turned to the assistant who was doubled up with laughter, holding his stomach with one hand and using the other one to support himself against the door-jamb.

'And you can stop that laughter or your bleeding head will be on display in the shop window after Christmas!' He wiped the sweat from his forehead. 'And no doubt you will still have your finger planted up that nose.'

He brought down the cleaver as hard as possible, burying its razor sharp blade some two inches into the wooden chopping block.

# Chapter Twelve

There were two things you could be certain of in the slums of the great city, a decent send off when you died and a great knees up at a wedding. The world and his wife turned up whether they had been invited or not. A wedding usually meant a real free booze-up. For weeks Martha had been buying either two bottles of beer or a bottle of cheap wine, neither of which she could hardly afford. Sometimes Alex helped her out and Harry ordered two barrels of beer from the pub where the reception was to be held.

Everyone turned up for a funeral, if only to prove to themselves that there was at least one person worse off than themselves. But even then, there would be someone in the crowd who would say, 'Lucky bastard, at least their worries are over!' Then cough blood into his or her handkerchief and wait their turn. Someone might then remark about the contents of their own pine box. Nevertheless, come funerals or weddings, life still had to go on.

The great day arrived. It was the wedding of the year, with an open landau transporting the bride, all dressed in white, along with her two bridesmaids, Karen looking as beautiful as ever and Polly, sitting demurely beside her.

A woman nudged her neighbour. 'She had to get rid of a kid, you know.'

'Who, the bride? And her dressed in white too.' she replied with a disgusted look on her face.

'No, the young one, Polly. Old Mrs Baker got rid of it for her. They say that dirty, fat bastard, Wally Hunter put her up the spout. You know, Martha went round for a showdown. Made old man Hunter pay up for Mrs Baker's services and Polly's loss of earnings for a couple of months.'

'Get away!'

'Yes, and that's not the half of it.' She was about to carry on with more street gossip, but just then the carriage passed. Her face changed to a sickly smile as she shouted, 'Good luck, Helen.' Then to her neighbour, 'I shall be watching her belly for the next few months. Being married in white don't mean much these days.'

The church was crowded. Harry had gathered a few distant relations. Some he hadn't seen for years but like the rest of the local populous they were there tempted by the thought of free booze and a meal in the offing. His own mother was much too feeble to attend, although a few friends from the undertakers had turned up, along with his boss, and his wife who was giving Harry a condescending smile as she sat behind him near the altar. The usual whispered jokes flew around the church. Helen's family and friends sat on the opposite side of the church. A distant uncle was giving her away. Alex and his friends were warned at the last minute to be on their best behaviour. To keep them occupied and out of trouble they were instructed to act as ushers.

The vicar rubbed his hands in satisfaction. It had been a long time since he had seen his church so full. The only time he witnessed such large congregations was at Christmas. Hopefully, this should yield a profitable collection. Perhaps, during the service, he would subtly let it be known that the church roof was in a bad state of repair. He might go so far as to let the organist play a couple of bum notes just to remind them that the organ had seen better days.

Alex and his friends were handed large, silver trays, but if the result of Alex's collection was anything to go by, the vicar was in for a rude awakening. It consisted of a shilling's worth of coppers, a worn down silver three penny piece, the inevitable trouser button and a couple of German copper coins. The vicar shook his head in disgust as he peered over the top of his glasses which were perched on the end of his nose. His audience was subdued, much too embarrassed to look directly at him. That was except for Arthur's father, who wore a satisfied smirk on his face, pleased in the knowledge that he had at last got rid of those German coins, he had tried every cigarette machine in the city.

The room over the pub was large, covering both the saloon and public bars downstairs. It was the only pub in the area that boasted a small stage along with an ancient piano in one corner. Ancient was the only way to describe it, with two ornamental brass candlesticks, one on either side of the marquetry panelled front. The keys could only be likened to a mouthful of rotten teeth, and covered in black cigarette burns. The only thing that could be said in the piano's favour was that it was tuned to perfection, having been well maintained by a blind piano tuner who was kept well supplied with beer by the pub manager.

Old Joe Masters was invited, as he always was to everyone's wedding, he could play the piano like a true professional. Although unable to read a note of music, there wasn't a tune he didn't know or, if in any doubt, he would ask someone to whistle a few bars and would then carry on from there. Before starting, he took out his false teeth and put them in his top pocket. Then with his jaws clamped together so that half his chin vanished, he ran the back of his hands along the keyboard. He played on and on, only slowing momentarily to a one handed melody, whilst he took a long drink from his special glass with a handle, which was standing on the top of the piano, constantly topped up.

'Joe plays a lot better when he's pissed,' said a fat woman, talking to no one in general and patting old Joe on the back. She winked at a man sitting near her whom she'd never seen before, guessing he must be one of the groom's friends or relatives.

'He always takes his teeth out. He went home once and puked, leaving his teeth in a pool of vomit up somebody's entry, and nearly lost them. His missus had to go and sort them out the next morning.'

Mrs Webb took the stage. Old Joe didn't ask the tune, he knew exactly what it was. He ran through the introduction of 'I dreamt I dwelt in marble halls.' She had a passable voice, and a respectful silence fell over the room. Arthur couldn't take his eyes off her breasts as they heaved up and down, as she reached for the high notes. As Mrs Webb left the stage, Arthur's father staggered up, unsteady on his feet and waving a half empty glass. He tripped over the stage, but managed not to spill one drop of the precious contents. Two of his boozing cronies rushed to his aid. Staggering to his feet, he held up his hand in the smoke filled room and mumbled something in old Joe's ear.

'Trust my old man to get into a party where there's free booze going,' said Arthur, spitting the words out to show contempt for his father.

He swayed on the stage and held up his hand once again for silence, then dropped it to his side. 'I'll sing a song we boys sang in the trenches the night before we went over the top.' He stumbled against old Joe. 'Play Joe, play, play - 'Keep the Home Fires Burning.'

Apart from a few rough edges, he had a reasonable voice. Crocodile tears rolled down his beer stained face, as the crowd joined in, softly at first. The Great War was still very fresh in people's minds and, before the second chorus finished, most of the elder people were dabbing their eyes. As the song finished, he collapsed into a heap on the stage floor.

'That's my old man making a prat of himself,' said Arthur, not making a move to help him to his feet. He had seen it happen time and time again, especially when there was free booze on offer. 'Just look at him. It's not nine o'clock yet. Just 'cause the booze is free he has to go and make a pig of himself!'

It didn't take long for Alex to take advantage of the situation. Most of the adults were doing a knees up and singing their hearts out, so no one noticed him and his pals vanish for a few minutes, taking back the empty beer bottles to the various pubs thereabouts. In their district there was a pub on virtually every street corner, and with a penny deposit on each bottle, they soon made a few shillings - that was before the pub manager caught them sneaking out, their pockets bulging with empty bottles.

The party started breaking up at midnight.

'Come and give me a hand to get your father home, Arthur. He's pissed as a newt.'

'He's been drunk since nine o'clock, Mom. Let the drunken sod find his own way home.' But watching his mother struggle to get his father to his feet was too much. 'Let him go, Mom. Me and Alex will get him home.'

They each took an arm and hoisted him to his feet, then walked him home.

'Have you noticed, Alex? The crafty old sod hasn't got a limp when he thinks no one is looking at him. If I had my way, I'd leave him in the entry till he sobers up.'

Next day was Sunday. Karen and Polly had a lay in. It was almost midday by the time they eventually sat down to breakfast when there was a loud knock on the door. They looked at each other wondering who was going to answer it. Whoever it was there, it couldn't be a close neighbour because they would have just walked in. It had been a long night and both of them were still undressed with just a coat over them. There was another loud knock. Cautiously, their mother got to her feet and opened the door a crack. Her mouth dropped open. At first, she didn't recognise the soldier standing there, resplendent in his blue walking out uniform. Two gold stripes adorned his arm and his shoes were so shiny you could use them as mirrors.

'Why, Mr Kingsley.'

His wife was clinging to his arm.

'Good heavens, fancy seeing you two here.'

She shook hands with him and put her arm round his wife's shoulder. Karen and Polly, on hearing a man's voice, knew their mother would invite them in. She never failed to invite everyone inside her house. They both vanished upstairs, leaving their half finished breakfasts on the table. Mr Kingsley lowered his head to come through the doorway, steering his wife in before him.

Seeing the half finished breakfasts he said, 'I hope we didn't come at an inopportune moment.'

'Don't be silly, you're always welcome. I was just a bit taken aback when I saw you both standing there, and you back in uniform. What happened?'

He lowered his voice to a whisper. 'You know I had that trouble, well they released me early. Said it was for good behaviour, but I think my old C.O. had something to do with it. I met you in the Bull Ring that day. You hadn't seen the wife for a while, but you thought she was living in Aston. When I found her, she burst out crying. She had been shacked up with some fellow. I didn't blame her for that. She needed someone, and he was very good to her. A nice quiet, decent fellow. We all went back to where they were living and acted civilised. It was no use losing our tempers.' A humorous glint came into his eyes. 'He was a lot smaller than me. He looked after my Nora and she didn't want to hurt him, so we thought it best to leave Brum and took off for London. We only had a few bob between us. A lorry driver gave us a lift. He even shared his sandwiches with us, before dropping us off at the Embankment in London. We lived rough for a few days.'

'I got a job carrying those billboards around. It wasn't a lot of money and one day, I was passing this recruiting office. It was an old shop with all the army adverts in the window, so I stopped to look at the posters, when the recruiting sergeant came out. It was my best friend from my army days in India. He had a word with the recruiting officer and they let us sleep in an empty room above the shop. He found us a couple of old army beds and blankets. It was a lot better than the Embankment. He must have asked around, 'cause one day our old C.O. turned up. One thing lead to another. He pulled a few strings; he had a bit of influence in the War Office. I would have loved to rejoin my old regiment but that was out of the question. My old C.O. must have had a few words in my new C.O's ear 'cause after six months I had two stripes. It's likely I'll be a sergeant before very long. The regiment is off to Egypt shortly.' He smiled down at his wife. 'We're looking forward to that. I don't think anyone minded me getting back into the army. They're taking on recruits as fast as possible. With this bloke Hitler, I wouldn't be surprised to see the world at war again.'

She didn't ask them if they wanted tea. She just took it for granted and passed them a cup each. Mrs Kingsley looked surprised. The last time she was in the house, none of the cups had handles and all were either cracked or chipped.

Martha saw the look on her face and laughed, 'Don't worry, Mrs Kingsley. Alex works on the china stall in the market, he also sells china.'

'Your Alex was always a smart lad, Mrs Edwards.'

'Yes, but it does worry me a bit. He's always working. He didn't get away from the wedding last night till after midnight, and then him and his mate Arthur helped someone to do a moonlight flit. Every Saturday he's up at six to go down the market. He don't get home till ten at night.' She looked through the window. 'Here he comes now.'

The door burst open and Alex sat down at the table before he realised that Mr Kingsley and his wife were sitting on the old sofa.

'Why, Mr Kingsley, how are you?'

'Fine, Alex. Haven't you made that first million yet? Ever thought of joining the army, Alex. We need lads like you. Make a nice drummer boy.'

'No thanks, Mr Kingsley. It must be a great life seeing all those different places, but I want my own business. I don't want to stay in this place all my life.'

'I suppose when we get back from Egypt in six years time, you will be a millionaire. How old are you now, Alex?'

'It won't be for the want of trying, Mr Kinglsey. I'm thirteen now. I leave school next year.'

They stayed for over an hour, talking over old times. Alex's mother didn't mind, but Karen and Polly didn't take it too kindly. What was left of their breakfast had now solidified into a greasy blob. Their mother made a fresh pot of tea.

'I thought they'd never go,' said Karen as she sipped her tea, 'we both fell asleep upstairs.'

'Is it any wonder? You didn't get to bed till almost two.'

Polly looked at Karen, a mischievous glint in her eye.

'I bet it was much later than two before our Helen got to sleep.' And they both burst out laughing, till their mother stopped them with a withering look.

Alex had another flitting job on that night with Arthur. It should have been done the night before, but he already had one on and he didn't start that till after the wedding. Tenants always flitted at the weekends. It gave them time to get as far away as possible, before the landlord or agent called on Monday. Alex went to see the man in the afternoon, to demand his two shillings. The man promised to pay them when the job was completed but Alex refused this offer.

'Sorry, mate. I want the two bob now. It's a bloody long way to Summers Lane, and me and my mate ain't pushing those barrows for sod all.'

'Bleeding hell, don't you trust me?'

Alex shook his head and gave the man an emphatic no. 'The landlord trusted you and now you're running out on him. Why should I trust you? I want my two bob now.'

He threw the man a contemptuous look. One thing his mother had taught him was to be honest and pay your way as you go. His mother had gone through every hardship imaginable, struggling to bring up four children with no support from her sick husband, but two things she'd never done were fail to pay her rent or make a meal of some kind for her children. Fortunately, she was a dab hand at making a nourishing meal in her large saucepan. Give her a few scraps of meat from the butcher's, two penny worth of mixed vegetables, and a lump of suet, and she could rustle up the best stew and dumplings you ever tasted. Now here was this man, standing before him, who could smoke a packet of fags a day, spend an evening in the pub, where he was regularly thrown out for being drunk, yet he couldn't manage to keep a roof over his family's head.

Alex watched as he took a handful of coins from his pocket and counted them out, a pleading look on his face as he said to Alex, 'I've only got one and eightpence, Alex. Can I give you the other fourpence on Saturday next week? You do realise of course that you are taking the bread from my kids mouths?'

'Come off it, mate. That one and eightpence was for your booze tonight. If your kids didn't have school dinners, they'd bloody starve to death!'

'You cheeky bugger. You can't talk to me like that. What the hell do you know about my family?'

'The whole neighbourhood knows. Don't get giving me that crap or any sob story. It's two bob or shift your own gear.'

He went to hand the money back, but the man shook his head. He was very near panic. Alex felt sorry, not for him, but for his wife. If he didn't move tonight or if he didn't have a couple of pints, he would punch her round the house.

'You're a right bloody Shylock. What synagogue do you go to, bloody little Sheeney?'

'Nothing wrong with the Jews, mate, at least they pay their way. You don't see them sitting in pubs pissing it up. Come on, mate, another fourpence or the stuff stays where it is.'

'Honest, Alex, that's all the money I have till I draw my dole next Friday.'

To emphasise his point, he turned his trousers pockets inside out. He was pleading. Any minute now, Alex felt he would start crying.

'I'm desperate Alex, the landlord is going to sue me and there is no way I can pay. I will end up in the nick. You know what my temper is like. If they send in the bums, I'll put one on them.'

Alex softened, not for his sake, he hated the sight of him, but his wife and kids would be the ones to suffer if he was banged up. The man was a rat bag. Alex went to school with one of his sons, and he hated his own father.

'Tell you what I'll do, mate. I'll take the one and eightpence for now, but when I come round Saturday for the fourpence I want another tuppence interest as well. If I don't get it I'll tell the landlord where you have flitted to.'

'Why you lousy little perisher, that stinks of blackmail. Don't worry, you'll get your sodding money.'

'It's not blackmail, it's looking after my interests.' Alex pocketed the money. 'I'll be round your house just after dark. Get it all ready and me and Arthur will bring the barrows.'

He could see the man was quite prepared to continue with the argument, so he turned his back on him and walked away.

He was still within earshot when the man shouted, 'Bleeding perisher, you will never starve!'

'I don't intend to, mate. I saw Mrs Tanner starve to death. Me and my family never will.'

# Chapter Thirteen

Karen blossomed into womanhood, hating every minute she had to spend in her squalid surroundings. She would readily have moved into a rented room of her own, but now that Helen was married she knew her mother needed every penny to keep the family from starvation. To leave now would be a bitter blow, although her mother frequently told her it was time she got married and settled down.

'One of these days, Karen, you will find yourself fancied by that boss of yours.'

Karen burst out laughing. 'You must be joking, Mom. He's sixty and married to one of the sweetest ladies you could wish to know. No, Mom, when I do marry it will be to someone I love. I have seen too much misery around these parts to choose a man just as a sleeping partner.'

She stood in front of a pock-marked mirror, making final adjustments to her blonde hair, which was her pride and joy. A frown furrowed her brow. Marriage was right. Was she setting her her sights too high? She was twenty-one now. Many girls from her area were married at twenty-one with a couple of kids. Perhaps she should start looking. There was that manager of the tool room, not a bad looking chap and one of the highest paid on the factory floor. He had made it clear more than once that he wouldn't mind taking her out, and several times she'd see him watching her from the corner of his eye as she walked through the tool room. Perhaps not, he gambles a lot and she couldn't make up her mind which was worse, a gambler or a drinker, with plenty of both in this street.

Perhaps she should wait. Young Alex was already standing on his own two feet and not fourteen yet. Sometimes he gave his mother as much for the family budget as Polly, and some weeks almost as much as herself. She smiled, there's a lad who'll never starve. She had taken a sneaky look in the Oxo tin, under the floorboards. It wasn't such a secret as Alex thought, although she had been amazed at it contents. She would most likely have fainted if she had also found out how much he had in the school bank and the Post Office Savings Bank.

'Your hair looks nice, Karen,' said Alex as he came into the room and watched her admire herself in the mirror. Alex didn't throw his compliments round often.

'Sorry, Alex, I can't lend you any money. I don't get paid till tomorrow.'

He laughed and emptied his pocket of coins onto the tablecloth and, sorting them into their appropriate values, he began counting. She watched him in the mirror. He looked like some miniature miser.

'How much you got there, Alex?'

'Just over five bob.' He emptied five shillings worth of copper into a blue paper money bag from the bank.

The door flew open and Horace rushed in all excited. He pulled a thick book from under his pullover.

'Look at this, Alex. I bought if from the second-hand book shop. Jane's Fighting Ships. He wanted a shilling for it but settled for nine pence.'

His excitement was infectious. Alex moved in closer to him and Karen looked over his shoulder.

'It gives the names of all the fighting ships including the foreign ones.'

But as far as he was concerned, the latter held no interest. He was calling out all the British ships listed under the letter 'R'.

'Rodney, Repulse, Revenge, and look at this one.' He flicked the pages over. 'This is the Hood, the greatest battleship in the world. Just look at those guns, Alex. Here's one named after our town, H.M.S. Birmingham.' He looked at it lovingly and held it at arms length. 'I would love to get on that one, Alex.'

His mind was miles away - sailing out of Portsmouth Harbour towards Spithead. He had never visited that port but there wasn't a thing he didn't know about it. He put the book down slowly on the table still staring into space as if in a trance.

'I think I'll go in the signals branch. I fancy that.'

'Bloody hell, Horace, make your mind up. Last week you wanted to be a stoker. The week before that a gunner, then a torpedo man. Make your mind up and stop living in a dream world. Your old man won't sign any papers so it doesn't matter.'

This brought Horace from his trancelike state. It was true, he knew his father would never sign his papers, for his father wouldn't even allow him to bring any naval books into the house, and the mere mention of enlisting sent him into a terrible rage.

'I'll get into the Navy somehow, Alex.' He started to whistle 'All the nice girls love a sailor.'

For months, Horace haunted the recruiting office. He and the recruiting officer were on first name terms. This was his last term at school. His father already had a position in mind for him, but just the thought of working in that filthy factory filled Horace with dread.

Alex and Arthur left school a couple of terms later. The three of them were celebrating their last year at school, with Horace waiting for the day he could join the Navy. Arthur was impatient to leave so he could get a job, and be old enough and big enough to punch his old man on the nose next time he hit his mother. Alex was waiting for the day he could leave school and get down to making some real money.

It was also the year they became mobile. Horace's father bought his son a cycle to appease him.

'It's a shilling a week, Horace. You can start paying me when you start at the factory.'

Horace had been brimming over with excitement of the prospect of getting a bike. Now the old man had put a damper on it by mentioning the factory. Horace should have known better. His father never did anything without some motive behind it. On the other hand, his father taught not only him to ride, but also gave Arthur and Alex instructions. He knew they would only try behind his back, so better he taught them how to handle a bike the right way.

Alex also knew he had to get mobile. The thrill of speeding along at five to ten miles an hour filled him with enthusiasm. He had heard rumours of green fields outside the city limits, some ten or fifteen miles away. He waited for his sisters and mother to go out, then lifted up the floorboard to get at his Oxo tin. It was overflowing, mostly with coppers. He counted out thirty shillings. Rather extravagant, but he knew he must have a cycle.

The cycle shop was on his way to the market. He'd seen several cycles hanging on hooks outside, all second-hand, renovated but in very good condition. Alex went inside. A man was kneeling down mending a cycle behind the counter.

'That B.S.A. tourer hanging outside, mister, thirty bob is it?'

The man didn't bother to look up. Not a day passed without a schoolboy day-dreamer visiting the shop. He removed the cigarette butt from his mouth, leaving a black greasy mark on his lips.

'That's what it says, son, that's the price.' He put the black butt back in his mouth.

'Take twenty-eight, mate? I have the twenty-eight shillings in my pocket.'

The man shook his head, and through a haze of smoke said, 'Nope.'

'I can pay, mister.' He rattled the coins in his pocket.

The man spat the cigarette butt to the floor. 'Nope.' He didn't take his eyes off the cycle he was repairing. 'This here is a real bike. A good solid tourer. Almost new.' He stood up. He was quite tall, standing well over six foot. Over the years the grease from the cycles had become engrained in his skin giving it a grubby appearance, making it look like he was sorely in need of a good scrub. He eyed Alex up and down a few times. 'Give me another tanner and you can ride the bike away.'

There was a determined look on Alex's face. The man knew he couldn't squeeze him for thirty shillings. Alex had developed the face of a poker player, the dealer hesitated, these were very hard times and he had only paid ten bob for the bike from some unfortunate man who needed a meal for his family. He had beaten the man down from the fifteen shillings he had been asking. A good clean up, the paint work polished, a touch of enamel here and there, and a few gold lines done with a steady hand, had brought the bike up almost like new.

'You're a hard bugger, son. Give me your twenty-eight shillings.'

Arthur had no intention of being left out of the cycle excursion they planned for the following Sunday. He had no bike and very little chance of getting one. If Alex could be described as poor, this was nothing compared to the poverty Arthur lived in. What little pension his father brought in went on booze and the horses. When he was sober, he was constantly looking for sympathy for his gunshot wound from the war but everyone knew it was self-inflicted and that only a sympathetic M.O. had prevented him being court martialled: His mother did a little cleaning, but that was barely enough to provide a couple of meals for the family. The only other income was from his elder brother and two sisters, all of whom were on starvation wages. But his elder brother did have a cycle. It was a case of paying one and sixpence a week to the tally man for the bike, being cheaper than the two shillings a week tram fares to reach his work place on the other side of the city.

Saturday night after they had finished their market job, they assembled in Alex's room to decide where to cycle to.

'Let's go to the Lickey Hills, there's a fair up there.'

The Lickey Hills, situated on the outskirts of Birmingham in the direction of Bromsgrove, was a popular place for picnics and days out. They were also famous for their walks, and well known by many a courting couple.

'Not the Lickey Hills, Alex. Let's go out to Stratford-on-Avon. See if we can see old Billy Shakespeare and his missus. Who knows, they might invite us to tea.'

'You'll be lucky, he's been dead four hundred years. His arse must be cold by now.'

'Shame, he was showing promise. Our teacher read us a bit from Hamlet the other day. I didn't understand all of it, but what part I did, I liked.'

'All right Arthur, you and your Shakespeare. You can't come anyway, you haven't got a bike.'

'Our brother has one, I'll borrow his. If we get off at seven like you say he won't know. He doesn't get up till twelve on Sunday, and by that time we'll be half way there.'

'He'll kill you when you get back. I heard him tell you if he ever caught you on his bike he'd cut your balls off!'

'So what? He'll have to catch me first. Anyway, he's seeing that tart of his. She's sleeping on the sofa downstairs. He doesn't get to bed till after midnight, so he'll be fast asleep when I leave the house.'

Horace was already waiting, sitting on his saddle with one foot on the kerb. Hardly a sound could be heard. What few birds ventured into the city, mostly pigeons and sparrows, were lined up on the roofs of the houses.

'I'm only giving him ten minutes, Horace. I bet his brother has locked his bike up.'

Alex looked down the deserted street then checked his tyres.

'Don't worry, Alex, here he comes now.'

Arthur was pedalling like mad on his brother's new Raleigh cycle, the chrome glinting in the early morning sunlight which shafted between the houses. He skidded to a halt beside them, leaving a black tyre mark on the road and the smell of burning rubber in the air. He was out of breath.

'Very nearly didn't make it, Alex. My brother's girlfriend, who was sleeping on the sofa, woke up just as I was pushing the bike through the door. She started shouting for my brother, lousy cow that she is!'

'Well, we'd better get moving now. Here he comes.'

His brother was tearing up the road, shirtless and holding his trousers up with one hand shouting, almost screaming, 'Come here with my bike, you little bastard! I'll kill you!'

The once silent street came alive. Bedroom windows flew open and the neighbours craned their necks to see who the hell was disturbing the peace so early in the morning. Sunday was the only day of the week they had a chance to lay in. Arthur, impervious to his brother's threats, shoved up his two fingers and started pedalling furiously, leaving his irate brother standing in the middle of the street waving his clenched fist at the departing cyclists.

What little traffic that passed didn't bother them as they pedalled serenely along the almost deserted roads. By ten the sun was boiling hot and they were sweating profusely.

They sat on the river bank at Stratford, stripped to the waist. Arthur hadn't brought any lunch with him because he'd left in

94

such a hurry, so they shared their own packed lunches with him. Contented, they lay back lapping up the sunshine. Birds sang in the trees. A man nearby had brought a small portable gramophone with a limited number of records. His favourite must have been 'Lazybones' because he played it over and over again. Men in punts, their girlfriends draped over the bows, drifted lazily by, while men on skiffs were showing off, seeing how fast they could row. There were children in canoes paddling by. It was an idyllic setting - that was until Arthur complained about the heat.

A small crowd had gathered on the bridge carrying the traffic over the main road. They were leaning on the bridge rails watching the boating fraternity.

'Couldn't half do with a swim, Alex. Wish I'd brought a cossie.'

'Go for a swim if you like. Just wear your underpants,' said Horace, laying on his back and staring up at the sun filtering through the leaves of a tree creating a mosaic of green and gold.

'Underpants?' Arthur sounded bewildered. 'Underpants? My old lady can't afford top pants, never mind underpants! I'll go in the nuddy.'

'Go on, I dare you,' Alex and Horace said in unison, jolting upright together.

Since his pubic hairs had started to grow, Arthur had become a little self conscious, but he put on a brave front.

'Don't worry about me, if I want a swim in the nuddy I shall have one.'

He hesitated again as the last bit of his apparel, his shorts, was about to come off. He undid the top button, and looked at the crowds picnicking along the banks of the river. He estimated the distance between himself and the water, six strides would do it. Then, without warning and in quick succession, he undid the remaining buttons, turned, and fled to the waters edge, diving head first into two feet of water. His bottom stuck out pointing skywards. A few seconds later, he surfaced his face covered in weeds and mud.

Alex and Horace nearly bust a gut laughing, and the picnickers roared. Those who had witnessed him enter the water hadn't quite got over the shock of seeing him in the nude. Those with small girls, had covered their little darlings' eyes, or pulled their daughters towards them, crushing them to their bosoms.

Always the ham actor, Arthur took a bow and struck out into deeper water, turning on his back and floating downstream with the placid current, his penis sticking up like a submarine's periscope.

There was a loud shout from the opposite bank. A red faced policeman was pushing a cycle along the towpath, a helmet perched on his head which, like the cycle, looked two sizes too small for him. He pointed his finger at Arthur, shouting all kinds of threats.

'Get out of that water, you horrible little boy, and get some decent clothes on. I'll be marching you down the police station.'

Arthur's response to this command was to roll over point his bottom in the air, roll over again and stick up two fingers. This, all amidst cheers from the picnickers. More people ran to the water's edge to see what was going on, and the main bridge was thronged with spectators. Arthur never worried about the outcome. He had an audience and he loved it. He swam towards his two friends.

'Take my clothes along the towpath till the copper gets fed up, then I'll get out.'

Horace rode along holding the Raleigh with one hand and steering his own bike with the other. Alex carried the bundle of clothes. The policeman's tactics changed. These were no local lads, these were city boys. Instead of pursuing them on the opposite path, he hailed two young men in a rowing boat.

'Try and get that damned swimmer. I want him out of the water.'

'We only hired the boat for an hour, constable. Our time is almost up.'

'Damn the time. I want that little sod out of the water. Now come on, pull for all you're worth.'

He stepped unsteadily into the boat. It rocked dangerously as he squatted in the middle. It was easy to see it was the first time the two men had taken to the water. In their excitement to get away from the shore, one of them dug too deeply into the mud with his oar. The boat shot out at an acute angle, slanting on its side. The policeman pushed down hard in a vain attempt to right it, but the weight of water pushed the boat down further and it sank in the middle of the river. Both rowers and the policeman were forced to swim for their lives.

By now, Arthur was safely back on dry land with his shorts and shirt on. The crowd was in an uproar. Without waiting for an encore, amidst claps and cheers from the crowd, the three of them pedalled like mad for the main road.

'That's us finished with Stratford. Our first day's outing on our bikes and we're already barred from the town. I bet if the sergeant had his way, he would have posters of us stuck up all over town - 'Wanted, Dead or Alive!'

Two miles on, Alex pulled off the road. 'We ain't out of the woods yet. In our hurry to get out of town, we've taken the wrong bloody road. We ain't heading towards Brum, we're going in the opposite direction towards Banbury and Oxford. We'll have to turn back and head the other way. The sergeant won't be there now, but I bet his mates will be on the look out for three cyclists. Let's go back one at a time. Ten minutes between each one. Horace is the only one with a watch so he'll have to time us.'

They all met up again under the viaduct that carried the canal barges over the road, a few miles north of Stratford going towards Birmingham. Well out of danger, the three of them burst out laughing.

On their return, Arthur's brother was waiting for them at the bottom of the yard, brandishing a broom handle in his hand. Arthur spotted him first and stopped.

'Christ, it's our kid.' He laid the bike on its side and started running in the opposite direction shouting, 'He'll kill me.'

That was exactly what his brother had in mind, as he chased Arthur, waving the broom handle and shouting all kinds of obscenities.

'Don't you dare come home, you little bastard!'

He brought the broom handle down hard on some iron railings with such a force that it broke in half.

'That's what I'll do to your neck when I catch you!'

Arthur retaliated by cupping his hands and shouting, 'Get a shave, shit face!'

There was no love lost between Arthur and his brother. Bringing up a large family in crowded surroundings, five to a room and in some cases three to a bed, brought out the worst in them. However, three to a bed in the winter was not only tolerable, but an absolute necessity as most of the bedclothes had generally made their way to the pawn shop. In the summer it was another matter. In a closed room with windows that wouldn't open, it was sheer hell.

His brother Ernie walked up and down the room, peering through the windows every time he heard footsteps.

'I'll kill him, I'll kill him!' He kept repeating over and over, 'Just wait till I get my hands on him, I'll kill him.'

His father was incapable of settling the matter as he lived in a permanent daze, his brain befuddled with booze. When his wife appealed for his help, he just grinned, 'Let them sort it out themselves.'

Alex and his family were sitting down to supper. There was a tap on the door. It opened slightly and Arthur's head peered round grinning.

'Can I sleep here tonight, Mrs Edwards?' he asked.

Karen and Polly burst out laughing.

'You haven't seen your brother then, Arthur?'

'I'm still alive ain't I, Karen?' He looked back down the yard. It was deserted, no one had followed him. 'Yes, but it was worth it. Seeing the lovely countryside and Stratford-On-Avon, and swimming in the river. Better than the dirty canal, eh Alex? You should have seen the beautiful flowers on the hedges, nearly all a bright yellow, and the cows grazing in the fields. Cows don't graze in Brum, Karen!'

'Thinking of becoming a farmer then, Arthur?' asked Polly.

'He couldn't be a farmer near Stratford that's for certain. I bet that police sergeant would get him hanged. You should have seen this copper, Karen. He was a big fat bloke and when he came up from the river his face was covered in green moss. If I could have stopped laughing, I would have felt sorry for him. I liked Stratford but it looks like we're barred from there now.'

'Never mind, Arthur, there's plenty of other places to go,' said Karen to console him.

Alex's mother informed Arthur's mother of his whereabouts, so she wouldn't worry any further, the argument had already taken toll on her lined face.

'We'll keep him a few days. He'll have to sleep on the floor.'

His mother was a thin little thing. A nervous wreck who was constantly looking over her shoulder. She had an irritating habit of starting a sentence in a normal voice and halfway through reducing it to a whisper. She never smiled, just twitched nervously.

'You sure you don't mind, Martha?'

'Anything to prevent a murder!'

But even this mild joke didn't bring a smile to her thin lips. He stayed for two weeks by which time his brother had calmed down sufficiently to strike him on the nose just the once. He bled profusely but retribution had been attained. Like a pair of duellists, blood had been drawn and the matter settled.

It was a hot summer. The air was stifling, the heat trapped between the tenement buildings. The neighbours sat on their doorsteps. Some of the boys were cooling themselves down at the communal yard tap by attaching a length of old hose-pipe to it and using it as a shower. The dustbins were overflowing and flies gathered in huge black clouds. Someone poured a bucket of strong disinfectant over them. This made them buzz round irritably for a few seconds, they became silent only to start again a few minutes later.

July and August were exciting months for the boys. Most of the men of military age were serving in the local Territorial Army. The family clothes lines could be seen festooned with army webbing equipment as they prepared for the annual camp. The wives were often glad to see the back of their husbands for a fortnight. Nevertheless they were just as pleased to see them return after picking up two weeks full soldier's pay plus their five pounds bounty. The men looked on it as a fortnight's holiday away from the wife and kids.

Alex was watching one of the men blancoing his equipment with all the enthusiasm of a regular soldier. Arthur tapped his friend on the back.

'All right isn't it, Al? I wish we could go.'

This comment caught the attention of the old soldier. He looked at both of them, sizing them up quickly.

'Why don't you join up then? You both look old enough and they're crying out for new recruits. Tell them you're seventeen. They don't give a damn so long as they can make up the numbers.'

What he omitted to tell them was that he got five pounds for each new recruit he introduced.

'You won't be able to get on this camp, but you will be certain for next year. Don't forget, we also have some weekend camps.

Come down to the Drill Hall next Tuesday. I'll take you to see the recruiting sergeant, and don't forget, you're seventeen.'

The following Tuesday, the old soldier was waiting impatiently at the gates of the Drill Hall, rubbing his hands and sending up a silent prayer.

'Ten pounds, the kids will have some decent clothes this winter.'

He was relieved to see them walking fast along the street.

The recruiting sergeant gave them a form each for their parents to sign, and told them to have a bath and bring it back on Thursday. They took the forms to Arthur's house. Ernie was sitting on the sofa with his girlfriend, twiddling the knobs of a second-hand wireless he had just purchased. All he was getting from it were some high pitched whines interspersed with the occasional flash of music.

'Got nothing on there yet?' asked Arthur.

The wireless emitted a piercing screech.

'No, piss off!' He concentrated on turning the tuning button, but only received more screeches. 'What do you want here, anyway? Why don't you go and drown yourself in the canal?'

'Can we borrow your fountain pen, Ernie? We've got some papers to sign.'

'Only if you promise to bugger off when you've finished. Me and Elsie are trying to listen to the wireless. I gave Mom fourpence for the cinema and Dad sixpence to get some beer, just to get rid of them. Now you two prats show up. Can't a bloke ever get any peace around here?'

'We'll only be a couple of minutes, Ernie,' pleaded Arthur.

Alex straightened out the forms. 'What's your old man's first name, Arthur?'

'Archie, but that's not what Mom calls him.'

Alex signed his application forms and passed his own to Arthur, both ready signed. He held them at arm's length. Ernie snatched the forms from Arthur's hands and burst out laughing.

'This is for the Terriers, you pair of silly sods. You haven't left school yet. You're no where near old enough.'

He burst out laughing again. Arthur wouldn't have the guts to do such a thing alone but he never doubted Alex's capabilities. If Alex had been applying for the Lord Mayor's job, he wouldn't have been surprised!

'I can hardly wait to see you pair in the Territorials.'

Arthur swore at him as they left the house. 'That Ernie will do anything to get rid of the family when his bird comes round. I reckon he gives her one when they're alone.'

That Thursday they became proud members of the Territorial Army. The sergeant hardly glanced at their papers. He took them along to see the medical officer who suffered from bad breath, aggravated by stale whisky. After a cursory examination, they were marched before an army officer who was dressed in full uniform with two rows of medals across his chest. He had a nervous twitch which he'd picked up in the trenches during the last war, one of the reasons he had been seconded to this job from his regular battalion. The more generous said to allow him to complete his pension time, though those less gratuitous said it was because, like the M.O, he was pissed half the time.

Along with two other new recruits, they were told to hold up their right hands and swear allegiance to H.M. the King, his heirs and successors. Then they were informed that they were now full members of H.M. Territorial Army known locally as 'Weekend Soldiers' - for the next four years.

Horace was working in the factory though not on the shop floor with his father, but in the tool room where he was serving an apprenticeship. As his father had said, 'It's a good steady job, Horace, and should there be another war, God forbid, you will be in a reserved occupation.'

So that was it. In case of war, he wanted to make sure his son wouldn't be labelled a conscientious objector like himself so he made certain Horace got a job that would warrant a reserved occupation without the stigma of the C.O. label. There was all this talk in the air of war once again with Germany, but Horace was no fool. He knew another war would encompass the civilian population; even his father would be involved. There was already a civil war going on in Spain and all the great cities were being bombed. Germany could easily bomb this country. No one would escape action.

Horace's father was due for a rude awakening. In another few months Horace would be eligible for boy service in the Navy and he knew he had two friends who would help him if they possibly could. Three years later, when he was eighteen, he would no longer need permission so even his father wouldn't be able to stop him then. Each night he would pour his heart out to Alex and his family, each day he spent at the factory was like a prison sentence. It was Alex and Arthur who finally sowed the seeds of an idea in his mind. If they could get away with enlisting in the T.A, why couldn't he do the same with the Navy?

'In the regular Navy, Horace, they will want to see your birth certificate. Bring it here Friday night. Our mom is going out and Karen goes to her friend's to have her hair done. Don't matter about Polly, when she gets her nose in a book she won't bother us.'

'It's no good, Alex, they know me too well at that naval recruiting office. I bet they could even tell you what time I was born. You have to be fifteen for boy service. They told me to get a job for a year then get a reference from my boss.'

There was little to choose between who was the most devious - Arthur or Alex - although Alex could be a little more subtle.

'Listen, Horace, I have read all those books with you. In boy service you will be lucky to get a shilling a day. If you are going to alter your birth certificate, why not join man service and get double the pay? Get that birth certificate and let's see if I can doctor it for you.'

'What about a reference? The recruiting officer said I would need references.'

Arthur as ever soon solved that little problem.

'Get pally with one of the girls in the office. Treat her real nice, like take her to the pictures or something. Then get her to pinch a sheet of the firm's note paper and I'll get Karen to type out a reference for you on her typewriter. Don't go to the local recruiting office. Get on your bike and ride out to the one in Coventry.'

'Our Karen will never type a letter like that. I would never ask her to,' said Alex.

'I bet she will. She has a soft spot for Horace.'

This was quite true. Horace was different from all the other local kids. He was always clean and nicely dressed, and had perfect manners. Horace was already looking and feeling a lot better since leaving school. He enthusiastically joined in with the preparation for the great forgery.

'That's great. Mom and Dad go to the cinema every Friday and it's their favourite this week, Gracie Fields. They usually stop and see it twice round, so I should have plenty of time. I know a girl in the office who started the same time as me. She stays alone in the office every dinner time to eat her lunch. She's got rotten teeth and freckles, but I'll put up with that to get my hand on two sheets of paper.'

So everything was set for the great forgery. Horace could hardly wait till his parents left the house. Once alone, he went to the cupboard where the family papers were kept in an old picture cake tin. His father was a very methodical man, so he made a mental note where the exact location of the tin was and the position of the lid. Inside, the papers were neatly tied. Insurance papers in one bundle, birth certificates in another. There were love letters written by his parents to each other and letters from his relations. The letter on the top of the bundle had the tip of a white feather sticking out and Horace wondered why he had kept it. Not many of his aunts and uncles ever spoke to his father. Carefully, he removed his birth certificate. It was as neat and as clean as the day it was issued. His parents marriage certificate fell out. He read it and smiled, then started counting on his fingers.

'Why, the crafty old sod. According to this they were only married six months before I was born.' He rechecked his birth certificate. 'Pompous old sod,' he said to himself as he folded the paper neatly and slipped it in his inside pocket. He replaced the rest of the papers back in the tin, making sure that everything was just as he'd found it.

The three of them gathered round the kitchen table in Alex's house. Alex laid out the birth certificate.

'Bloody hell, Horace, where does the old man keep this?'

Carefully, Arthur rolled up a piece of bread and gently rubbed the last two figures of the birth date. It didn't remove them completely, but Alex superimposed a new date over it. They waited for the ink to dry then held it at arm's length. It didn't look right. They crumpled the paper up to age it but then fate stepped in. As Arthur leaned over to take it from Alex, he knocked over a cup of cocoa which spilled all over the certificate.

'That's ballsed it up now,' said Horace.

Alex tried to dry the paper and smiled. 'No, it hasn't. Just take a look at it.'

The cocoa had dried in a long streak covering the figures, but the date was just discernible. Horace's face lit up. This part of the scheme was cut and dried.

'Now for the firm's note paper.'

It was a fortnight before he came into Alex's house, a broad smile on his face. Karen was there with her mother and Polly. Alex was doing a little job with one of his barrows.

'Could I see you alone, Karen?' He looked at her rather nervously.

She frowned and lead him to the door. It was a warm night so they sat on the doorstep.

'Will you type me a letter?' He hesitated, 'Well not really a letter, more like a reference.'

'What do you mean, a reference?' Her brows knitted, the V between her eyes deepening. 'I don't understand you, Horace, why the secrecy? I can soon type a letter saying I know you, that's no trouble.'

'It's not exactly like that.' He took the firm's note paper from his inside pocket. 'It's on this note paper.' He looked round to see if Polly or her mother were within earshot. 'Just say that I have worked here for four years and all the usual stuff; I am a good worker.'

'I know how to write a reference, Horace. I've done enough.' She stared hard at Horace. 'I know which two put you up to this. It's against the law to give a false reference and stealing the firm's paper. I'm sorry, Horace, as much as I like you, I can't do this.'

He put his arm round her shoulder. Something he would never have done until he'd come under the influence of his two friends.

'Please, Karen, I hate that factory and I'm starting to hate my father for making me work there. It's only your brother and Arthur who save me from blowing my top.' He tightened his grip on her shoulder. 'Please, Karen, I can't wait another three years. Every time me and Dad leave the house for work, I feel like punching his grinning face. Always telling me I'll be better off in the tool room. I don't want to be a conchie like him if war breaks out. He tried to drum it into me that my job will be a reserved occupation. Do you know, my father hasn't got a friend in the world? No one wants to talk to him. I don't want to end up like that!'

Horace appealed to her better nature. She knew how the family had suffered over the years and now his father was prepared to watch his own son suffer the same fate. Should Horace marry and have children of his own, it would be like history repeating itself. All this talk of war might come to nothing, but had she been born a man, she would do exactly what Horace was doing. Join the Navy and see the world. He'd won her over but she mustn't allow him to see she had given in so easily.

'Let me think about it, Horace. Leave the papers with me. If I type them for you, you must swear to me that you won't breathe a word to anyone. Not your family, my family, or friends, and should anyone discover the forgery, I'll deny it. I will say I hardly know you. I won't use my typewriter at home. I'll take it to work to do.'

Blushing a deep, beetroot red, he kissed her on the cheek.

The next night after work, Horace called round to see Alex. The family were all sitting down to tea. While no one was looking, Karen passed Horace a long, brown envelope. He didn't open it till he was alone in his bedroom later that night. She had given him a glowing reference. With that I should make admiral in six months, he thought. He carefully hid it where his mother would never find it.

Alex was negotiating another moonlight flit when Horace called the next day.

'You want three barrows, Mr Tomkins. Me and Arthur will push two, your Tony can push another. Say about ten on Saturday night, there might be a few drunks about. Your Tony goes to our school. Pity to take him away, he's a pretty bright lad.'

'Yes, it's a shame about that, Alex, but it can't be helped. There's a school right next to the new house. It's a better area too and the rent's cheaper.'

'That shouldn't make any difference to you, Mr Tomkins, you never pay any rent! How many times have you moved in the past two years?'

'About three times. But that shouldn't worry you, it means more in your pocket.'

They met at his house on the Saturday and piled the three barrows high. Mrs Tomkins walked behind with her pram full of bedding and curtains. The streets were very quiet, apart from a few drunks and people coming out of the cinema. They passed several policemen on their beats, but they didn't take any notice. People flitting at night was a common sight thereabouts and it wasn't unknown for a policeman to help a flitter push a barrow up and down the kerbs, no questions asked.

# Chapter Fifteen

It was late September and the country was basking in an Indian summer. Alex didn't know why it was called an Indian summer and doubted if his mother knew either. He was sitting on the doorstep, fanning himself with a piece of paper, eyes half closed, when a long black shadow fell across him. It was Horace's mother. She tapped him on the head and he could see she'd been crying.

'I suppose you knew all about it,' she sobbed, but before he could answer she vanished inside the house and broke into more sobs. 'It's my Horace, Martha. He's gone and joined the Navy. His father's doing his nut. It looks like he went to another town to enlist. His bike, his savings, his spare clothes, they've all gone. What shall I do, Martha?'

'Well, the best thing to do is sit down and take it easy. Crying won't solve the problem.'

She made a fresh pot of tea and poured them both a cup. Tea was the first answer to any problem in the neighbourhood. Horace's mother sipped and sniffed alternately.

'He said he was going to work. He works in a different part of the factory from his father. They said cheerio at the gates, then, as soon as Alf's back was turned, Horace must have gone the other way. He didn't go into the factory, he just vanished. I couldn't believe it when his father came home without him. At first he thought Horace must have come on alone. We searched the house. Horace is always neat and tidy. He'd make his own bed so at first I didn't bother. Later, when we went into his room, we found this letter.'

She handed it to Karen who read it aloud.

'Dear Mom and Dad. I have joined the Navy. Don't try and get me out. If you do I'll just join the Marines, or the Army, or the Airforce. You both knew my heart was set on joining the Navy, but you wouldn't even let me bring any Navy books home. If you succeed in getting me out, I will never speak to either of you again. I love you both, but you cannot keep ruling my life. I an no longer a little boy. For years I have had to live with the stigma of Dad being labelled a conchie. I don't blame him, every man has the right to do exactly what he wants to do and never allow anyone to intrude on their private lives. I will give you a couple of months to cool off before I write to see if you want me to come home. I love you both. Please don't stop me from doing what I have always wanted to do. Love Horace.'

When Karen put the letter down, she was crying and wondering if she had done right, typing that reference. Horace's mother put her head on Martha's shoulder.

'It's his father, Martha, he's going absolutely mad. I'm sure he will do something very stupid.'

'The stupidest thing you can do is interfere with Horace's life. He wanted to join the Navy. You should be proud of the fact he can do this for himself. I bet within a year you'll both be very proud of him. If you have any sense, you will talk to your old man before doing anything. As Horace says, if you get him out he will only try the Army next then the Airforce. I know how you feel but all boys are adventurous. Take Alex, I never expected to see him in uniform but when he goes out of here on a Tuesday and Thursday in khaki, I can see his father. From the back, I can hardly tell the difference. Let the lad go, he'll be all right.'

Horace's mother didn't get over the shock of her son doing a flit without confiding in her. Every night for weeks, she cried herself to sleep, refusing to speak to her husband unless it was absolutely necessary, or just to blame him for their son's disappearance.

'It's all your fault, you and your damn conchie ideas. You were scared to fight for your country and your son and I have suffered all these years because of that. The poor lad had to change school several times till he met the likes of Alex and Arthur who looked after him.'

'It's them two sods I blame for putting ideas into his head!' he retaliated, raising his voice for the first time in fifteen years of marriage. 'They encouraged him, and them in the Terriers when they haven't left school yet. I bet if the army knew their real ages, they would get kicked out. I have a good mind to inform on them, bloody little perishers. I shouldn't have let Horace go out with them in the first place.'

'Go out with them? My God! It was them two that saved him from being bullied at school, and it's them that made a man of your son, and without any help from you. If you go anywhere near that Drill Hall, I will never speak to you again. All you advised Horace to do was get a job in that stinking factory of yours. He hated it from the minute he stepped over the threshold. Take a trade, that was the only advice you gave him. Not to better himself but to prevent him being called up in the services. Just like you, save your skin and let some other poor mother's sons do the fighting for you. You bloody disgust me!'

He looked at his wife in disbelief. All the years they had been married and she'd never before spoken to him in that tone. Inwardly, over all those years, was that what she had really

107

thought of him? He stared around the room, so nicely furnished. They were the envy of the neighbourhood, the first family to have a wireless. Now the rug had been pulled from under his feet. All this had been for nothing. His inner self told him she was right. He hadn't been a conscientious objector on any religious or political grounds. The truth was he had been dead scared. His heart had been in the right place when the war started. He was as patriotic as the next man and a staunch royalist. But then the casualties began arriving. He was at the railway station the first day they arrived. Men so badly wounded they could neither walk nor talk. Some blinded or with limbs missing, not just an arm or a leg, some were completely limbless. He didn't sleep for weeks. The nightmare of what he'd seen completely took over his life and his patriotism vanished. He wasn't married then, and when they finally came for him, he cowered in the corner of his mother's room and had to be dragged away to go before a board. He was made to work in an ammunitions factory and labelled a C.O.

Horace kept in touch with Alex from the start of his basic training, and always put a letter inside the envelope for his mother. Not once did he divulge his address, not even the town where he was stationed. He settled down from the start. Alex laughed when he wrote and told him he'd finally made his mind up to go into the signals branch when he'd completed his basic training.

'It's everything I expected, Alex. You wouldn't believe it, but I've put on a stone. The training is hard, the food basic but good. Mind, tell your mum they don't make suet puddings as good as hers, and they won't let me scrape the white cloth with a knife like your mother used to. I will get shore leave shortly, and two weeks' leave when I finish my training, so if the old man has calmed down I'll come home on leave. I went out with a couple of lads the other night. I only had a couple of pints and believe me, I was pissed to the eyeballs! It was the first time and the last. I can definitely repudiate what they say about drunken sailors. From now on I'm strictly T.T.' His letters were always filled with enthusiasm about his life in the Navy.

Alex and Arthur left school. Arthur worked with his brother in a metal polishing shop. He hated it. The money was good for a school leaver, sixpence an hour, but the conditions were abominable. It was a filthy job. Each night he would return home covered from head to toe in a fine, sooty substance. He complained to his friend.

'Horace knew what he was doing when he joined the Navy. This job is just the limit, stuck in that filthy, polishing shop all day long. The dirt penetrates everything, even my ears and nose get bunged up. We can't leave the shop for a tea break. We have to make our tea on a gas ring and when you put your mug down, before you get time to drink it the tea is covered with a film of metal dust. Forty-eight hours, plus two hours for cleaning down your machine, and you don't get paid for that, and all I get to take home after stoppages is just over a pound. There has to be an easier way of making a living than that.'

There was a bitterness in his friend's voice he'd not heard before. He looked at him carefully. Only three months in that factory and the dirt was already engrained in the pores of his face. Alex certainly had no intention of going into any factory while he still kept his Saturday job in the market with Mr Fleming. Sometimes he would pick up various items of housewares himself.

His greatest ambition was to get a shop of his own. He had managed to rent an old, empty chapel. The owners had long since given up the idea of getting any lost souls in that area to repent, leaving it vacant for some time. Alex approached them and they agreed to let it to him for a few shillings a week, on the condition that he didn't retail from there.

This didn't stop him from organising some of the factory women to act as his agents. They formed clubs for him and he allowed their customers to buy a pound's worth of china and pay back twenty-one shillings at a shilling a week. The agents kept the extra shilling, and if they wanted any goods themselves, they got another ten per cent knocked off. It worked very well. In no time at all, he had over twenty agents bringing in between two and five pounds a week. Thursdays, the agents would arrive with their orders. Fridays, Alex would go round the various factories with the goods and on Saturdays the agents would go to the chapel to pay in the money. Karen became his part-time bookkeeper, while Alex kept his Saturday afternoon job in the market learning the china trade from Mr Fleming, and a lot more besides from the chests of china that were delivered. When they arrived, Alex would tear off the labels showing the manufacturers' addresses in the Potteries and keep them for future reference.

'Why don't you start up on your own, Arthur?' asked Alex one day feeling sorry for his friend who'd come home looking more like a Kentucky minstrel, moaning as usual about his job in the polishing shop.

'I'm not like you, Alex. I haven't got your head for business, I wish to God I had.'

He sat on the edge of a table Alex used as a desk, and looked round the chapel.

'Do you remember when we attended chapel on a Sunday here, Alex? We used to come for a couple of weeks to get a card and a couple of attendance stars. Then we'd cut a star in the end of an old potato to make a star stamp, and filled the card just so we could go to the Christmas party.'

While Arthur reminisced, Alex was thinking up ways to get him away from that factory. It was another two weeks before he came up with an idea. Alex called at his home to find him stripped to the waist, washing himself in a bowl of warm water. Arthur's father was sitting on the sofa, bleary eyed, watching him.

'That's a good job, son. Over a pound a week. When I left school, I was lucky if I got five bob.'

'You was bloody lucky you got a job at all. I bet you were pissed before you left school.'

'Why, you cheeky little bastard. I've a good mind to put my hand across your gob.'

'Yea, I'd like to see you try it. I wish I was a bastard, I wouldn't have you for an old man!' Arthur looked at his mother, who was ironing some clothes on the table. 'Are you sure you didn't go wrong, Mom? Tell me you did and I will give you an extra five bob this week.' He knew his father wouldn't retaliate too much. Arthur occasionally gave him sixpence for his beer out of his wages.

'Can I have a few words with you, Arthur?' said Alex, as the argument hotted up.

They walked slowly towards the chapel.

'It's like this, Arthur. You know old Solly. He sells those second-hand clothes down the market. He told me he's packing it in.'

Arthur looked a little doubtful.

'I was chatting to him on Saturday. He's had enough. He goes totting round those big houses by Cannon Hill Park. Practically gets the clothes given to him. Must do all right 'cause he lives in a big house and both his sons went to college. One of them is a doctor now. Why don't you go out with him for a few weeks? Get to know the job. You can use the chapel for storage. There's still two or three empty rooms. You can have them rent free till you get on your feet. One condition. When you bring in some decent clothes I get first refusal. I need a good overcoat and a decent suit.'

'Do you really mean it, Alex? I wish I had your bloody brains for business. You could fall in a barrel of shit and come up smelling of roses!'

'Come off it, Arthur. We went to the same school, had the same teachers, so don't talk a load of crap. Use your loaf. No one

110

in this district can afford new clothes so they have to buy second hand gear. I've seen queues round Solly's stall. He always gives them a good deal. Like me. I sell seconds in china because people can't afford first quality. They save up to fifty per cent on shop prices. Some of my agents are earning five shillings a week and I've one woman who earns ten.'

'Do you think Solly would let me have his business, Alex? That would suit me.'

He felt a flood of relief surge through his body with the thought of leaving that factory. He couldn't understand how his brother had survived so long, he was always complaining about his chest and coughing up black phlegm.

# Chapter Sixteen

Arthur visited Solly. Although they had never met previously they took to each other straight away. Several weeks before he was due to retire, Arthur accompanied old Solly on his rounds so he could learn all the tricks of the trade.

'When they give you a bundle of clothes, never, and I mean never, offer them any money. Start walking away. If they want cash they'll soon ask you. Up in the big houses they very rarely ask. They're too toffee nosed. Once you get clear of the house always search through the pockets. If I told you what I've found in some of them you'd never believe me!'

So old Solly retired much to the relief of his long suffering wife, he should have done it years before. He wasn't a poor man. Over the years he'd made enough to keep them in comfort for the rest of their lives.

On his very first house call alone, Arthur could hardly believe his luck. Perhaps it was an omen for the future. At first he had his doubts. He rang the bell and a lady came to the door crying. She blew her nose in the tiniest handkerchief he'd ever seen. He went to walk away.

'I'll call later, madam.'

But she called him back. 'Come for some old clothes, son? Well, follow me.'

It was a beautiful house, all richly carpeted, with electric lights all over the place. It had toilets and bathrooms both downstairs and upstairs. She was dressed in a fine, pink silk dressing gown. She lead him upstairs. He hesitated at the bedroom door, as she opened a wardrobe that took up one complete wall of the room. It was full of men's suits, overcoats, dressing gowns, sports trousers, jackets and raincoats. He'd never seen so many clothes belonging to one man.

'Take the damn lot, son.'

She started pulling out drawers from the dressing table and chest of drawers. They were filled to the brim with freshly laundered shirts of every colour, underclothes, pyjamas, socks and shoes of every design imaginable.

'Yes, take these damn things as well. I never want to see any of them again.'

She started throwing them on to the bed with a vengeance. Arthur protested. He didn't have enough money to buy all these clothes. There must have been hundreds of pounds' worth. The bed was draped with a silk bedspread which sagged under the weight of all the clothes piling up on top of it.

'I don't want your damn money. Just get them out of my sight!' Her tears had stopped, as anger welled up inside her. 'They are my husband's. Get rid of every single item.'

She took a bundle of pound notes from the top drawer of her dressing table, peeled off a couple and thrust them into his hand.

'The bastard has shacked up with that little blonde secretary of his. I didn't trust the bitch from the day she took the job. I almost caught them at it once when I turned up at his office unexpectedly. He has run off to Portugal with her. He has another business over there, but I don't give a damn. The business over here belongs to me. It was left to me by Daddy.'

'I'm very sorry, lady.' Looking at the pile of clothes heaped up on the bed helped to sooth his sorrow. 'I mean, running off with that blonde bitch. Perhaps he'll come back.'

'Come back!' she screamed. 'Come back? Why I wouldn't have him back if he came crawling on his knees. Go on, sonny, take the lot. I was only going to burn them this afternoon.'

The door bell rang. She ran downstairs in her dressing gown and flung open the door. A tall man stood there, distinguished looking, dressed in a light grey suit, a camel hair overcoat thrown over his shoulders. He sported a pencil thin moustache, and wore a grey trilby that matched his suit. Elegant would have been a better way of describing him. He was smoking a cigarette, held in a long ebony and silver cigarette holder. He leaned on a Malacca cane as he lifted his hat. Her attitude immediately changed.

'Oh Jack, you're here. Thank God for that.'

Arthur's heart sank. What clothes that had been piled on the landing, he started replacing in the wardrobe. He was in the midst of hanging up the suits and putting the overcoats back on their hangers when the lady returned smoking a ghastly smelling Turkish cigarette.

'What the hell do you think you're doing?' she asked, looking at him and then at the clothes he'd put back in the wardrobe. 'Do you want the damn clothes or don't you?' She began emptying the wardrobe and threw the clothes back onto the bed. 'Get the damn things out of my sight, if you want them'

'But your husband, lady.'

The words trailed off. Arthur was no fool. Even at his tender age he knew enough about the facts of life, and here he was just about to get the greatest lesson of all. He stared hard at the woman. Then he quickly started to throw the clothes down the stairs before she changed her mind.

The man returned and had changed into a deep blue dressing gown. He put his arm round her waist from behind, and peered over her shoulder at Arthur and smiled, revealing two rows of gleaming, pearly white teeth.

'Is that little urchin still here, darling?' he asked, in a long drawn out, affected voice. 'Damn me!'

'Not for long, Jack, darling.'

She stepped inside the bedroom and started flinging the remainder of the clothes on to the landing.

Arthur stood for a few minutes, his eyes glued to the bedroom door, scratching his head and wondering if he would ever understand women. He could hardly wait to tell Alex all about it.

'You should have seen them, Alex. When she opened the door to me, she was crying her eyes out. Then this bloke comes along, and before I realised what was happening, she couldn't get me out of the house fast enough and this bloke into the bedroom. When I left, she was screaming and giggling, and this posh chap was grunting. When I'd finished loading up, I went to the bedroom door to tell the lady I was leaving and this posh tart shouts at me to piss off!'

Both of them sorted through the pile of clothing. Alex picked out two suits of the finest cloth and a camel hair overcoat with a fur collar. The clothes were too big for him but a tailor friend would soon alter them. He tried on several pairs of shoes. One pair had never been worn, but were no use as they were far too big.

'He had sodding big feet, Arthur!'

It is said that a man's life can be changed by being in the right place at the right time. This was certainly true in Arthur's case. His big break had come when he'd knocked on that lady's door, for from that day onward he never looked back. Even the boyfriend, Jack, had arrived at just the right moment, as his appearance had changed the lady's anguish into joy and she couldn't dispose of her husband's clothes fast enough. Arthur was now the proud owner of several hundred pounds' worth of clothes, most of which were still in perfect condition, almost as new. As for women, he doubted if he would ever understand them fully. Still, he could relax now as this amount of stock would give him a decent standard of living if he sold just one item a week. Alex was just as pleased, his friend would no longer have to work in that stinking polishing shop.

Unfortunately, secrecy had become a part of their business. When Alex had taken on the lease of the chapel, he was told that under no circumstances was he to use the premises for retail, so all his dealings were sworn to secrecy by word of mouth. Word soon got round but they still worked under the constant threat of exposure to the chapel authorities.

Arthur, on the other hand, had just one worry - being haunted by the spectre of his father, continually on the scrounge, his limp being more pronounced when he visited the chapel.

Sidling up to Arthur he would lower his voice to ask, 'Got a couple of shillings to spare, Arthur? Your mom wants me to get her a loaf of bread and half a pound of marge.'

'Cut the crap, Dad. I took Mom a basket of groceries yesterday. Dad, you're a drunken old sod and a damn liar!'

It was then that his father would go into his old routine - it was the likes of him that fought in the trenches, so he could have a decent business. The plain truth was that the entire neighbourhood knew that he could have the limp come and go at will, just to suit his needs.

Arthur slipped his father two shillings.

'Go and get yourself a couple of pints, Dad. I can't understand why you don't get yourself a job. There are one or two jobs flying around but just don't give me that crap about the family is starving!'

'Who wants a cripple like me? Some day the pain is so bad I can hardly stand. You don't know what it's like to suffer. I only get my bit of pension and I have always done my best for you kids.'

'Done your best! You lying old hypocrite. Why I've seen you take the last few coppers from Mom's purse just to buy a pint and there's been no grub in the house. For heaven's sake, Dad, get out of my sight before I take the two bob back.'

His father passed Alex, limping as usual. Alex smiled to himself and shouted to Arthur, after his father left the hall, 'Been on the scrounge again, Arthur?'

Arthur shook his head in disgust.

'Silly old sod. I have just listened to another version of the wound saga. What my old lady ever saw in him, I shall never know.' He sat on the edge of the table, staring into the distance. 'Wouldn't it be nice to learn my old lady went astray and my real father were to turn up? Say he was the Duke of Norfolk, or somebody. Even a dustman, anyone but that silly old sod!'

In contrast, relations between Horace and his father had improved somewhat. It had been two years since Horace joined the Navy, and over a year since his last leave. After his first leave, his father had realised there wasn't anything he could do about the situation. His son seemed to have settled down in the career he had chosen, and he grudgingly admitted to himself that there was a marked improvement in his son's attitude, along with both his mental state and physical appearance. His mother was just pleased to see him. So pleased in fact, that the day he knocked on the door of his home and she saw him for the first time in uniform, she fainted.

So it was some surprise when Horace walked into the chapel one day. Alex was busy sorting out some fresh supplies of china, while Arthur was rearranging a fresh batch of clothes on the racks.

A voice boomed out, 'You wouldn't have a pair of size ten shoes with rubber soles, I suppose?'

They both recognised his voice instantly, but he had changed physically. His face was as brown as tanned leather and his chest had taken on beer barrel proportions. After all this time, they were once again together. They started pumping Horace with all sorts of questions. One thing he was adamant about, he had never regretted joining the Navy.

They did very little work that afternoon. Horace said he would spend a couple of days with his parents, and they would have the day together on Sunday. Alex and Arthur were going on weekend camp with the T.A, but they reckoned they'd be home early on the Sunday afternoon and arranged to meet up in the centre of the city, all three of them in uniform.

Horace was getting plenty of attention from the girls. It was the custom to touch a sailor collar for luck. He encouraged them, although what really took his fancy was a neat little blonde sitting alone on a bench, pretending to read a book, occasionally, casting a sly look in Horace's direction. Their eyes would meet, then she immediately glanced downwards again at her book. The three of them were laughing and joking although it was obvious that Horace's mind was on other things. As they came abreast of the young girl, he winked at her. She blushed and bent her head. Taking the initiative, he walked over to her.

'Interesting book, Miss?'

She smiled and her whole face lit up. She dropped her book to her lap.

'Not really, there isn't a lot to do, but I do like to come here and read a book or watch the birds. I work up at the hospital and have to be on duty at six.'

She picked up her handbag, slipped her paperback inside, then stood up and adjusted her clothes.

'I'll walk you back, if you don't mind?' he said.

She replied with a bewitching smile, 'What about your friends?'

'What about them? They're capable of looking after themselves.'

He boldly took her arm and walked towards the churchyard entrance, putting two fingers up behind his back as he passed his friends.

They walked from the heat of the city and the park into the hospital. The nauseous smell of antiseptic filled Horace's lungs. He hated hospitals. It reminded him of the time he cut his leg open and Alex and Arthur had taken him to the hospital. His mother had been alarmed when she'd seen his leg bandaged, and both of his parents had forbidden him to see his two friends again. He retaliated by refusing to speak to his parents. It was two weeks before they relented.

Alex stared at Arthur as he saw Horace and the girl disappear down the path, out of the churchyard.

'Was that really the shy kid we knew two years ago? We only had to mention girls to him then and he would blush to the roots of his hair. Karen and Helen would tease him blind.'

They hardly saw Horace again till the following Friday. He walked into the old chapel and tossed his cap on the table.

'Can I use your phone, Alex?' He didn't wait for an answer and started looking through the directory. 'They don't give the Stratford-on-Avon numbers here, Alex.'

'No, you have to ring enquiries. What do you want Stratford for? Going to apologise to that copper after all these years?'

Horace laughed. The thought of that police sergeant wading in the weeds, brought back memories.

'Christ, I'd almost forgotten that, when I suggested going away for the weekend with Carol. She said it would have to be somewhere out of the city so Stratford was the first place that came to mind.'

'Carol, who the bloody hell is Carol?' He stopped dead in his sentence and stared at Horace. 'Not that lovely blonde girl we met in the churchyard last Sunday?'

'Yes, that's the one and only.'

But someone was answering the telephone now. He spoke into the mouthpiece.

'Oh yes, is that the hotel? My son's in the Navy and has just got married. We have planned a surprise honeymoon and want a room for the weekend.'

# Chapter Seventeen

Anyone studying from the outside would think that Alex's movements were carefully planned. On the contrary, lady luck was shining down on him from every angle. He had decided to buy himself a small van to travel to the Potteries. Going up by train and then travelling from one factory to the next on foot was time consuming, especially as the whole of the Potteries covered five towns. What took two, or sometimes three days, could be covered in one if he had his own van. Time spent there would be more profitable.

The next time he visited the Drill Hall and read the notice board, he could hardly believe his eyes. They were actually calling for volunteers to learn driving and mechanics which would be badly needed when the battalion was mechanised. Alex wasted no time in submitting his name.

This was to result in a lecture from the officer in charge, a toffee-nosed captain with a bushy moustache and sporting a monocle. He was sat at his desk, smoking a foul smelling cigarette held in a discoloured, bone cigarette holder. He screwed the monocle into his eye and looked Alex up and down a few times.

'Bit young, my man, but let's say the younger the better.' He removed the holder from his mouth and flicked the ash towards a makeshift tray. This missed and the ash flew across the blanket covered table. 'Ever driven a motorised vehicle before, Edwards?'

'No, sir,' replied Alex as he studied the top of the officer's head thinking what the hell do you think I'm standing here for you stupid idiot. You asked for volunteers to learn to drive.

'Do you think you're capable of handling a three tonner?'

'See no reason why not, sir. Once I learn to drive, I suppose I will be able to drive any vehicle.'

The officer was impressed by the confidence in Alex's voice. Out of the forty or so volunteers, he was one of the six men selected for the first batch. The next few Sunday mornings, a time when Alex was normally busy in his own warehouse, were taken up with driving instructions. He knew that in a few weeks this would pay dividends. He was getting lessons for nothing and being paid for it, so he saw no reason to worry. It would just mean he would have to work a bit harder on Mondays.

The war clouds were gathering fast, and Alex was reminded of Horace's parting comment, 'Don't make any long term plans.' The Germans had already walked into the Rhineland without a shot being fired. Rumours were spreading through the battalion faster than a bush fire. The more experienced old soldiers, survivors of the first war, guessed there was something in the air.

'Mark my words, there's something up. We don't get all these lorries and new equipment for nothing. It's the regulars who get them first, then the T.A. The last war, we went to camp for two weeks and it was four years before the remnants of the battalion returned!'

The old soldier pulled the stub end of a Woodbine from behind his ear and lit it, staring into space as he recalled those four dreadful years. But the annual camp came and went without a hitch. The old soldiers sighed with relief, while the younger ones cursed, inwardly thinking they had been robbed of a romantic adventure, but not daring to voice these opinions in front of the old soldiers. They had, no doubt, joined the T.A. for the extra few pounds it brought into the family kitty, and not from patriotic ideals alone.

Horace came home on leave regularly before he was drafted overseas. A posting would make him absent from home waters for at least two and a half years. He visited his two friends whenever Carol was on duty at the hospital. On occasions, Carol would visit him in Portsmouth. He passed his signals course with flying colours and was soon promoted to Leading Hand, and displayed the single gold anchor on his arm with pride.

Alex bought his new van with Karen's help. She chose the colour and arranged all the monthly payments.

'Karen, you know that old empty shop in Gooch Street? I saw the agent today.'

'That dump, Alex? It's been empty for years and it's in a hell of a state.'

'I know. They want a pound a week for it. I got the key from the agents and had a look inside. There's old papers two feet high, everywhere's covered in dust, and it smells, but underneath all that dust it's in good condition. I wiped one of the shelves and it looked like polished oak.'

Some kids had shouted through the open door, 'Eh mister, this place is haunted!' Alex wasn't superstitious. He guessed the sinister, scratching noises the kids had heard through the letter box, were just coming from the rats. The place was infested with them. Even while inspecting the basement, one ran over his foot, but he omitted to mention this to Karen.

'I told them I would take it for fifteen shillings a week, but I must have the first year rent free. The agent looked relieved that he'd finally found a tenant foolish enough to take over the empty shop. He said he would have to approach the owner, but the look on the agent's face told me there would be no objections.'

The following day, the agent had the lease all ready for him to sign. 'It's a nice property, Mr Edwards, once it's been cleaned up.

119

That flat above it is nice and clean, and you can be assured there's no damp at all in the premises.'

Alex spent the next morning going over the property. As he walked through the front door, the rats, disturbed by this intruder, scampered in all directions. The whitewashed windows afforded very little light. He walked to the other end of the shop and opened the french doors. Light flooded in bringing a comforting breath of fresh air into the musty interior. The doors lead to an outside toilet and a garden that stretched right down to the River Rea. It was a long garden, shoulder high in weeds and unkempt grass. At the bottom was a square, brick built building with a flat concrete roof. He nodded his head with satisfaction and stepped back into the shop. With more light, the shop looked even more dilapidated, like a throw back from the Victorian era.

The shop itself was about forty feet long with an oak counter stretching the whole length of the building. Two old cash tills had been left behind. Both made of steel and brass, they must have been the previous owner's pride and joy, but were now more suited to a museum. On one till, two white tickets showed the last sale was eleven pence and three farthings, whilst the other till displayed the 'No Sale' sign. He pressed one of the keys and a bell rang sharp and clear. On each side of the shop, shelves stretched from floor to ceiling in two foot intervals. There was one thing in its favour, the owner had installed electricity. He pressed a switch but nothing happened. The first thing to do was to get the place cleaned up, then call in an electrician.

He inspected the flat. There were three bedrooms, an inside toilet, a bathroom, kitchen, and the biggest living room he had every seen. Strips of paper hung from the walls. He lay his hand against the wall, but couldn't feel any damp. The owner had left an old gas stove behind. He turned on a tap and there was a sudden hiss of gas that quickly fizzled out.

Four men were standing on the corner, outside the shop.

'Hallo, chaps. Looking for a bit of casual work?'

They had all been smoking the same cigarette, passing it from one to another. Alex handed around his packet, which they viewed with envy. He nodded towards the shop.

'I want that cleaned out and scrubbed till it shines like a new pin. I'll give you half a crown a day, no questions asked. The windows are whitewashed, so if the men from the labour exchange come snooping, they won't be able to see through. The place is full of rats, but you can soon sweep them down to the river. I'll get the gas put on, you can boil some water upstairs, and I'll leave tea, milk and sugar. There are several buckets and brooms, and plenty of rags. I want the shop ready in a week. If

120

you finish before, I'll still pay you for the seven days.' He gave them half a crown each and the unfinished packet of cigarettes to share between them.

When he drove up in his van the next morning, they were already waiting for him, anxious to start work. For half a crown a day, old Nick himself wouldn't have prevented them from starting, let alone a few old rats. They set to with relish.

'There's a cellar to do, but I want the shop done first. I'll pay you extra for the cellar and the flat.'

One of the men made a flat scoop by nailing a three foot piece of wood to an old broom handle, and both the rubbish and the rats were scraped unceremoniously along the shop floor and out into the garden, and then into the river. By the end of the first day, the shop was rid of the worst debris. The gas company had re-connected the gas meter, making sure first that there were no leaks. By the end of the week, the shop looked like it had only just been vacated. For some extra money, the men set about cleaning out the basement, having a good old time chasing the rats and killing them with the flats of their shovels.

Alex called Karen in. She shook her head in disbelief.

'You've done wonders, Alex. These shelves look as though they've just been put up.'

'That's nothing, Karen, come upstairs.' He lead her up to the flat, their steps echoing on the bare, narrow wooden staircase. 'My luck was in, Karen. One of those chaps who helped me clean the place out was a bit of a decorator. He got me some very cheap wallpaper.'

Karen felt despondent as she said, 'Does this mean you're going to live here, Alex? We'll miss you at home.'

'You must be bloody joking! No, this is for the family. You and Polly can have your own room. Mom can have another, and I'll have my own room. I tell you Karen, we will have this place looking like a palace, but don't you tell our mom. I want it all finished and ready for her to move into first. Then I'll give her the surprise of her life.'

For the first time he could remember, Karen hugged him round the neck and planted a kiss on his cheek. There was a trace of tears in her eyes.

'Alex, you're one in a million!'

'Sod off, Karen.'

They had never been an over affectionate family, kissing and slopping over each other, their love for each other was deep and sincere. A far reach from the time he was a little urchin with a constant candle beneath his nose. He wiped his cheek with the back of his hand, took out his wallet and handed her a bundle of notes.

'Go down the furniture shop with this. I want four single beds, a three piece suite, a table and four chairs. If there's anything left, get a bit of lino for the sitting room. We'll get the rest of the stuff as we go along.'

Karen did wonders with the money Alex had given her, adding to it another twenty pounds of her own which she had so laboriously saved over the years. She had intended to use it for a holiday in Blackpool, but after seeing Alex's great effort, she could never have taken a holiday with a clear conscience. She bartered with the owner of the furniture shop, doubting if he had ever had a cash customer with that amount since the day he'd started his business, and all folding money. The following evening, when the furniture was delivered, the owner himself came along to supervise the carter unloading it from his horse and cart.

By the following Sunday, everything was in readiness to spring the great surprise on his mother. Karen had kept the secret to herself, never daring to mention it to Polly, who she knew couldn't keep a secret whatever the circumstances, so it would be just as big a surprise for Polly as for her mother. Alex's mother had often volunteered to help him clean the shop, but he adamantly refused, saying he had sufficient help.

So it was a surprise for her to see Alex on the Sunday morning, as he was usually busy with some job or other. She was just putting the roast beef joint in the oven, having already prepared the vegetables.

'Leave that, Mom. I want you to come round the shop and see it now all the shelves are filled with china and glass.'

'Can't it wait till after dinner, Alex? I've almost finished getting the dinner ready.'

Polly was stretched out on the sofa reading her penny romantic novel. 'Can I come, Alex?'

'Certainly, I want you both there.'

He finally convinced his mother. She looked around the shop and sniffed.

'Smells like something cooking, Alex?'

'Yes, it's coming from next door. The manager has moved in with his wife and kids,' he lied. 'By the way, Mom, you never did see the flat, did you? The landlord said I could have it for another five bob a week but I wanted your thoughts about it first.'

He led his mother and sister up the narrow, creaking staircase. His mother puffed and wheezed. She was a big woman and Alex wondered if he had made a mistake.

When she stepped into the large room that smelt of new furniture, she exclaimed, 'Oh my God!' Then doubt immediately crept into her mind. The same idea came to her mind as it had done with Karen when he had first mentioned to her about decorating the flat. Was Alex about to move out of the old house and set up in his own flat?

'How do you like it, Mom?'

'Very nice, Alex.' She cast a critical eye over the polished table and sideboard. 'When are you moving out, Alex? I mean, moving from our old house. I guessed you'd be going sooner or later. Sleeping on that old sofa doesn't befit an up and coming business man. You deserve this, son, you've worked very hard.'

'Oh shut up, Mom, you silly bugger. It's not just me that's moving, you are and so are Karen and Polly. This is your new home now.'

She was overcome with emotion when Karen caught her arm and gave her a guided tour of the flat.

'This is your own bedroom, Mom.'

She turned down the sheets and blankets, and made her mother sit on the bed. All her life, Martha had never owned a new bed. The feather mattress she slept on now was second-hand when she bought it just before she married, and could easily have passed through several families before she owned it, along with the furniture. Now she had a new bed with a spring interior mattress. She was led from room to room, and finally into the bathroom. Another first in her life, as previously she had always used a long, galvanised bathtub set in front of the fire, or taken a bath at the public baths. Karen turned on the gas geyser above the bath. It hissed for a few minutes, then lit with a slight bang. She jumped backwards, then, after the initial shock, she felt the hot water.

'God, Karen, what will they think of next?' She returned to the sitting room and looked around. 'I don't know where I will be able to put my furniture. It will look so decrepit amongst this new stuff.'

'Over my dead body, Mom. You're not bringing that stuff in here. What do you think I bought this furniture for?' He led her to one of the big easy chairs and made her sit down. 'It's time you took it a bit easy.'

She tried to struggle. 'What about my dinner? I shall have to go back and see to that.'

'Don't worry, that's all been taken care of. Helen is looking after that. Karen is just cooking dinner here. After dinner you can go home and pick up a few of your personal things, but not too much. The picture of our Dad. I know you want to keep that, but

I don't want that old furniture here. You can give it to one of the neighbours. Your dinner has already gone to that little old lady that lives alone. We know you often send her a dinner on a Sunday. Well, today she is in for a treat. She can have the pudding too.' He smiled, for he knew his mother always boiled his favourite spotted dick on Sundays.

The table was set for six people, complete with wine glasses and shining new cutlery. There was a banging on the shop door. He looked out of the window. Helen and her husband, Harry, were waiting outside.

'Well, Mom, how do you like your new home?'

The emotion was too much for their mother. She burst into tears, but tried to pass it off by saying, 'You buggers, fancy playing a trick like that on me. I could have had a nasty stroke or a heart attack!'

Next morning, Alex made a sentimental visit to his old house. He sat down on the edge of his mother's old iron bed, the same bed he and his sisters were born in, staring round the bare walls. They had never seen wallpaper or paint as far as he could remember. Neither had the old fireplace in the bedroom seen a fire since the day his father died, but his mother had black leaded the grate till it shone like burnished steel. In front was the loose floorboard under which he kept his Oxo tin, dropping through pennies and the occasional silver coin. He lifted the floorboard. The Oxo tin was still there. He picked it up. Beneath it was a very thin Victorian penny, the old Queen's head rubbed smooth and hardly discernible. He pictured the old woman standing at the door, the thin penny in her hand. 'Can you change this for me, Alex? Give me a thicker one. You get more gas.'

He smiled to himself as the ghostly memory disappeared. He put the penny in the tin and took it with him. When he arrived back at his flat, he placed the tin safely away in his new sideboard.

# Chapter Eighteen

Alex was confident from the day he opened the front door of the shop it would be successful. He was giving people what they wanted at a price they could afford, and for those who coudn't afford to pay outright he allowed them one pound credit paid back at a shilling a week for twenty-one weeks. He spent his time at the Potteries, searching for job lots and seconds. There was a market for everything at the right price. He also had twenty agents working in the factories and could have had twenty more as everyone was interested in making a few shillings on the side.

Karen was secure in her own job as a secretary to her boss. Her money was good, far above the average, so she was reluctant to give it up. She kept Alex's books in her spare time and typed his letters; a typed letter always looked superior. Polly jumped at the chance of handing in her notice at work. She hated the factory. Her clothes always stank of industrial suds and she hated the work, so when Alex offered her a job for twice the money she was getting, she threw her arms round her brother's neck and kissed him. Alex wiped his cheek and laughingly threatened her with the sack if she kissed her boss again.

Much to Arthur's relief, Alex decided to keep the old chapel going for storage and packing his agents' orders. Arthur was doing well with his second-hand clothes stall in the market and trading illegally in the chapel. He also discovered several warehouses that supplied new children's clothes, and the market inspector allowed him another stall next to his own. Alex had certainly instilled his friend with ambitions.

On occasions when she had the day off, Karen would accompany Alex to the Potteries. He was teaching her to drive and soon gained so much confidence in her, he would let her drive home while he caught up on his sleep.

Karen was getting more beautiful as she grew older and had a figure that turned men's heads, staring unashamedly as she passed. Alex was quite proud to take her round the factories, especially one pottery. It was a factory that specialised in the better quality goods, not exactly Wedgwood, but employed a hundred men and women. The owner, some fifteen years Karen's senior, took a fancy to her and naturally Alex took advantage of this, buying most of the seconds and rejects. He was getting a good name in the trade for his honesty and always paying in cash.

'I think Jeremy has taken a fancy to you, Karen,' he told her one day when he returned from the Potteries. 'He asked about you and looked disappointed when he knew you wasn't with me. He's a widower, you know. Lost his wife about three years ago.

He has a little boy of five. You'd be all right there, Karen, he's got pots of money and you'd have a ready made family.'

'Bugger off, Alex! Let's get that van unloaded, and give me your invoices.'

She blushed deeply, but Alex could see she was flattered.

The threat of war hung over Europe like a gigantic storm cloud. Tales were coming out of Germany of concentration camp horrors and Jew baiting was openly shown on the newsreels in the cinemas. Jackboots were goose stepping once more, and Hitler was shouting for expansion of territory. Posters were going up all over Birmingham for volunteers for the R.A.P, Red Cross and special constables. Training was stepped up at the Drill Hall. The old Vickers machine guns were called in and new Bren guns issued, which were more accurate, lighter and could be fired faster. War talk was the topic in all the pubs and British Legion clubs. It was no surprise when, one day the property owners agent called in. Alex waited for him to make the first move.

'Don't be a bloody fool. Tell the owners all I am prepared to pay is two hundred and fifty pounds. He can take it or leave it. He gets fifteen shillings a week for this place. That's equivalent to eight years rent, so he can think himself lucky. Have you seen the posters all over town asking for volunteers for the R.A.P. You know what that means?' He answered the question himself. 'It means the war, when it comes, won't be trench warfare like the last one. No, sir. Every man, woman and child will be in this one, and that means bombs, so if this is still standing after the war he will be bloody lucky!'

'But four fifty, Mr Edwards is a fair price for a shop in this condition and in this location. Can I tell him you will offer three hundred, I'm sure he'll settle for that?' 'No, and I mean no. Two fifty is my offer. This is only a nice shop because I made it so. When I came here it was overrun with rats and in a filthy condition. It took four men, my sister and myself to lick this into shape. I have spent pounds on the premises and haven't asked the landlord for a penny. New guttering on the roof and the outside walls pointed. If you had offered this for sale before I took over, you would have been lucky to get a hundred. Now you must excuse me, I have a lot of work to get through.'

As the agent left the shop, Alex looked at his mother, who had been helping him to wipe some of the china, and winked his eye.

'Bet you a couple of shillings to a penny, he'll be back before the day's out.'

His mother laughed.

It was just after lunch when the agent returned. Alex was on top of a flight of steps stacking away and displaying tea and dinner sets. He looked down on the agent. He knew he had the advantage so he didn't bother to climb down.

'I don't wish to haggle with you. I suppose you have seen the owner. My offer still stands, two fifty. You must be a busy man and as you can see so am I, so let me know what the position is.'

The agent had already had several dealings with Alex. The owner of the shop had seen the improvements made to the premises and then explored every avenue looking for a loop hole in the lease to increase the rent, but the agent had likened the outcome to hitting his head against a brick wall. Alex may be very young for a business man, and although he was described as hard, he also had a reputation for being fair.

'I also have to tell you, Mr Edwards, that the premises next door are up for sale. Mr Maynard, as you know, has a very successful hardware and tool business, but he wants to retire. Both his employees are in the T.A. If the war breaks out they will be the first to go and he says that at his age he'll never manage on his own. His daughter lives in South Africa, he plans to settle there.'

This was one bit of news that Alex hadn't anticipated. Mr Maynard was an institution in the street. No one could remember the street without him. In fact, when anyone enquired where Alex's shop was, the answer would always be, 'next door to Maynard's.' True, Alex didn't know much about the hardware trade but he hadn't known anything about the china trade till he went to work in the market. Perhaps he could work out a deal with Mr Maynard. He didn't fancy handling tools, that was a specialised job, but hardware mixed with household goods, he could make a go of that. Already he was visualising a part of the wall that separated the two shops, vanishing. He already had eight hundred square feet of selling space and by making some quick mental calculations he reckoned that he could double that to sixteen hundred.

'In that case, I'll give you five hundred for the two. If that's satisfactory, we can get it finalised by the weekend. You should tell the owner he's lucky to get a deal straight away, no one with any sense is buying property these days.'

Alex closed his ears to anything the agent was saying, as he babbled on in his phoney pound note accent. He was already making mental calculations as to how he was going to set out the property.

'You may tell Mr Maynard there's no hurry for him to vacate his premises. I'll give him time to dispose of any stock I don't want. Now, if you don't mind, I'm sure we both have plenty to do without wasting time on small talk.'

The agent was about to open his briefcase, when he noticed that Alex had turned to carry on with his work. He thought better of it, snapped the briefcase shut and walked out of the shop.

'Bought old Maynard's shop today, Karen,' said Alex, as they sat down to tea. 'Also bought this shop. No good paying rent to someone else all our lives. Got the pair of them for a song.'

'How much?' Karen put down her teacup and stared hard at him. 'And what do you intend doing with it? We are already bursting at the seams with china. You have the basement full, and shed at the bottom of the garden, and the old chapel. I think it's time we stopped buying and sold off some of the stock.'

'What, and miss seeing that boyfriend of yours?'

'He's not my boyfriend.' She blushed deeply, but couldn't help but smile as Alex stared at her over the top of his teacup. 'He's a very nice man and acts like a gentleman.'

Everyone knew the war was inevitable, but still they turned their backs on the fact, so preparations were very scant. But Alex was an exception. He converted the garden end of the basement into a self-contained air raid shelter. He double bricked the section and fitted it out with six ex-army beds he'd bought from the local ex-government store. He hoarded stacks and stacks of tinned food, tea, sugar and tinned milk. The toilet was just outside the back door. 'If Arthur's or Horace's mother wish to stay they may, but whatever you do, don't let Arthur's old man near it or you can say goodbye to the bottles of brandy!'

He set out instructions for the use of the shelter. At least he would have some peace of mind while he was away. Britain was an island so every drop of fuel had to come across the seas, and he was aware that the tankers carrying this would be prime targets for the enemy submarines. He took the precaution of building up a store of petrol using the brick shed at the bottom of the garden. He employed a couple of men to dig down two feet and concrete the sides.

'Building an inside swimming pool, Mr Edwards?' asked one of the men.

Alex burst out laughing. It was best not to let anyone know his precise intentions. 'You could say that, I suppose.' He handed them a cigarette. 'No, it's an air raid shelter for my sisters and mom. I shall be away early with the Terriers.'

'You reckon there will be a war then, Mr Edwards?'

'Certain, its as plain as the nose on your face. Believe me, when it starts there is sure to be air raids and Brum, being an industrial city, will be a prime target. Haven't you done anything about it?'

They shook their heads. 'It's all talk. It's more than he dare do. I would pay old Hitler to drop a few bombs on some of these decrepit old buildings. That's all they're fit for.' This was a sentiment shared by thousands of people living in back to back houses, that should have been demolished previously.

Once the workmen finished, Alex started to store away the two gallon cans of petrol he had been collecting over the past few months. He covered them with the soil which had been dug out, then laid planks of wood over them. Like his air raid shelter, only a direct hit would destroy them. Used sparingly, the petrol should be sufficient to take Karen to the Potteries for a few months at least. Unfortunately, there'd be no joy rides or trips to the countryside for his mother or any members of his family.

If anyone was prepared for war, it was Alex. When it did arrive that fateful Sunday morning and the air raid sirens sounded after just a few minutes, the family was secure.

Alex and Arthur departed, their battalion joining the B.E.F. in France, but for months nothing happened. When it finally started, with the might of Hitler's armour ploughing its way across the countryside, both the French army and the B.E.F. were totally unprepared, overrun, and within weeks were beaten back to Dunkirk.

'Just take a look at this lot, Arthur.' Alex said, as they reached the outskirts of the city.

Abandoned vehicles of every description stretched for miles, all totally disabled, their engines ripped out and petrol tanks bashed in, some had been set on fire. A black solid smoke settled over the area like a thick London fog. Military policemen were directing them to the dunes on the beaches.

'Disable that vehicle and carry weapons.' He looked them up and down. 'You infantry, how many there?'

'A sergeant and eight men, two Bren guns, the rest riflemen,' the sergeant answered, sweat running down his grimy face.

'You have to report to the officers over at the house.' He pointed to a large building, which was temporarily being used as G.H.Q.

A mixed bag of infantry regiments were formed to hold a perimeter around the city, while the bulk of the expeditionary force were being taken off the beaches in any kind of craft that floated. Alex and Arthur were detailed to hold a small section of a side road. They stood behind a stone garden wall reinforced with sand bags.

'How long do we have to hold it, Sarge?' enquired Alex.

The sergeant sighed and shrugged his shoulders.

'Buggered if I know. Make sure you have plenty of ammo. Frankly, Edwards, I doubt if you'll be getting off. We have to keep them away till most of the troops are evacuated.'

For two days, they held the post without anything happening. A battery of twenty-five pounders set up in the field behind the house, and more infantry men took up positions. Troops kept pouring in. After two days, the incoming troops became a trickle. By the third afternoon, hardly any men came in, just an occasional straggler. One man came in riding an old fashioned 'sit up and beg' ladies bike, his rifle strapped across the handlebars.

'Any grub, mate?'

Alex gave him a tin of bully and a couple of biscuits. Arthur handed him a mug of lukewarm tea.

'How far behind are they?'

'Buggered if I know, mate. I was kipping in this barn last night and could hear their guns. You couldn't see my arse for dust! I haven't seen my regiment since Arras.'

Later that day, they heard the faint crump of the enemy guns. Alex stood behind his Bren gun, his finger curled around the trigger. Patrols were sent out and reported back with the information they could hear tanks in the distance.

It was daybreak when the first shells started falling.

'Keep your eyes and ears open, men, they'll be sending patrols and recce parties out. If you see them, make sure they don't get back to their lines.'

He inspected their Bren guns and ammo. 'You'd better go and get more ammo, Edwards, and a few hand grenades, if I were you. Good luck, lads.'

Suddenly Alex was in the thick of it. Shells were dropping all round his post. Arthur went to fetch more ammo. As Alex turned, he saw Arthur running towards him, his hands went in the air and he dropped the ammunition he was carrying and slumped to the ground. Alex touched an infantryman's shoulder in a slit trench next to him.

'Ever handled a Bren gun, mate?' He didn't wait for an answer. 'My mate's been hit. I'm going to fetch him in.'

'You won't stand a chance in this lot.'

But before the man could stop him. Alex was sprinting across the ground. He knelt beside his friend. The left foot was now hanging by a couple of tendons, blood gushing from the wound. Picking him up, he lifted him over his shoulder and ran in a crouching position, back to his post. The man on the gun looked at Arthur's foot and threw up. A medical orderly nearby tied up the wound, stemming the flow of blood.

130

Arthur suffered incredible pain and, without any pain killing drugs, occasionally dropped into a deep coma-like sleep, only to wake with a sudden jolt, look at his foot, and burst out laughing. The medic gave him a sip from a bottle of brandy but Arthur almost choked on it as he burst out laughing. The medic shook his head.

'He's going round the bend. He should have hospital treatment, can't we get him back?'

'Right, you lads, hold the fort here.'

Alex recognised that voice booming out as if he were on a barrack square. The big man came striding up. If there were any enemy snipers near, he would make a prime target but it didn't seem to worry him.

'What have we got here? God, man, can't you stand on one foot? The Jerries will be down any minute.' He looked at Arthur then at Alex. 'What the hell are you two men doing here?'

'Holding this post, sergeant.' He bent down to examine Arthur's foot. The medic was nearby. 'What do you make of this, medic? In a bad way?'

'He should have medical treatment, Sarge. I've done all I can for him. The wound should be cleaned and stitched up. Could lose his leg or his life if it isn't attended to.'

'Right, laddie, get him over your shoulder and down to the boats. Try and get him evacuated as fast as possible.' He helped to get Arthur across Alex's shoulders and whispered in his ear. 'And give my love and best wishes to your mother, Alex.' He put a letter in Alex's top pocket. 'See my missus gets this, Alex.' He tapped his back and shouted, 'Get that man evacuated as soon as possible.'

Alex smiled to himself. So it was Mr Kingsley. He hardly recognised him with all that filth and sweat on his face, but there was no way he could forget that booming Sergeant Major's voice.

The sand dunes and shore were crowded with troops, some up to their necks in water. Ships of all sizes were running into the beach, picking up troops and ferrying them out to larger ships. It looked hopeless. He laid Arthur down as close as possible to the sea, then went in search of a small craft. But as soon as a boat beached there was a mad rush. Arthur kept bursting out laughing. The men waiting for a boat looked at him and shook their heads sadly.

'Poor bastard is doing his nut,' said one.

'He'll be all right as soon as I get a boat for him,' answered Alex, but his face told a different story. He was panic stricken at the thought of losing his closest friend. 'You stand as much chance as an ice cream in hell, pal! Anyway, they won't take him. Can't you see he's snuffing it? Poor bastard's delirious.'

'He'll be all right when I get him back.' He lifted Arthur's head on to his knee and gave him a sip of water from his water bottle. 'You'll be all right, Arth, we will get a boat soon.'

'You're wasting your time, mate. Tell the bloke the truth. He's finished, like us. They don't give a toss about us. We may as well put our hands up and let Jerry take us. They'll look after your mate.'

'No Jerry will take us, mate, and he ain't going to die, even if I have to swim with him on my back.'

'That's the only chance you've got,' said the man in a light blue airforce uniform and walked away to the doubtful safety of his shallow slit trench.

Alex saw a small launch coming towards them. He swam out strongly towards it, thankful for those days they'd spent swimming in that filthy old canal, dodging the flying lumps of coal from the bargees. Several other men had the same idea. Alex held on to the boat's gunnal.

'Take me and my mate will you? He's badly wounded and needs medical treatment. If you can't take me, take my mate or he'll die.'

'We'll all die if I don't get some fuel. I must have a petrol leak somewhere. I won't make it back to England.'

He helped Alex and two other men on board. Alex examined the engine. A heavy smell of petrol filled the small compartment. The boat itself was only thirty feet long. A sergeant was waiting, knee deep in water, for the boat to beach.

'How many can you take aboard, mister?'

'About a dozen if I can get some fuel. I've promised this man I'll take his friend who is badly wounded, but I've a bad fuel leak.'

Alex lifted Arthur on to the small cabin roof, then set about locating the leak. He found a small fracture in a copper tube.

'Send half a dozen men to get some petrol. There must be gallons laying around. Meantime, I'll try and fix this leak.'

He rubbed the copper tube dry so he could cover the split with a piece of elastoplast he'd got from a medic's haversack. Then he realised that this would be useless as once the plaster got wet it would fall off.

'Anyone got any chewing gum?'

They found an airforce man chewing gum, his jaw frantically going up and down like a neurotic engine piston. At the promise of a lift home, he removed the lump of gum from his mouth and several sticks from his pocket. Alex plastered the tiny crack and the medic bandaged over the whole lot. The men were returning with a dozen cans of petrol and in no time the small boat was heading for home.

They landed at a small port, west of Dover. The owner of the boat was a fresh water sailor who normally just cruised the Thames every summer weekend, where the only taste of danger was accidentally smashing into a bridge or hitting another vessel. Now, the owner's face told its story, lined with fear at the sound of exploding shells crashing outside the city or the lone German place straffing the beaches. When the coast of England had loomed into view, it was not the white cliffs everyone expected to see. They landed further west along the coast, where a handful of women had been waiting with hot tea and sandwiches. Everyone congratulated the weekend sailor and the lines of fear on his face disappeared as he smiled with pride.

Two hours later, they were whisked away in an army lorry, and Arthur was despatched to the local cottage hospital. Alex managed to get through to Karen on the telephone. She was relieved to hear his voice, knowing that he was safe and sound.

'But I have some very bad news. Arthur was badly wounded. He's lost a foot and it's probable he may have to have some more of his leg removed. We managed to get him on what must have been one of the last boats to leave France. Remember Mr Kingsley? We met him, he was the one who got us away. I don't know what happened to him. The last I saw, he was waiting for Jerry behind a Bren gun, a rifle with fixed bayonet by his side. I have no idea when I'll see you all. It looks like leave is out of the question at the moment.' His money ran out and there was a queue of men waiting to use the phone.

It was two months before Alex got leave. He was mentioned in despatches for saving Arthur's life, and promoted to corporal, then posted to a depot near his home town. After Dunkirk, people became very wary. Would it be their turn next? Property prices slumped, houses and business premises were going for a song. Karen cashed in, buying property left, right and centre, exactly as Alex had instructed. When he went through his books with her, he was amazed at how much property they owned.

'You've done well, Karen. We can't have a lot left in the bank.'

She smiled. 'You'll be surprised. Business has really taken off. Buying all that china paid dividends. I go to the Potteries about once a month, and our own petrol store is still untouched. The government give us a little allowance but I don't think that will be for very much longer now, we're losing quite a bit of shipping. China is no problem, Jeremy sees I get plenty. He's a bit worried though because most of his men have gone in the services and a few of his women have left. Some to go into the forces, but a lot of them have gone into munitions where they can earn twice as much as Jeremy was paying them.

Alex visited Arthur at the hospital near Hastings, using some of his precious petrol to get there. It was the first time he'd seen him since Dunkirk. He took Arthur's mother and Karen along. Arthur was sitting up in bed, supported by a wall of pillows, his face ashen and drawn. He brightened up when he saw them enter the ward, shaking hands warmly with Alex. Karen and his mother kissed him. There was a metal cage over his legs. He patted it.

'They've taken my leg off below the knee. Bloody ironic, isn't it? My old man puts a bullet in his foot during the last war and I get mine blasted away in this. I couldn't stop laughing when I saw my foot dangling off.'

'So that's why you kept laughing when I took you down to that boat. Everyone thought you were delirious.'

'How has Dad been, Mom? Still on the booze? Whatever you do, don't let him get near that bleeding chapel or there'll be sod all left when I get back!'

His mother didn't say anything. That was just what his father had been doing. Going to the chapel and selling bits of clothing to pay for his beer. He'd been having a grand old time.

'Don't you worry about a thing, Arthur. You just get yourself well. I suppose this means the end of your army career, thank God. It could have been worse, like some of those poor men that's left behind. When they discharge you, you'll be able to look after the business yourself.'

She was overcome with emotion and burst into tears, burying her head in the bedclothes. She had to keep the real truth from him. He patted the top of her head, her hair long since turned grey, years before its time.

'Don't worry, Mom, I'll sort it out when I come home.'

He burst into a hysterical laugh again, laughing so much that the tears rolled down his face. It was several minutes before he regained his composure, and repeated himself. 'Bloody ironic, isn't it? The old man puts a bullet in his foot to get out of the war, and me, I wanted to stay in and not content with just a bullet, I end up losing the bottom part of my leg.' He laughed again.

The ward nurse came to his bedside to see what was going on.

'He goes like this now and again, but he's harmless.' she said as she adjusted the bedclothes, then walked away smiling.

They stayed with him for over two hours, Alex relating how they managed to get across in a small boat; Arthur with only the slightest idea what had happened. He knew that Alex carried him from the perimeter they were holding and made sure he was on the boat, but the smaller details were lying dormant in his sub conscious. He looked a lot better by the time they left.

'I don't know what I will tell Arthur when he comes home. His father has been selling his stock for booze. It's got to stop, Alex. I've got myself a job in the factory now they're on war work. There will be no beer money for his father. If he wants money he'll have to work for it.'

'I'll put a pair of heavy padlocks on the doors tomorrow. That'll stop him getting in again,' said Alex.

But she was deep in thought. 'I could have broken my heart, seeing poor Arthur laying there helpless. What kind of father is he, Alex? What manner of man can openly rob his own son while he's away serving his country? That miserable swine even had to mutilate his own body. I have put up with that sham for twenty-five years. Believe me, Alex, when we get back there's going to be some drastic changes. He'll get a job if I have to drag him to the factory. He isn't much good, but put a broom in his hand and he can sweep the floors and do a bit of labouring, and just let him complain once more about that foot of his and I promise you, I'll twist it round and stick it up his behind!'

She was as good as her word. As soon as Alex dropped her off, she stormed in the house, a determined look on her face. Her husband was stretched full length on the old sofa in a semi drunken stupor.

He opened his eyes and in a slurred voice said, 'Hello, Doll. How's our little son?'

She looked at him with contempt, grabbed him by the feet and spun him round. He sat up with a jerk, trying to put on a pained look, but saw his wife's face and just stared at her. All the years they'd been married, he'd never seen her in such a mood. Now he was in for a shock.

'Why you lazy, good for nothing bastard!'

He sat up straight for this was another first. Never before had she used such strong language.

'You lay there, pissed to your eyeballs on money you've stolen from your own son, while that lad had fought for his life for months, and he's not out of the woods yet. Now I'm going to tell you what you are going to do. In the morning you're going down to get a job. They're short of men so they'll take on anyone, and you fit the bill. Each week you'll get a pound of your wages. The rest will go into Arthur's bank account to help pay for what you've stolen. And don't your dare come home with that wage packet opened!'

'But, Doll, my foot, no one will take on a cripple like me. Who wants a cripple hobbling about their factory?'

She lifted her handbag as if to strike him. 'Your foot, you lying bastard. There's sod all wrong with your foot. Men have worked with worse injuries than that. If I hear one more moan about that rotten foot of yours, I'll chop it off and stuff it up your rear!'

He stared at her, bewildered. She was actually swearing at him. He had never heard her utter a swear word before, although he had made up for that. 'But, Doll.' he tried to protest.

'Don't you Doll me. Get a job or bloody well get out! You have two sons in the services, one badly wounded, and a daughter in the army. It's about time you did your bit for your country and the family. You've been scrounging off them all for years.' She looked at him. His eyes were half closed. 'Are you listening to me?'

'Yes, Doll.'

To make sure, she took the kettle off the gas stove and poured the contents over his head. Luckily the water was cold, but it brought him to life. He knew she meant business.

The next day, she went to her job in the munitions factory, and he got a job as a labourer. Not once did he dare go home with his wage packet opened. She went round to see Alex's mother on the Saturday.

'I should have done it long ago, Martha. Strange isn't it, he's hardly said a word and brings his wage packet home unopened.'

On the Saturday, Alex rang Jeremy at the Potteries to ask him to open on the Sunday as he was on leave and very busy. Jeremy was only too willing to oblige.

'Why don't you come over tonight, Alex? The boy is at boarding school out in the country and it gets very lonely up here. I could do with a bit of company. All my friends are in the services.' There was a slight pause. Alex knew what was coming next. 'Why not bring Karen along? I'm sure she could do with a break.'

She blushed when Alex asked her but didn't put up much of a protest. She was curious to see where Jeremy lived but more than surprised when she saw the house. It wasn't quite what you would call a house, especially when she'd been born in a house with just three rooms and no electric light, gas or indoor sanitation. This was a mansion, standing in ten acres of its own grounds. The lawn was neatly manicured, when they arrived the sun was just setting, throwing a golden light over the beautiful stone work.

'God, Alex, look at that!' Karen exclaimed as Alex stopped his van on the long drive leading to the house.

Jeremy was delighted to see them. They could see he was very proud of his house.

'My grandfather built the house. We have nine bedrooms and six bathrooms. It was his father and grandfather who started the business. They lived in that small cottage over there. They were both farm labourers but the son was a clever lad, and ambitious. First they started making clay pots in the cottage. They then discovered that the young lad's mother, my great grandmother, was a bit of an artist. The son gave up his job and went to work in an old pottery. He went out of his way to learn everything about it. They built a kiln in the yard. Just a small one, and it progressed from there. Before the war started, we employed over a hundred men and women. Now we're down to forty. I've lost three men in the war so far. One was killed at Narvik, another at Dunkirk, and this morning I heard another was killed, his ship sunk by a U boat.'

He gave Alex a telegram. 'His mother brought it over about an hour ago. She was distraught, and dropped the telegram.'

Alex read it, then handed it to Karen. She stared at it, her mouth wide open and gasped. 'Oh my God.' Her face turned white.

'Is something the matter?' asked Jeremy.

'Yes,' said Alex. 'Horace, my best friend, was on that ship. Do you know if there are any survivors?'

'No, I don't think so.'

Karen sat down in the overstuffed armchair and buried her head in her hands. Her body shook with sobs. Jeremy handed her a glass, a drop of brandy spinning round in the bottom.

The news ruined the weekend, which was to be a social occasion as well as business. On the Sunday, Alex conducted his business as fast as possible.

'I'm sorry, Jeremy, perhaps the next time I'm on leave.'

'I hope so, Alex. Karen, you're welcome to visit anytime you wish. Perhaps one day you could bring your mother for a day out.'

They shook hands. His eyes lingered on her face as he held her hand much longer than a normal handshake.

When they arrived back at the shop on the Sunday afternoon, Polly responded to her knock. She was crying so Karen put her arm round her.

'We heard the news when we were at Jeremy's house. It's terrible, Polly.'

This brought on another bout of hysterics. It was some minutes before she calmed down. It was their mother that filled them in with the bad news.

137

'Horace's mother was over here. She was hysterical. The telegram said he had been killed in action, his ship sunk with no survivors. His mom and dad are in a terrible state. Someone will have to tell Carol, his mother's in no fit state to go to her house.'

Karen was the only person who seemed to have kept her cool and was in a fit state to break the news to Carol. She jumped into the small van, still loaded with china. Arriving at Carol's house, she was just getting out of the van when Carol came to the door. She looked at Karen, her hand trembling on the door latch.

'It's Horace, isn't it Karen? I know, I had this terrible premonition, I never slept all night. I just kept tossing and turning, and when I did sleep I was continually waking up. Is he dead?'

Karen nodded her head. She was lost for words and felt that if she tried to talk she would burst into tears. She put her arms around Carol's neck.

'His parents received a telegram saying he was killed in action. They're in a hell of a state, will you come and see them?'

'Of course I will. I was just off to the cinema to try and get rid of this depression. They took Dad back in the Navy yesterday. He was in the first war and he's been pleading with them to take him back. Mom called him all fools possible, but she knew she never stood a chance and always played second fiddle to the Navy. He reckons he'll get a shore job, but knowing my dad he'll be in the thick of it before very long.'

They knocked on Horace's door. There was no response. They opened it quietly. His mother and father were sitting in the armchairs facing each other. They didn't look up as Carol and Karen walked in. His father looked worse. Always meticulous in his dress-as a rule, he was staring into space, his boots unlaced and his shirt wide open. He hadn't shaved. Carol put her arms round his mother.

'Come on, Mom, pull yourself together. Shall I make you a nice cup of tea?'

She didn't answer, so Carol made tea, lacing it with plenty of sugar and milk. She held it to his mother's lips and she sipped slowly.

'What shall I do, Karen? They are such lovely people when you get to know them.'

'There's nothing you can do. Only time will heal a wound like this, although I doubt very much if they will ever get over it. Horace was a great lad, we all loved him. It was me that wrote that reference for him, and Alex and Arthur who doctored his birth certificate. Please don't ever let his parents know. I feel so damn guilty.'

'I shouldn't feel guilty, if I were you. He used to tell me all about it and me, and Mom and Dad, we'd have some good laughs. He thought the world of your family and would always say he had two moms, a brother and three sisters. He will never know he was going to be a father. I think I'm in the family way. I've got to see the doctor on Tuesday. I told my mom. She's over the moon. She loved Horace as much as I did. I'll tell Horace's mom and dad as soon as I've seen the doctor. It may help to soften the blow. Horace used to say, when we are married and have kids, and we have a boy, for God's sake don't name him Horace. But believe me, Karen, if it is a boy he will be named Horace, because as far as I'm concerned, Horace will never be dead.'

Karen was surprised how coolly and calmly Carol had taken the news. Any other girl, especially if she was pregnant, would have had hysterics. It was later the tragic news hit Carol when she returned home alone to an empty house. She threw herself on the bed and sobbed. Which is where her mother found her the next morning when she returned from her evening shift at the factory.

# Chapter Twenty

Horace's parents didn't get over the shock of losing their one and only child. They retreated inside a shell. His father, who in the past had always taken a pride in his appearance, had gone down and down, hardly bothering to wash or shave for days on end. He never changed his shirt or underclothes from one weekend to another. The only thing that didn't suffer was his work. His firm had gone over completely to war work and he now worked as he'd never worked before, cursing and muttering under his breath. Alex visited them, but they hardly bothered to talk, as if they were silently blaming him for their misfortune. Alex's mother and Carol visited them frequently, cleaning up the house and doing their washing.

Two months later, when Carol was certain she was pregnant, she broke the news to them and for once his mother looked up, tears in her eyes.

'Horace will never be dead, Ma, not while Horace junior is here.'

She patted her still flat stomach and put her arms round his mother. They both cried together.

'Oh God,' she sobbed, 'you must come and live here, Carol, at least till it's all over and you will bring him to see us often?'

'Don't be silly, Mom, of course I will. But I can do even better than that. After the baby is born I will have to return to the hospital to work so I'll leave him here all day, and nights when I'm on duty.'

If they needed a tonic, this was it. From that day on they talked of nothing else but the baby, knitting and buying him baby clothes, sacrificing their own clothing ration coupons.

Alex was recalled from leave a few days before it was due to expire. His heart sank as rumours were flying around that the battalion was to be reformed and sent to the Middle East. It wasn't quite that disastrous. He was promoted to sergeant (acting unpaid) and ordered to get a new platoon into shape. The rumours of the battalion going overseas still persisted with the Middle East being the favoured destination. In the meantime he managed to get home most weekends.

Alex's mother was serving in the shop, when a young V.A.D. nurse walked in and looked around, inspecting several tea sets. She turned and smiled.

'Mrs Edwards?'

Her heart missed a beat. She thought the young nurse was about to break some bad news to her. Her voice was quiet and didn't lack education, but still bore traces of a Birmingham accent. She held out her hand and smiled.

'You don't remember me, do you?'

She stared at the young nurse. There was something familiar about the girl. She took off her small blue cap. Her hair, which had been tucked beneath it, fell to just above her shoulders like a golden waterfall.

'There is something familiar about you, but for the life of me I can't put a name to it.'

'Perhaps Victoria will help?'

'I only ever knew one Victoria. A little girl who lived facing us in our other house. She had a sister, Veronica, but they ...'

Her voice broke off as she recognised her.

'Good heavens, fancy that, after all these years. I can seen now, still the same golden hair and blue eyes. I shall never forget that day when that dreadful woman came and took you away. Your screams haunted me for weeks.'

'Yes, that dreadful woman, she showed no compassion whatsoever. She caned us when we arrived at the children's home. I shall never forget that day it was terrible. The only good thing that could be said about it was we had wonderful food, but after what we lived on for years, any kind of food would have seemed wonderful.'

Curiosity got the better of her. For years she had wondered what had happened to them. Where they went could only be an improvement on the squalid conditions they had been living under, only one decent meal a day, and that was at school. Just a few weeks previously, the family had been discussing the old street and the names of the two girls had come up with Alex wondering what had been the outcome.

'I think we had better go up to the flat. We can talk in peace there.'

She called Polly over and introduced her. She hardly remembered her.

'We're going to the flat, Polly.'

She led her up the stairs, now richly carpeted. Victoria looked around her.

'It looks like you've done very well, Mrs Edwards. A nice shop and this beautiful flat.' She noticed it was all pretty new furniture.

'It's Alex, he's away in the army depot. He's a sergeant now,' she said with pride in her voice. 'But he comes home most weekends. They're reforming his battalion and he reckons they will be sent overseas when they're fully trained. He doesn't seem to mind though. Karen had more or less taken over the business. I'm expecting her to come home any day and say she is getting married. Her bloke's a few years older than her and owns a pottery factory. Alex tells me he's crazy about her. But you'll meet them all soon. I must say, Victoria, you're looking well. Tell me what happened.'

'It's a long story.'

'So what, we've plenty of time. Polly can manage down in the shop and the one next door almost looks after itself. I still love a good gossip. So start from the beginning, while I make us a nice cup of tea.'

'From here they took us to a home. We were there for six months. It was out in the country, the other side of Bromsgrove. Once that horrible woman had dropped us there and hit me with the cane, we hardly ever saw her again - only when she brought in other children. One day, Veronica and I were playing in a field in front of the home, when this couple kept looking at me. The matron called me over. The man had a lovely face, and the matron said he wanted to adopt me and take me home. I burst out crying. I wanted to go but not without Veronica. Eventually they relented and said they would have both sisters. He was the type of man you wanted to call father from the start, he was so good and kind. Turned out he was a doctor with a practice in Harley Street, a specialist. He also had a small practice in the village. He sent us to a private school quite near. The school normally only took boarders, but as he was also the school doctor and a very persuasive man, they made an exception in our case. We both had ponies, there was nothing that was too much trouble, and we wanted for nothing. We were idolised by him and Mother. Veronica hopes to become a doctor. She can twist father round her little finger. I was hoping to become a teacher, but when the war started I joined the Red Cross. I'm in a hospital not more than ten miles from Birmingham. I would loved to have seen Alex, he was so kind to my mother. I used to watch him and his two friends in the yard with their home-made barrows.'

'Yes, that would have been Horace and Arthur. Horace was killed when his ship was sunk. It broke his mother's heart. Arthur has lost his leg. He's in hospital on the south coast. Both Arthur and Alex were in the very last small boat to leave Dunkirk.'

They were still talking when Polly closed the shops and came into the flat with the day's takings from both shops. A few minutes later, Karen arrived and was introduced.

'It's lovely to see you again, Victoria. Pity Alex isn't here, I'm sure he would loved to have seen you again. Where are you stationed?'

'About ten miles from here. There's a small military hospital where they treat crippled soldiers, not very big, there's about

142

forty patients. I have a few days' leave so I thought I'd try and trace my roots. Things haven't changed much.'

'No, still the same old bug and flea ridden slums. Pity they don't evacuate the place and encourage Jerry to drop a few bombs on it.'

Karen nodded her head, agreeing with every word her mother said.

'Where are you staying, Victoria?'

'Queens Hotel.' She looked out of the window. It was getting dark and Polly was preparing to put the blackout shutters in place. 'I hate this blackout.'

'Stay here, Victoria. It would be nice to have some company for a change. You can have Alex's room and Polly will be going out soon as she's had a bath. It takes her almost two hours to get ready. Her boyfriend's just been called up, so they're spending as much time together as possible. Then I can tell you everything that's happened here since you left and you can tell me all about your new life.'

In a casual manner Karen turned to her mother and said, 'By the way, Mom, I was up at the Potteries today and Jeremy asked me to marry him.'

Victoria was beside herself with the news.

'At least that's one bit of good news, Karen. Are you going to accept?'

'I don't know. He is fifteen years my senior with a ten year old son. It's rather a big step. I told him even if I accepted I couldn't go to live there till after the war. I just couldn't let Alex down. The rumours are rife at his depot that they may be going to the Middle East.'

Inwardly Karen was excited about her recent proposal and could hardly stop talking, unusual for her, as she was usually quiet and reserved.

'Do stay, Victoria, we have chicken for dinner. I've been thinking about it all the way from Stoke. Mom is still a good cook and there's plenty to go round.'

She didn't take a lot of coaxing as rationing had now begun to bite, and chicken was a rare treat. She was also keen to see Alex again.

'But I'll have to go to the hotel tomorrow to collect my case and pay my bill. If you don't mind, I'll use your phone to ring them. The hotel is very full and they may want to re-let my room.'

Alex came running up the stairs on Saturday morning.

'Had a hell of a job getting a lift this morning.' he shouted to Karen who was working at the top of the shop. 'I walked three

143

miles before anyone stopped and that was a battered old farm lorry.'

He stopped dead as he opened the lounge door and saw Victoria sitting at the table having breakfast. His forehead creased into lines forming an inverted V above his nose.

'Who are you?'

She smiled and a flicker of recognition flashed across his face.

'If you are who I think you are, I just can't believe it. You are Victoria, that little girl who lived opposite us. Well I'll be damned. Why only the other night, we were talking about the old house and your name crept into the conversation.'

'I know, your mother and Karen have told me. Strange that you remembered my face after all these years. I was so thin and scraggy then.'

He could have told her, he would never forget that face and those blue eyes. Neither would he ever obliterate from his memory those screams that echoed in that entry as they dragged her away.

'Well, believe me I am so pleased to see you again, and looking so well.'

They shook hands. He sat at the table and poured himself a cup of tea.

'I hope you will stay for a few days.'

'I've been here three days already, and sleeping in your room. Where will you sleep?'

'On this settee. I've slept in many worse places than this in the last few months. You certainly won't be putting me out. It'll be nice to have some company. But what brings you to this neck of the wood?'

'Sentimentality, I suppose. We all like to return to our roots, even if they do hold only bad memories. I went round to the old house. I cried a little. In one way, I didn't want to go, but it drew me like a powerful magnet. At home I used to dream about it often, waking up in the night screaming. They were bad days, Alex. Very bad.'

'I can agree with you there, Victoria. How people survived I will never know, starving in houses that were condemned before the last war. What with unemployment and the Means Test, the few coppers they handed out were barely enough to keep the wolf from the door. Then suddenly war breaks out. There's full employment with good wages, and they soon found the money to keep millions of men and women in the forces. Do we have our priorities right? I knew, since the day I pushed my first home-made barrow to collect a twenty-eight pound bag of coal, and earned my first few pence, that one day I would get rid of those shackles that kept me and the family on the poverty line.'

'Yes, Alex, and I am sure you will make it. You've done wonders with this shop. Your mother told me about the chapel you've rented. Was that the chapel where we went every Sunday to make sure we could go to the Christmas party at the end of the year?' She smiled. It was one of the few happy memories she had of her childhood. 'I was very sorry to hear about Arthur and Horace. I wonder how many more hearts will be broken before this is over?'

Alex never took his eyes from her face. Her expressions changed with her moods. Her skin was flawless and her eyes the deepest blue he's ever seen, staring at her unashamedly. He knew there would never be any other woman for him.

They were sitting alone together, the family had retired to their own rooms.

'I don't suppose you have any idea where my mother is buried, do you, Alex? I would love to see her grave. Her life was hard, but we both knew she went without food to give to us. On Sundays we could smell everyone cooking roast beef and we used to sit there with just our bread and jam, no butter. Sometimes, we would go for a walk in the park, just to get away from the smell. One Sunday, we watched this old lady feeding great chunks of bread to the ducks, while we sat there licking out lips. Poor mother, she was always coughing up blood. She had T.B. then, but never told us. We wouldn't have known what it was if she had. We were sitting on the park bench one Sunday, it was very hot and we hadn't eaten since Friday's school dinner, when a man came up and whispered in our mother's ear. She got up from the seat and went away with him for a few minutes. When she returned she had half a crown in her hand and she was crying. I didn't know what she had done at the time, but as I grew older I realised she had sold her body just to get us a meal. She didn't eat anything, she just cried and cried. She must have been deeply wounded.'

She brightened up as she recalled another day.

'We were walking through the park, when Veronica spotted this piece of paper against a hedge. She ran over to pick it up to put in the bin, but when she got hold of it she found it was a pound note. We looked around. It was a cold day and the park was deserted. Believe me, Alex, we lived like royalty that week. Can you imagine it? Mother got fifteen shillings a week out of which she paid five shillings rent. That only left ten shillings to feed and clothe all of us and buy fuel in the winter. I hated the long school holidays. Veronica and I never got dinner then, but that pound note, it was like an angel had thrown it down just there for us to find.

You know, Alex, I would never forget you and that barrow of yours. I heard later that it was you that wheeled my mother home that day, and lit a fire for her, then tried to give her hot milk. You and your mother were always kind to her. I used to look out of the window and envy the people you delivered those sacks of coal to. We used to have to burn paper and any old scraps of wood we could find in the streets. One day, we were lucky enough to find several lumps of coal which had dropped off a coal cart. We had no bedclothes so we all slept between two old feather mattresses. We would take it in turns to sleep in the middle. Mother used to make a joke of it, keeping a roster, but really it must have been tearing her apart.'

'Yes, I remember the mattresses. But you, I just can't believe how you've grown up. You mother was a very sick lady. You must be very proud of her. I know she would be very proud if she could see you now.'

'She does see me, Alex. She watches over the both of us. I can feel her presence constantly, and when ever I have a problem, I sit alone and think about how she would have handled it. That's why my greatest wish is to see my mother's grave. Do you think I have a chance? I wouldn't ask your mother or Karen. They've enough to worry about.'

Next morning, Alex spent several hours with Karen, going over the books and encouraging her to buy as much property as possible. He picked up the newspaper and ran through the property for sale advertisements.

'Property prices are still falling. I see the old chapel is up for sale.'

He read the advert with the final lines - 'Let to a reliable tenant.' He smiled.

'Go for it, Karen. It's not right to mix business with sentiment, but it's a very useful building, quite roomy. Make a nice storeroom.'

He slammed the large ledger shut.

# Chapter Twenty-One

If there was anyone who knew the location of the grave, it would be Harry. He paid him a visit.

'I don't know, Alex. She was buried in a pauper's grave. I remember, I collected her body from the morgue. We had three pauper burials that day. I know it was Witton Cemetery. I don't suppose you remember what year it was?'

'No but I'll try and find out. Anything else you need to know?'

'If we can get the date she died, I can go through the boss's ledgers. The supervisor at the cemetery owes me one or two good turns, as I always give the bereaved a gentle hint that it's customary to tip the diggers, and they in turn drop some to the supervisor. It's all swings and roundabouts, Alex. Get that date and I'll see what I can do.'

Alex rang the hospital and told Victoria he was making progress. It was really an excuse to speak to her.

'You are absolutely certain that was the date?'

'Believe me, Alex, I will never forget it. Of course I don't know the exact date of the burial.'

'That's all right, Victoria.' He lowered his voice as he plucked up courage to tell her the real reason he had telephoned. 'Will you be down next weekend? I can get away Friday evening.'

'Of course, Alex. I'm longing to see you again.'

His heart beat a little faster, he'd thought of nothing else since the previous weekend. Worse was to come. Rumours of the impending departure overseas were growing stronger. They were taking bets in the sergeant's mess as to where and how soon. The Middle East still seemed the most favoured destination now that Italy had joined in the war.

Harry had the information ready for him.

'It was very difficult, Alex. They bury as many as possible in a pauper's grave. Fortunately, she was the last one in.'

He gave him a piece of paper with the number of the grave, her age, the date she was born, and the date she died.

'She was only thirty years old, Alex. She died on her birthday.'

The note read - Rosalind Tanner, born 16 October 1898, died 16 October 1928.

'Knowing you, I suppose you will be putting a stone over it. The supervisor said he will put a wooden marker there and a pal of his will do a small headstone cheap. They reclaim some stones and re-polish them.' He gave him the name of the monumental mason whose workshop was just outside the cemetery gates. 'Nip over and see him this afternoon. He's a friend of mine. Tell him I sent you.'

Alex didn't tell Victoria he'd located the grave. The mason promised him the stone would be in place the following week, and he wanted it to be a surprise.

They spent the weekend together. She took him to the park and showed him where she and her sister had sat, enviously watching the ducks being fed.

'Look, Alex, that's the very same bench we sat on. I know it's that one because someone had carved their initials on it and they're the same as mine, V.T.'

She threaded her arm through his as they sat down. An old woman was feeding the ducks. She wondered if it was the same old woman. It was getting dark when they returned home. She had to return to the hospital that night as she was on duty. Alex took her to the railway station. As the train was pulling off, she leaned through the carriage window and kissed him gently on the forehead.

'I'll see you next week, Alex, I've got a long weekend then. Perhaps you would like to go down and visit Arthur. It's been such a long time since I saw him last, I doubt very much if he will remember me.'

Arthur was overjoyed to see his old friend Alex again. He vaguely remembered Victoria but couldn't understand how she could be this beautiful apparition now standing before him. He still recalled her from her childhood, as the spindly legged girl with streaky blonde hair.

'Oh yes, Arthur, I remember you all right. You used to swear a lot! I also remember that time you and your two friends went to the cinema matinee to see a Tarzan film, and then went home and painted that little blonde girl from head to foot with that black polish. You said she had to be a zulu if she wanted to play.'

Arthur laughed as he remembered his childish prank. Then looked at Victoria and stammered, 'That wasn't you, was it?'

It was her turn to laugh now. 'Thank God it wasn't. My mom could never afford soap and I would have gone to school looking like a zulu for three or four weeks. I do remember the girl's mother going to Alex's house and threatening to ring the three of you by the neck. I was in the same class as that poor girl. She had traces of that black grate polish in her ears and round her mouth for weeks.'

By the time they'd left, Arthur had shaken off his melancholy mood as they reminisced about their childhood pranks. Unfortunately, Victoria's only happy childhood days were those spent watching the other kids at play as she looked through her window.

'Do me a favour, Alex, when you get home. Tell my old man, if I hear him complain once more about that bloody foot of his, he'll have to go to hospital to have my other foot removed from his rectum!'

'I don't think you will have to, Arthur. Your old man is a reformed character now. Your mother laid the law down to him. He's working now and seems to be doing all right. Your mom only lets him have a pint every night and a couple on Sundays, and he's tidied himself up. I thought your mother would have written and told you.'

'She can't write, can she? And I can't understand my old man's writing. He sent two letters but I didn't bother answering them. It's about time our mom laid the law down to that old bastard.' He hesitated and put his hand over his mouth. 'I'm sorry, Victoria, it just slipped out.'

'Don't worry, Arthur, I have heard worse than that.'

They said their good-byes. Victoria leaned over the bed and kissed him, whilst Alex shook hands.

'We may be off shortly, Arthur. I'll try and get down to see you again when I get embarkation leave.'

On the way back, Alex tried to apologise for Arthur's outburst of bad language but it hadn't bothered her.

'His old man was a swine, Victoria. All he ever thought of was booze and that saga of his war wound. He must have told me at least a dozen different versions of how he came by it. There was hardly a person in the neighbourhood who didn't know it was a self inflicted wound.'

They drove along the almost deserted roads, stopping a couple of times to eat the sandwiches they brought with them, and once at a transport cafe for a hot drink. The air inside the cafe was thick with cigarette smoke. Fifty pairs of admiring eyes followed Victoria as she walked from the door to a seat. She took off her hat and shook out her shoulder length blonde hair. The men, soldiers and civilians alike, licked their lips and cast an envious eye at Alex, as he placed a thick china mug of tea before her.

'Fancy a bacon sandwich like that one over there?' He nodded towards a middle aged civilian lorry driver who had two enormous thick slices of bread with a couple of rashers between them, dripping with bacon fat and tomato ketchup.

'Why not?' replied Victoria, proving that the change in her fortunes and lifestyle hadn't turned her into a snob and she was soon tucking into a large sandwich. The silence now broken, the crowded workman's cafe once more hummed with conversation.

The following Sunday, a surprise awaited Victoria. After lunch, Alex suggested a walk. It was hardly a day for walking. Heavy clouds hung over the city and the roads were continually being washed by sporadic bursts of rain. Most of the factories had turned over to war work, their chimneys belching out black sooty smoke. Victoria didn't object, she liked to be alone with Alex. She slipped her arm through his and slid her hand into his greatcoat pocket.

'The sky is brightening a little now, Victoria.'

She looked up at a break in the leaden sky, where two shafts of sunlight, like giant searchlights, fingered the rain sodden earth.

They stopped at the cemetery gates, while Alex bought a bunch of flowers and a vase from an old lady selling flowers and china flowerpots. The vase had 'Mother' inscribed on the side in bold black letters. He got the old lady to wrap it up so Victoria wouldn't see it. She walked on, but noticing the parcel wrapped in newspaper under his arm, her forehead creased into lines as she looked askance at him. She slipped her arm through his again, as they walked together up the path between the rows of graves.

'Is your father buried here, Alex?'

'Yes, but I don't remember him at all. I was quite young when he died, but I do have a dear friend buried here. He died from wounds he got in the first war and he was badly gassed. I would always talk to him. Strange thing is, he never talked to me. He couldn't. But he understood every word I said, and I knew what he meant by the look in his eyes.'

He told her of the long conversations he used to have with old Mr Fisher.

They turned and walked towards a flattened plot with just a few raised mounds and only one grave, which had a small marble stone at its head. She turned to him, her bottom lip trembling, her throat dry as she tried to speak.

'Is this it, Alex?' she finally said, moving slowly towards the solitary headstone, her legs barely under control.

He put his arm around her tiny waist to support her. She clung to his shoulders.

'Take it easy, Vic.'

As he said it, another shaft of sunlight broke through the clouds and struck the marble headstone making it shine like a diamond under bright light.

She stood motionless at the foot of the grave, looking at her mother's name. Gradually she sank to her knees, oblivious to the wet soil. She put her head in her hands, her body shook uncontrollably with sobs.

'I shall never forget you, Mother, never. You did all you could for my sister and me. Rest in peace, Mother, you deserve it.'

Alex took the vase and went to the solitary tap at the end of the row of graves, taking his time to allow Victoria a few moments alone at her mother's grave. He broke down the stalks of the flowers and arranged them in the vase. When he returned some twenty minutes later, she was still on her knees but in a different place now, her arm around the headstone.

'I shall never forget you for this, Alex. I loved you before we came here but now I love you even more. Will you marry me, Alex? I have just told Mother,' she said, pointing to the headstone, 'I intend to marry you. I know you will be going away shortly but I have asked Mother to watch over you. You'll be back one day.'

He took her by the hands and lifted her to her feet. Her knees and one side of her bottom were covered in mud. He took her in his arms and kissed her.

Quietly he said, 'Look Victoria, I don't want you to marry me just because I arranged this for you. Wait till I return to England. It will only be for a couple of years. It'll give you time to think really hard about this. I love you too but I want no regrets afterwards.'

'No, Alex. I loved you from the first time you walked into the lounge of your flat. I want to marry you and I want to marry you now. Of course you do realise that Karen won't be with you all the while. She wants to marry Jeremy.' His eyebrows raised. 'Don't look surprised. We will get married in a couple of weeks time. I have already told my adoptive parents that I have met the man I want to marry.'

For the first time since they'd stopped at the grave, she gave a wicked grin.

'Well, if that's the case, we had better marry straight away. We can't disappoint your parents.'

Like a teenage couple who had just discovered love for the first time, they stood either side of the grave, holding hands over the headstone, and swore an oath over her mother's grave that they would be true to each other forever.

He looked directly into her eyes and said, 'I promise you this, Mother, that she will never want for anything in her life while I am able to provide it.'

Then they kissed across the headstone.

Alex's mother and sisters were overjoyed at the news.

'I wanted her to wait till the war was over, Mom, but she was insistent we marry straight away.'

He visited her parents and sister, the following weekend, and received a warm welcome. Veronica was out riding her horse, when she saw the small van coming up the drive. She raced after it her long hair blowing in the wind.

'She rides well, Victoria.'

'Too damn well. One of these days she will chance her luck too far. She's a real tomboy. It's a rare sight to see her in a dress. At home she's always out riding. Father just laughs when I bring the subject up. They're as thick as thieves.'

Veronica entered the room breathless, kissed her father and mother affectionately, then looked Alex up and down.

'He's not bad looking, Vic.' She looked at the three stripes on his arm and pulled a face. 'A sergeant, eh? Thought you would have brought home a captain at least!'

She kissed Alex, then returned to where her father was sitting in his winged, easy chair. She put her arm round his shoulders.

'What do you think of your future son-in-law, Father?' She poured herself a sherry and her father a brandy and soda. 'Do you drink, Alex?'

'No thanks, can't stand the taste of the stuff myself.'

She shook her father's shoulder. 'I asked you a question, Father. What do you think of having a sergeant for a son-in-law?'

'He could be a dustman as far as I'm concerned. All I ask is he makes my daughter happy, and woe betide him if he doesn't.'

'That's what I wanted to hear.'

She raised her glass towards Alex. 'Welcome to the family, Alex, and may you both be very happy. What do you say, Mother?'

'I agree with both of you.' She went to raise herself from the armchair. 'I must see that lunch is prepared, then Alex can tell us all about himself and his ambitions for the future. Excuse me, Alex.'

Alex was surprised but not the least bit embarrassed at the explicit questions her parents asked him, going into the tiniest details. He left nothing out. His life as a child, the hardships the family undergone during the great depression, making money as a child with his home-made barrows. They laughed at some of his exploits, her mother nodding her head with approval as he related the saga of his childhood.

'What about the future, Alex? Victoria has led a sheltered life. By what you have told us here and being so forthright, I'm sure you have ambitions for when the war is over?'

'I certainly have. I want to be a millionaire before I'm forty.' They looked at each other across the table. 'Then I hope to go into local politics. The first think I want to do is help get rid of those vermin infested slums. No person should have to live in those conditions. I already have two large shops and about ten properties. My sister is acting on my behalf while I'm away. Property is cheap at the moment, everyone is scared in case the bombing starts.'

Victoria interrupted the conversation. 'Mother, you should see the air raid shelter Alex made for his mother and sisters. It would take a direct hit from one of Hitler's bombs to destroy it.'

Victoria's parents must have been more than satisfied with Alex's answers, for the next thing he knew, they were discussing wedding arrangements. Karen, Polly, Veronica and one of Victoria's friends, were to be bridesmaids. Her father's friend was the local vicar so he made all the arrangements for a special licence.

They were married the following Saturday. The whole village turned out. At first his mother felt embarrassed out of her own social environment although Victoria's mother soon put her at ease. Alex's sisters and mother arrived and were made as welcome as Alex. A large marquee was set up on the lawn outside the house. Alex was only pleased he was in uniform as most of the guests were in top hat and tails, including Victoria's father.

Whilst on honeymoon, they made a point of visiting Arthur again. He was sitting up in bed, without the cumbersome big cage round his legs.

'So you finally went and done it, Alex, and you always said we would be best man at each other's wedding.' He looked at Victoria, a cheeky grin on his face. 'In a bit of a hurry, wasn't you? Not pregnant are you?' His face very serious.

'No, I am not.'

Victoria tried to sound innocent and hit him playfully with her handbag. It was the happiest she'd seen him. The colour was back in his face, and he laughed and joked.

'Should be getting my wooden leg shortly. The sister said my stump is healing nicely, although to be honest, I can't look at the damn thing.'

After hearing Arthur's story from Alex, her father had given them a bottle of champagne and a box of cigars to take to the hospital. There were three other men in the ward so Arthur shared the drinks and cigars amongst them.

The honeymoon was over all too quickly. Victoria was very sad when Alex said goodbye at the house.

'Don't come to the railway station. I hate station goodbyes.'

She cried when she heard the shop door close behind him.

# Chapter Twenty-Two

All the rumours that were flying around the battalion finally came to fruition at the end of the month, with Alex finding himself in an overcrowded troopship sailing in convoy heading East. It was another three months before he confirmed it with a letter from the Middle East and giving his address as Middle East Forces. At the same time every national newspaper was telling the world of the advances and retreats of our forces up and down the Western Desert with monotonous regularity, sometimes only warranting a small column in a back or middle page. So far all the local populace had been fed defeats and set backs. It was Alex's first letters that revealed the whole truth - sand, sand and more sand, flies, flies and more flies, but worst of all the complete boredom only relieved with the humorous antics of the men of his regiment.

Whether this was to help to keep up his family's and Victoria's spirits they could only guess as he never mentioned the active side of life out there. Victoria was no fool, she had witnessed the serious and dangerous side of the war in her small hospital.

The highlight of Alex's life was when he received his letters from home. Victoria wrote every day and these he sorted from the family letters to read later when he was alone. Karen always wrote on their mother's behalf as she always professed she was no letter writer. However there was one good bit of news from the family. Jeremy had popped the question of marriage for the hundredth time and she finally agreed.

'However, Alex, do not worry. I will stay and look after your business until you return, although I must add that Victoria has been a tower of strength to us, when she is off duty she always spends her time with us. She is a lovely girl, Alex, and she really is one of the family.'

He could always tell when Victoria was on night duty, her letters were always long, lengthy and passionate.

'I write this in the ward when the patients are fast asleep and the countryside is quiet. I have a good lot of patients here, with the exception of one man, he snores loudly, so I couldn't sleep if I wanted to.'

Polly remained unmarried, her boyfriend had been called up six months ago. He came on leave for two weeks and the next letter she received from the Red Cross, he had been captured in Burma, since then no news. Victoria told him she had receded inside her own shell, she hardly spoke at all. Since the episode with dirty Wally she had never trusted another man, till she met her boyfriend, now he had gone, languishing in some Jap hell hole.

Alex had been in the desert a year when the war out there took a turn for the worst for the Third Reich, which was to have lasted a thousand years. Hitler and his allies were driven from North Africa, his invincible army in Russia was chased out of Stalingrad. The American 5th Army and the British 8th Army had taken Sicily and were soon on the mainland heading north up the tip of Italy. Mussolini and his mistress were swinging from a lamp post in a most undignified manner. While fighting through the mud of Italy they were rewarded with the great news that the invasion of Normandy was in progress and gave themselves the title the 'D Day Dodgers' but it brought the war to a glorious and victorious end. Alex, with the remnants of his platoon, got blind drunk and suffered two days of severe headaches, vowing he would never drink again.

Alex's mother and family, with Victoria, were in the shop when the phone rang, it was Saturday morning and they didn't get very many calls at the weekend. They looked at each other and it was several seconds before Karen picked up the phone and almost dropped it when she heard the voice at the other end.

'God, Alex, we thought you were still in Austria.'

She handed the phone to Victoria who rushed to her side. She put the ear piece to her ear as tears started rolling down her cheeks, he heard her sob at the other end and burst out laughing.

'Well, I should be home in a day or two, perhaps then you might be pleased to see me.'

'It doesn't matter, Alex, I am leaving tonight, I know a small hotel near your depot. Let's see.' She looked at her small wrist watch. 'It's twelve now, I will throw a few things in my bag, the Midland Red buses do a regular run to your town, that will take at the most two hours, by the time I book into the hotel and sort things out, let's say I will meet you at the barrack gates by five.'

She turned to his mother and putting her arms around her, hugged her tightly. 'He is home, Mother, safe and sound. For three damned years I have lay awake in bed wondering and praying if he will come home all in one piece, or if he would come home at all. Every time I saw a telegraph boy on his cycle with that little leather bag strapped on his belt I used to shudder. One day I saw him coming towards the shop and looking at the house numbers. I froze. He went straight past but I didn't stop shivering for almost an hour.'

'You don't know our Alex,' Karen said. 'I never had the slightest doubt that one day he would come sailing through the door. If you only knew what him, Arthur and poor Horace got up to when they were kids you would know he would be back. Swimming in that filthy canal, chasing round that damn train marshalling yard, picking up lumps of coal, and then playing on that old corporation rubbish tip, it's a wonder they didn't die with some kind of fever. Don't worry about the bus, Victoria, I will run you up there in the van, that's the least I can do for my little brother.'

Karen stepped from the van and slammed the door angrily behind her.

'Trust the damn van to play up now, just look at that steam.'

Victoria wished she had come by train or bus, the journey seemed to be taking ages. She frequently looked through the rear view mirror, making sure every hair was in place and just the right amount of lipstick, she knew Alex hated too much lipstick. She had left her V.A.D. cap behind and as the sun struck the windscreen her beautiful blonde hair glowed in the brilliant sunshine. Five minutes later, but what seemed to be hours to Victoria, Karen stepped back into her seat, her fingers covered in a black sooty oil.

'Damn radiator was dry.'

The town was filled with returning soldiers and Victoria tried several places before she found an obliging lady that would take them in for the night. It was a small house, just two up and two down, she would have preferred a hotel but those had been well booked in before the troops arrived. However Mrs Bates was a pleasant woman in her early forties whose husband was still overseas and she was glad of the company.

Alex was waiting at the barrack gates impatiently pacing up and down, he spotted her from a distance and when she saw him she rushed into his arms, tears rolling unashamedly down her cheeks, oblivious to the glances of the passing troops.

Mrs Bates was not at home when they arrived back, the door was locked and Alex heart slumped. The next door neighbour came running out and gave them a patronising smile, the key to the house in her hand.

'Mrs Bates has been called away to one of her relatives in Birmingham, she won't be home tonight, you are to go in and make yourself at home.'

She gave them a knowing smile.

'I couldn't tell you before, Alex, you had enough on your mind. My father died while you were away. I miss him terribly.'

She sobbed. Alex didn't say anything but left her alone with her memories.

'Yes, nothing snobbish about him. When I asked if I could marry you I expected to be thrown out on my neck, I think he had better things in mind than an army sergeant.'

'No, Alex, he admired you as he admired any man that was making a name for himself. He visited your mother and sisters several times while you were away. Both Karen and your mother went to his funeral. No, I am afraid the only snob in the family is my sister, Veronica, she has turned out a real madam. She takes her finals next year and becomes a fully fledged doctor. But the death of her father broke her heart. They were so close and he would have been very proud of her. She has become a real snob with real snobby friends. She hates being reminded of her past and refers to you as 'my sergeant hubby.' But she will make a very good doctor, she wants to be a surgeon.'

That night alone and in each other's arms she whispered, 'I want to have a baby, Alex, all the while you were away I wished that I had fell for a child on our honeymoon.'

'We must wait first, Victoria, we will have to see how things are. I mean, can we really afford to take such a step? I have to get the business going first, babies are not a cheap commodity.'

She burst out laughing. 'You are joking, Alex? Hasn't Karen told you? You own dozens of properties all over Birmingham, Karen has been buying them up at give-away prices. She married Jeremy and he has been keeping her well supplied with china, not from his own factory alone but seeing that all his friends in the pottery trade keep her well supplied. His son calls Karen mother and they are devoted to each other. He says he can't wait to meet you, he tells everyone his uncle is a Desert Rat. Don't worry about money, Alex, Father left us comfortable.'

The thought of living on his wife's money, money that was rightfully hers, filled Alex with horror. Brought up in a world of poverty and a world where it was a man's right to provide for his family, if only on the bread line, so be it.

'It wouldn't be right for me to touch that money, Vicky, it rightfully belongs to you. I can understand your father leaving it in the will to both of us, he was that kind of man, but it's my duty to support you.'

'Oh don't be such an old fashioned man, Alex. One thing about this war it's put men and women on more equal terms. What am I suppose to do with all that money? Put it under my mattress and give it to the children when I die? The will was quite clear about it, "to my loving daughter and her dear husband, Alexander Edwards, I leave the sum of fifty thousand pounds and my holiday cottage near Littlehampton on the south coast with the one provision, my wife have use of it while she lives." Now that is quite

157

specific. He left Veronica the same amount and a choice of any of his three cars. The residue of his estate he left to Mother with the provision that she leave any remainder on her death, together with the house to his two daughters. But let's hope she lives to a great old age.'

He learned from the day he was married it was impossible to argue with her when she made up her mind and all he could answer was, 'We will wait and see.'

She smiled to herself knowing she'd won the argument.

Back at his depot he was promoted to Company Sergeant Major. The C.O. was hoping he would stay on but since his four year term with the T.A. ended during the war, nothing would stop him returning to civvy street. He helped to form new platoons and companies and watched with a leaden heart as they marched through the depot gates on their way to the Far East campaign. Fortunately the Japs capitulated during the outward voyage. Arriving home on his demob leave he was embarrassed to see the front of the shop decorated with red, white and blue balloons, garlands and a large 'Welcome Home' sign. His mother and Vicky were there with their arms round each other, both had been crying.

Karen, at least six months pregnant was with Jeremy, his son standing in front of them. Arthur was there with Carol and her son one side and Polly the other side. Horace's mother and father were also there clutching their grandson's hand. They greeted him with warm smiles and handshakes.

Horace's mother said, 'We are glad to see you back safe and sound, Alex.' She stifled a sob. 'I am only sorry my Horace isn't here to greet you.' She dabbed her eyes with her handkerchief but rallied round when her grandson caught her hand. 'What do you think of little Horace?'

'A grand lad, Ma, he's the double of Horace.'

He shook hands with Arthur and was greeted with, 'So they made you a sergeant major, you old bastard. Never thought I would live to see the day.'

'That was just a bribe to try and keep me with the regiment. No thanks. Six years of war was quite sufficient for me. I served my country now its down to business. That can come later. Let's go to the flat, Arthur, and have a good talk.'

Arthur had no trouble negotiating the narrow twisted staircase. Alex went forward to give him support but Carol held him back and put her finger to her lips and nodded her head. Alex realised what she was trying to tell him and stood back. It had been over four years since he lost his foot and part of his leg and felt that independence was the only way he would master it. He was still having trouble with his false leg with the stump rubbing raw.

Everyone crowded into the sitting room. Arthur sat in one armchair with Carol sitting on the arm. He noted for the first time how protective she was towards Arthur. He sat facing him on the other arm chair with Victoria sitting close, her arm round his shoulder.

'How's the business, Arthur?

'I have hit the jackpot, Alex! I can't collect any clothes, everything is rationed tightly but remember all those wedding dresses I collected and could do nothing with them? Well, it was Carol's idea. I started loaning them out. No girls could afford to buy new dresses and even if they could they couldn't get them, everything was rationed, so we started hiring dresses. I am booked for months ahead, all these chaps coming home now that the war is over are eager to marry and settle down. I am making hay while the sun shines, I suppose when everything is off ration and gets back to normal I will be out of business. I charge the wedding dresses at five pounds a time and a dress and four bridesmaids at fifteen pounds. Of course everyone wants the dresses on Saturday and I have to tell most of them it's booked so quite often they change it to during the week. Carol cleans them and repairs them if necessary.'

He caught Carol's hand and squeezed it. 'You haven't heard the good news have you? Carol and I are getting married.'

Alex looked at Horace's mother. She smiled, making it apparent she agreed.

As much as he liked to see all his friends, he wasn't sorry to see them depart one by one, leaving his mother, Karen, her husband and Victoria. Polly had been depressed for days. She knew the war in the Far East was at an end but she had heard nothing about her boyfriend, all she knew he was taken prisoner but that was over two years ago, since then no word. Victoria had contacted the Red Cross on her behalf but to no avail. Seeing the troops returning from the Middle East and Europe she was growing more depressed as the days passed.

They talked well into the night, Karen and her husband were staying at a hotel in town, the boy was sleeping in Karen's old bed. Thoughtful as ever his mother had bought and put a double bed in his own room.

'Bring all the books in tomorrow, Karen, let's go through them.'

She smiled. 'I think you are going to be pleasantly surprised, Alex.'

He was greatly relieved when he heard the shop door close behind them and his mother slide the heavy door bolts home. It had been at long hard day.

# Chapter Twenty-Three

When Karen arrived, Alex was sitting in his favourite armchair, wearing civilian clothes for the first time in five years. Her husband had returned to Stoke with his son. She was carrying a large briefcase then went down into the shop and returned with more ledgers.

'I keep these under lock and key in the basement. I don't want any snoopers round. I haven't told Mom where they are in case she takes them out and leaves them laying around.'

'Why all the secrecy, Karen?'

'Since you went away and left me in charge I learnt one thing. Never let the left hand know what the right hand is doing. In this war it's been a case of dog eat dog. Most of those who dodged war service, have been making a fast buck, and believe me, they've succeeded in making the black market thrive. They didn't give a tinker's cuss about our boys out there.'

She opened the first ledger and spread it on the table. 'This is the property you own.'

He scanned down the list and whistled through his teeth as he muttered, 'Bloody hell!' He re-read the list and counted them. 'That's twenty-two, Karen, and mostly business properties.'

'Yes, and we only lost three during the bombings.' She put her finger on the list. 'This one and this one are let and bring in a decent rent, and I've already received several enquiries from men who've just been demobbed. One man wants this one for a fruit and veg shop. His father ran one before the war. He used to work for him then but his father died while he was away, so his mother had to sell up. Since the war ended, I've had several enquires as to whether we want to sell for quite an enormous profit but I think it's best to hang on till things get back to normal.'

They studied the ledger for over an hour, going through each property in detail. Alex continually nodded his head in satisfaction.

'You certainly lost no time in buying these places, Karen. The shop must have been doing better than I thought. You managed to get your supplies all right?'

'Yes, Jeremy saw to that. He kept me well supplied.'

Alex smiled and looked knowingly at her swollen abdomen. 'So I see. I hope he kept you well supplied with china as well!'

'Don't be bloody cheeky, Alex!' she exclaimed playfully swiping him across the ear. 'Jeremy is a wonderful man. I really want for nothing. He may have been born with a silver spoon in his mouth but he's well educated and a thorough gentleman. Also, he's well liked in the trade. One word from him, and I had all the supplies

161

of china I needed. The other local shopkeepers would come round here and buy from me. I only gave them ten per cent discount, so heaven knows what they charged their customers.'

'I see we still carry a very good stock. According to your books, we hold over ten thousand pounds worth and are well into the black at the bank.'

'Yes, I've made arrangements for you to see the bank manager next Friday. He reckons you should open a separate deposit account as it should be earning interest. I also have to tell you, Alex, that I can only work for another month. Jeremy wants me home now that you're here. I have been grooming Victoria to take over and she's quite happy but it won't be long before you'll need a full time secretary. I've been considering making that large front room over the next shop into an office. You'll have no trouble getting a good secretary.'

Arthur wouldn't get married until he could walk up the aisle on two legs, albeit one false one. He would practise for hours in the old chapel, trying out the false leg. His face would distort with pain every time he put it to the floor.

'I will make it up that bloody aisle, Alex, if it kills me. Trouble is, if I pad it too much, it makes me limp. I want to be able to walk straight without a limp.' He burst out laughing, more like his old self again, as he said, 'My old man did his damnedest to perfect his limp for over twenty years, and here's me, I've just spent the last few years trying to walk without a limp.'

'By the way, Arthur. I forgot to mention it before. How is your old man?'

'A reformed character. Our mom rules him with a rod of iron. She's limited his beer to one a night and three on Saturdays. Some nights, he doesn't even drink that. He washes regularly now, and goes to the local baths once a week. He always wears a clean shirt and well pressed clothes. You wouldn't know him now, Alex. He's got a regular job and hands over his wage packet to our mom every week. She buys him twenty ciggies a day. She should have done it years ago. He sold a lot of those clothes I left here but Mom made him get a job and he's paid back every penny. He often comes in but not to scrounge, so I make sure I have a few packets of fags handy. He gets on fine with Carol and she loves him. She should have seen the old Dad. He takes her little boy over to visit his grandparents.'

It sounded strange to hear him sing his father's praises.

'I wish Horace had seen his boy. At least no one can say it isn't his, he's the double of him.' Arthur hopped over to the window and stared out for several minutes. 'It's a strange old world, isn't it, Alex? There's me wishing Carol had met me first, now poor

162

old Horace is dead, and Carol will soon be my wife. I didn't want it this way, Alex.'

'I know that, mate. I know if Horace is watching over his family, he'd be tickled pink to know you'll be looking after his kid. We can't live with the dead, Arthur. Just be good to her. I know you'll both be very happy. Little Horace seems to have taken to you. Apart from Vicky, I don't know of a better girl than Carol. Good luck to you both and don't forget, I'm going to be best man.'

'That goes without saying, Alex. And another thing. Carol won't be getting married in one of my hire wedding dresses. I've found a woman that does dressmaking, and her and Carol have designed a knockout dress. I'll see you later, Alex.'

Alone in the street, Alex walked round some of his old haunts where he used to play with his two friends. He stood on the bridge, watching the barges on the canal loading and unloading, the water still covered with the same old, green slime. There was still the hole in the fence of the railway marshalling yard. He laughed to himself as he noticed two boys jeering at the train driver, while the fireman was throwing pieces of coal at them. A young boy was pushing a home-made barrow, laden with dirty rags and jam jars. It could have been Arthur there, the same cheeky face and tousled hair. He stopped by the park and looked through the iron railings. The kids were still playing the same games he'd played all those years ago with his two friends. A hand fell on his shoulder.

'Hallo, Alex.'

He turned round sharply, staring in disbelief into the face of Mr Kingsley. He was still in uniform, and wore the insignia of a Regimental Sergeant Major, and two rows of medal ribbons.

'Bloody hell!' he gasped. 'I was just taking a walk down memory lane. The last person I expected to bump into was you. I honestly thought you had either been captured or killed when we left you at that machine gun post.'

Mr Kingsley bent his head backwards and roared with laughter. Passers by looked round to see what was happening.

'Didn't you know, Alex lad? Old soldiers don't die like that, they just fade away.' He put his leather covered swagger stick under his arm and shook hands warmly. 'I was captured and was marching back to Germany when I saw a chance to escape. I fell into a roadside ditch, and the lads pulled up great clods of earth and grass to cover me. I waited till dark, then made my way across France into Spain. I was picked up by some Basque separatists when I crossed the Pyrenees. Their leader had a daughter in England. She'd been evacuated there during the Civil

War and was well looked after, so he took me into Spain and then across the Portuguese border and handed me to the British embassy. Then it was back home and into the Commandos. Bloody good war, Alex. Raided Norway and France. Served with the Long Range Desert Group, Salerno, D. Day, and across the Rhine. Picked up a couple of gongs and one from old De Gaulle himself. Dirty sod kissed me on both cheeks. My lads never let me live it down. How about you, Alex?'

'Usual, North Africa, Italy and Austria, then home. Made Company Sergeant Major. I was demobbed a few months ago. I'm married now. She used to live near us but I don't think you know her.'

He sat on the low wall, his back against the iron railings.

'Of course, my mate, the one with the foot wound. He had half his bloody leg off. And Horace, that other lad we knocked about with, he was killed in the Navy. His ship was sunk with all hands.'

'Yes, Alex, that's the only trouble with war. People get killed. I reckon all wars should be fought with balloons and sticks.'

'I couldn't agree more. You must come and see our mom.' He wrote down his address on an old envelope. 'Bring the good lady.'

'I would, Alex, but she was killed in an air raid. I was just off to the cemetery to visit her grave, when I spotted you. Tell your mother, I will pop in and see her one of these days.'

He never did. They found him next day, slumped across his wife's grave, his medals across his chest. He'd shot himself through the temple. At the inquest, they discovered he'd been discharged from the army. The army had been his whole life. A soldier through and through, the war had been both his salvation and his downfall. When they'd told him his wife had been killed by enemy action, the bottom fell out of his world. Yet when he'd met Alex, there was nothing in his manner to indicate that he was about to take his own life. Alex and his family were terribly upset when they read about it in the newspaper. For the last time, Alex put on his uniform to attend the funeral. He knew R.S.M. Kingsley would have approved. Arthur was there as well.

'The war still has its casualties, Mom,' Alex said, as he took of his uniform on returning home.

# Chapter Twenty-Four

Alex couldn't remember when he felt as elated as he did now. The war had been over for almost three years, and although rationing wasn't completely over, things were beginning to settle down to normal again. It wasn't as if the shortages had affected any of his china and glass trade. Jeremy had made sure he never went short, and inside information told Alex whenever there were any job lots or clearance lines available.

Karen had her baby daughter and was pregnant again. It was obvious that Jeremy was making up for his years as a widower. Alex again enlisted the aid of his women agents selling in the factories, and recruited some twenty-four. Instead of giving samples now, he had catalogues printed. Not just for his agent, he also had them distributed round the houses. Giving the local scout troop the job of distributing them paid off a hundred fold. With the aid of a local district map pinned to his office wall, he made sure that each road was only supplied once.

He'd now become the scout troop's patron. When he was a boy, neither Arthur nor himself could join the boy scouts as their mothers couldn't afford the uniform. Now he could make sure that any boy who wanted to join could. He supplied the money and they paid him back, a token penny or tuppence a week. No one ever let him down and they were the best turned out troop in the city.

Arthur's former gloomy predictions, that things wouldn't improve before the end of the rationing, were proved wrong. His wedding dress hire business was now flourishing. Instead of the few tatty wartime dresses, he had several new dresses made up for both brides and bridesmaids, along with some men's dress suits. He rented a shop from Alex, just a few doors from his own shop. It was richly carpeted and Carol, now his wife, being very artistic, had dressed the bridal dummies with great expertise. Customers came from all over the city to hire the exclusive bridal wear, most of which was designed by Carol and Victoria. Arthur's leg gave no trouble. He mastered the false leg and walked with only the hint of a limp. His ambition was to own a couple of Rolls Royce cars.

Young Horace was eight years old and getting more like his father every day. With the shop taking up more and more of Carol's time, it was a good excuse for his grandparents to take him over. They doted on him, fetching him from school and taking him straight to their house. Carol collected him at nine every evening - that was if he wasn't asleep, for invariably when she arrived he was asleep in his father's old room.

'I swear those pair of buggers put something in his cocoa at night, Arthur.'

They both burst out laughing.

'I wouldn't be surprised,' he replied.

Arthur never allowed Horace junior to forget his father, although he called Arthur 'Dad'. He had a huge coloured photograph of him taken from a small postcard, and hung it on the sitting room wall, with the two medals the admiralty had graciously sent, and a picture of his ship, alongside. Arthur spent hours with him, telling him over and over again what he, his father and Alex had got up to when they were children, occasionally altering the story where he thought appropriate. It wasn't Arthur, but Horace who'd floated nude on his back down the Avon at Stratford. Horace would roll over and over on the settee, laughing and getting Arthur to repeat the story to him again. Arthur always made Horace, his father, the hero of their childish capers.

Carol would give a stern look of mock disapproval. 'If that boy is ever caught swimming nude in the river you'll be to blame!'

He had bought himself a small delivery van, and several times little Horace had insisted that he took him to the places he had visited with his father. Arthur would stand on the bridge, his arm around Horace's shoulders, and give him graphic details, pointing out where he floated and where the policeman had toppled into the water. On their return home, he had to stop the van under the bridge where they'd all met up and go over every detail once more.

'Why didn't my dad join the army with you and Uncle Alex?'

'Well, he wanted to be a sailor.'

Then Arthur would have to relate all the story of how they'd altered his dad's birth certificate, and how Karen had written out a reference, not daring to leave out a single detail.

'Your dad insisted we alter the certificate. No boy service for him on a shilling a day; man service paid two shillings a day.' He winked his eye at Carol, behind Horace's back. 'No, just fifteen and he was a real man.'

Carol smiled. She loved Arthur and the way he treated Horace, always making his dad out to be the real hero. She knew the true story of how shy and reserved he had really been as a boy, and it was Arthur and Alex who had talked him into enlisting in man service. She leaned over the boy's head and kissed Arthur.

'You and his bloody grandparents spoil him. You'd better change your tune soon, cause I don't want him going in either the Navy or the Army.'

'Carol, he'll be like his father. He will please himself what he does and where he goes but I hope he'll take over the business eventually.'

Polly's boyfriend had returned from the Far East a total wreck. He was taken prisoner at Singapore and worked on the dreaded Burma railway. A robust young man when he left, he was six stone when he was released, and now three years later, he was still a wreck weighing barely eight stone. He worked for Alex on his delivery van but Alex made sure all the parcels were light. He refused to marry Polly.

'I'm just a wreck, Polly. If I reach ten stone, I will think about it then, but look at me, Polly, all skin and bone. I had beriberi, dysentery, tuberculosis and I still suffer from a mild form of nephritis. Let's wait and see what happens.'

Deep down inside, he knew he would never reach thirty. Victoria knew it, and so did Alex and his mother. She cooked him tempting dishes of roast chicken, fresh fish, jellies and fruit, but he just picked at them, never finishing a meal completely. Polly would watch him then go to her bedroom and cry.

Every month without fail, Alex and Victoria would go to the cemetery to attend her mother's grave and place fresh flowers on it.

'I think we will get another headstone here, Victoria, a nice Italian white marble.'

Anger flashed in her eyes. He realised he must have said the wrong thing as she exploded. Since the day they'd first met, he'd never seen her so cross.

'Don't you dare touch this headstone, Alex.' She knelt beside it and put her arm over it. 'I wouldn't part with this stone for all the money in the world. This stone taught me what a gentleman you are, and it really brought us together. From the moment I saw it here, I knew one day I would marry you. To me, this is the most beautiful headstone in the cemetery.'

She was crying softly. He lifted her to her feet and kissed her gently. The only way he could demonstrate his love for her was by blowing gently in her ear. She loved it and responded with a passionate kiss.

'I think this is the best time to tell you, Alex, here over Mother's grave. You're going to be a daddy.'

He scooped her up in his arms, hardly daring to believe his own ears but after the initial shock he regained his composure.

'Are you certain, Vicky? I mean we've had so many disappointments.'

'Absolutely. Three months. The gynaecologist confirmed it last Friday. He said everything is quite normal.'

167

'That's absolutely great. I just can't believe it. Just wait till I tell Mom. She'll be over the moon. So will our Karen and Polly.'

'Don't bother. I should think by this time, they already know, and if I'm not mistaken, Mother will have told the whole neighbourhood. She came with me to the doctor's.'

They burst out laughing.

'Why the crafty old bugger. She hasn't said a word to me,' said Alex.

'Well, I suppose she thought it best if I tell you myself. I will warn you about one thing, Alex. We're only having one.' She tapped her stomach. 'This is it, the first and the last. I've been going through hell with morning sickness. You don't know anything about it. You're out of the house by six, so I suffer in silence.'

She insisted that she kept on looking after his books and collecting the money from his factory agents each week. All the property that Karen purchased during the war was now let and bringing in a comfortable income. Alex had the flat above the next shop knocked through to his own, making one large flat. He kept one room as his office and another room was made into a nursery. He now had two more bedrooms and an extra large dining room and lounge. Jeremy often visited with Karen. His own son was away at boarding school, much against Karen's wishes.

'You have done wonders, Alex,' remarked Jeremy, when he inspected the new flat. 'These buildings must be very old but looking inside here it's so very modern. Two bathrooms, and look at the way you've converted that old kitchen into a nursery.'

'That was down to Carol and Victoria. When those two get their heads together, there's no telling what they get up to. They don't give a toss how they spend my money.' He winked his eye at Jeremy and poured him a brandy. 'Of course you know, I suppose, they've asked me to stand for the council? I don't know what to do. Once you're in politics, people think you are there to feather your own nest.'

'Why not give it a go, Alex? You've always said you wanted to get rid of those slums. If you get on the council you might actually get the chance to do something. Karen took me round to see your old house once. My God! However did you manage to survive? Those places should have be raised to the ground before the first war. Some of the bricks in that yard are actually crumbling. It wouldn't surprise me to read in the paper one day, that the damn buildings have fallen down!'

'Yes. That's caused by the chemicals from those factory chimneys. They've been discharging their filth for years. When I was a kid, we would get this awful stench. It wasn't till I was grown up that I realised it was damn sulphur amongst other poisonous fumes.'

'Well, here's your chance to do something about it. I only wish I'd lived in the city and had that chance. Give it a go, Alex. I know one or two council chaps, so I could always put in a good word for you. Perhaps help you get on the housing committee.'

Alex was too preoccupied to give it much thought, what with Victoria expecting the baby. She wouldn't be able to work for very much longer now so he would have to find himself a secretary. He needed someone he could trust, perhaps a woman in her forties, they were more reliable. If he was lucky he might find one who could type well, as Victoria wasn't exactly a wizard on a typewriter, more like a one fingered job, which made typing a long letter quite a laborious job. He advertised in the local paper and within a week, with Victoria's help, had managed to find a forty year old war widow who was anxious to start work. Victoria was staying on for a couple of months to show her the ropes but in less than two weeks the new secretary was quite competent, you'd have thought she'd been doing the job all her life. She hardly talked, and when she sat down to type with her rimless spectacles perched on the end of her nose, she looked the model of efficiency. Fortunately, she didn't object to working late on a Friday night, when the agents brought in their collections and new orders. Sometimes, it would be well past ten o'clock before she left. Alex would run her home in his car.

'I don't mind working late, Mr Edwards. I only have my lonely, bed sitting room and I do enjoy the company of your mother and sisters when they pop in the office. You have a wonderful home, Mr Edwards.'

Alex was at the Potteries when Victoria went into labour. They knew her time was near but she had insisted he go about his business as usual.

'Women have been having babies since time began, and its not as though I'll be completely alone. Your mother's here, and she must have seen more babies born than you've had hot dinners. You go, Alex, I'll be just fine.'

He arrived home late that afternoon to be greeted by a smiling mother and sister.

'You have a seven pound baby girl, Alex, and she's the spitting image of her mother.'

Polly looked at her mother in disgust. 'How can you tell, Mom? They all look like skinned rabbits when they're born.' She turned to her brother. 'She is lovely, Alex, and she does have nice blue eyes but she's as bald as a coot.'

Alex wasn't listening. He was on the phone to the nursing home, then he phoned Karen, and Victoria's adopted mother.

'That is wonderful, Alex. I shall be down at the weekend.'

'Why wait for the weekend? Come down now. I will get your room ready. I know Victoria would love to see you. I haven't seen the new baby yet. I'm just off to the nursing home now.'

He didn't stop to wash or change, just jumped in his still laden van, stopping only at a flower shop which he found was closed. Luckily its proprietor was one of his tenants, and was only too happy to open up and serve him on this special occasion. When he arrived at the nursing home, he found Victoria was still a bit tired. He waited quietly by her bedside, holding her hand till she wakened. She gave him a drowsy smile.

'Are you all right, Victoria?'

She nodded. The ward nurse, seeing Alex, wheeled in a small satin covered cot, and placed it beside the bed.

'God, Victoria, she is beautiful.'

She smiled and clenched his hand.

'She's like a skinned rabbit. That's what Polly said.'

The nurse removed the baby from the tiny cot and placed her in his arms. He felt terribly emotional and, for the first time in years he felt like crying. The nurse laughed at Victoria, seeing the effect the baby had on Alex.

'Strange, isn't it, Mrs Edwards? All the new dads get like that. You would think it was them that did all the work. I bet if he had the next one, you would have the third but you could bet your life's savings there would never be a fourth!'

Everyone was excited, waiting for the day when the new baby would arrive home. Alex felt the proudest man alive. Everything he'd set out to do had finally been achieved, well almost. His one great ambition left now was to see those slum dwellings collapse to the ground.

# Chapter Twenty-Five

Neither Alex nor Victoria had ambitions to increase their family, quite content with what they had already achieved. Victoria was a model mother, and although Alex said they could easily afford to employ a nursemaid, she wouldn't hear of it.

'She's our baby, Alex. Why employ someone to have the enjoyment of bringing her up? She needn't tie us down, if we ever want to go out your mother will be overjoyed to look after her. She had three daughters of her own, so I'm sure she can manage. After all, she didn't make too bad a job of them.'

Alex knew it was impossible to win an argument with her. She would always listen to reason and accept any advice, so long as it was good advice, but she didn't suffer fools gladly. He looked at her with a new kind of love, unlike the time she'd asked him to marry her. Then he had a slight feeling of doubt. True, they both came from the lowest level of society, but at a tender age her guardian angel had looked down upon her and her sister. Her new adoptive parents had brought them up in a society that they could never have dreamt of as small children, educating them to a standard far above their birthright. Then, after all her parents efforts, when she wanted to marry into the society she had originated from, they raised no objections. On the contrary, once they'd met Alex, they eased her way into marriage. Her father was a far seeing man, and he immediately realised Alex was an ambitious man with a great future ahead of him.

Veronica was a fully fledged doctor with an important post in the small cottage hospital. She had also taken over her father's practice but she had ambitions too. Unlike Victoria, she could be quite a snob at times and referred to Alex as the Army Sergeant. This made both Alex and Victoria laugh. In return, Alex had special note paper printed, just for her benefit, headed: Sgt. Alex Edwards (Ex-Royal Warwicks). Eventually, as he progressed in business, this became a standing joke between them. She visited them a couple of times, and hinted that Victoria had married beneath herself. In return, Victoria took her round to the old yard and pointed out the house they had lived in as children.

'Alex is a wealthy man now, and a generous one.' She pointed to the old house. 'That's where we came from. We were very lucky, we were adopted and loved by wealthy parents. What Alex owns, he made on his own, with a bit of help from Karen.'

'Are you sure it wasn't with the money Father left you?' she replied sardonically.

Veronica could be real bitch when the mood took her. Victoria didn't answer but went straight to her room, returning a few minutes later with her bank statement folder. She opened it at her latest statement.

'Father left me fifty thousand.' She pointed at the entry further back, then to the last entry. 'It has gained five thousand in the last few years, all my own, and invested on Alex's advice. He won't allow me to put a penny either on the home or in his business, so don't make stupid accusations.'

After that slight argument, Veronica didn't come to the flat again till she was invited for the baby's christening. She wasn't even moved when the vicar named the baby Rosalind, after their own mother, but she brightened a little when he announced the second name, Patricia, after their adoptive mother. She had barely shown any emotions but Victoria doubted if her sister could even have remembered their own mother. After all, she was only seven when they were taken away. Perhaps it was one of the episodes of her life that she'd deliberately blotted from her memory.

When they returned to the flat, Veronica cast an appreciative eye around it. Alex had extended it, since her last visit, and for the first time, she threw him a compliment, albeit reluctantly.

'You have done well with this old building, Alex.'

'Well, I can't take all the credit for it. Victoria and Carol designed most of it. Carol is quite artistic and Victoria has the bright ideas. Between them, they make a perfect team. You should see some of the wedding dresses they design. Customers come from all over the city, and sometimes from other parts of the country. They've even had their dresses pictured in one of those society magazines you read.'

'Really! I shall know where to come when I need one.'

Victoria tried to press her further, to see if there was another marriage in the air but she became tight lipped.

Victoria was pleased to see her sister return home, and breathed a sigh of relief as she watched her car turn the corner. She stood with her arm round Alex.

'I'm afraid my sister is getting a real snobbish bitch. Pity Mother didn't come. She had a bad bout of 'flu and was afraid of passing it on to the baby. She wants us to spend the weekend with her in a couple of weeks' time. She'd like your mother to come too, they get on so well together.'

The shop on the other side of his first premises was about to become vacant. It was an old fashioned menswear shop that had been there through two world wars.

'It's time I packed in now, Alex. Men are not bothering to wear the old flat caps anymore. Those alone would keep me going in the old days. Lads of today won't wear them. Do you know, the other day I saw these two young boys with shoulder length hair. My father would have shaved mine right off if I'd gone out like that.'

'I know, Bill. Fashions come and go but we just have to accept it. Before very long, all the lads will be wearing long hair and the girls short hair.'

'But the kids have no respect, Alex. I took my caps out to show some lads the other day and they started taking the piss. No, Alex, I've had enough, I want to get out. Make me a fair offer for the property, Alex. What stock I have is already out of date. Buy the property and you can have the stock for sod all.'

Alex made what he thought was a good offer. Ten years previously, he would have got it for a tenth of the price but he had ideas for the shop. Arthur wanted to move his business next to him. Carol wanted Vicky as a partner in their bridal hire.

Arthur realised his ambition, more than he'd ever dreamed of. He now owned four Rolls Royce cars and several large Jaguars as well, and he had a vintage car for brides who wanted that something a little bit special. He also had arrangements with Harry, who was now a director of the local funeral parlour, to hire out an open landau carriage and two white horses. Carol was left to manage the entire dress hire business.

Bill and Alex shook hands on the deal, and within a week Alex had the builders in, stripping the place right out. Carol had the flat renovated. Bill had never lived there as he had a place on the edge of town. Apart from decorating, there was little else to do. Horace junior was almost twenty. Both his grandparents had died, his grandmother first and then his grandfather a few days later. It had hit Horace hard, and it took him months to get over their deaths. He became an engineer, travelling all over the world with his job but he never intended to marry.

Carol had the shop decorated and done out with gold fittings and a rich royal blue carpet on the floor. She had plush velvet curtains across the fitting cubicles, and old fashioned gold painted chairs with blue velvet seat pads. At first, Alex thought it looked too ornate for the area but times were changing. Television had opened up new prospects for the ordinary man in the street. No longer satisfied with a bit of cheap old lino on the floor, men were spending more time at home watching television, instead of vanishing to the pub night after night. They wanted more comfort in their homes. Public houses were going out of business and the larger pubs were being modernised. Out went the old sawdust covered floors, spittoons and dusty pianos. Now it was all chrome and plastic, with juke boxes and one armed bandits.

Alex had been on the council for four years and finally achieved his life long ambition by getting on to the housing committee. His first speech was to inform the committee members of a promise which had been made to men going off to the first world war - that they would return to houses fit for heroes to live in. It never materialised. No councillor had been near his old district for years, so he employed a professional photographer to take hundreds of photographs of the old tenements. He pinned these on the housing committee's walls. It proved the point. A party of councillors visited the area and within a few months, the tenants were being re-housed in properties on the fringes of the city. Decent houses with bathrooms, inside toilets, gardens, and in some cases a small drive on which to park a car.

'Well, Councillor Edwards, we start demolishing your old district next week. We, the committee, would deem it an honour if you would knock the first wall down. You have been so persistent, and worked so hard to see the people housed in better conditions, it would be only fair if you struck the first blow.'

Whilst the majority of the residents were overjoyed and keen to get away, a few of the older ones were reluctant. One woman had lived there for sixty years. She had been born in the house, married, and had then taken over the tenancy from her mother some thirty years ago. She broke down and sobbed as the removal men moved in, and sat stubbornly in the doorway. Alex was sent for.

'Look here, Mrs Thompson, we have a nice house for you. It's all modern with a bath and hot water, and a nice garden.'

'What do I want with a garden, Alex? I've lived with bricks all my life. It's forty odd years since I saw you born. I remember when you didn't have two ha'pennies to rub together. I saw you go to school swearing on the first day. I've watched every movement you've made since your first home-made barrow, and now it's you that's doing this to me.' She clung on to him. 'I don't want to go, Alex. I don't care about electric lights and an inside lavvy or bathroom. What can I do with a bathroom? And the rent's too high, four times what I'm paying here!'

He gave her a reassuring hug. 'All right, Mrs Thompson. I'll see what I can do. I have a small house I can let you have but it's just as bad as this one and it won't be long before they'll be pulling that down.'

'Two years, Alex, that's what the doctor has given me at the most. Just let me have it for two years.' She whispered in his ear, 'I have cancer, Alex, so let me have the house.'

'All right, you stubborn old bugger. Give me a chance to have it redecorated but if you won't go then, I shall come round myself and carry you out in one of my old flitting barrows,' he told her jokingly.

A ceremony was laid on for the demolition. Alex, a supporter of the local scout troop, was honoured with the drum and bugle band. (He had paid for the instruments.) The housing committee and a few council members, as well as a few of the old tenants, had come to pay a sentimental visit for the last time. Alex walked down the entry with Victoria, surprised to see so many people gathered in both yards. Children sitting on the wall separating the two yards. A cheer went up as he took hold of a heavy sledge hammer which had a chromium plated head, specially made for the occasion. A silence fell over the crowd as he lifted it over his shoulder. He gave it a determined swing and there was a whoosh as it cut through the air. It made contact with a brick below the window, sounding like a bell tolling a death knoll, which really it was. The death of an era, one most old tenants were pleased to see come to an end. The assembled crowd roared and a lone scout bugler attempted to play the last post but made an awful hash of it.

The window above the brick shattered, and Alex looked inside. The ghosts stirred. The old gas stove was still there and so was the old meter. 'Can you change this thin penny for a thick one, Alex? I get more gas with a thick penny.'

It wasn't the same old table they had used but it was woodwormed and the tenant had decided not to take it with her. Horace, Arthur and Karen were sitting round it, altering Horace's birth certificate.

'Why not man service, Horace? Fourteen, fifteen, eighteen, what does it matter? May as well get shot for a sheep as a lamb!'

'Yes, Martha, them are the wheels off my babby's carriage. My old man painted them.'

The memories all came flooding back. Someone was holding his arm.

'Have you finished, Alex?'

'No, Victoria.'

He handed her the solitary brick he'd removed, and lifting two children clear of the wall, eased himself over. There were more cheers from the crowd. Gripping the sledge hammer, he took a swipe at Victoria's old house. The brick crumbled as he eased another out with his bare hands.

One of the old tenants took it from him, wrapped it in a piece of newspaper and smiled as she handed it to him. 'Good luck, Mr Edwards and bless you.'

175

It had been the best day of Alex's life. While he couldn't say his childhood was unhappy in spite of the poverty, looking back now at the conditions they'd been brought up in, it was a wonder any child survived above the age of eight. Every time he walked down the street, he was filled with nausea as he'd watched each generation battling to survive. True, since the end of the second world war, conditions had improved slightly but most of that could be put down to the German Lufftwaffe. The bombed areas were reconstructed with prefabricated houses, complete with bathrooms and inside sanitation, but the slums still abounded in the industrial areas. He had made a solemn vow that one day he would see them demolished and decent houses erected. That vow had finally materialised.

He returned to his flat and Karen, who, with Jeremy, had made a special trip to see the commencement of the demolition. He poured out two brandies, his favourite drink. He sipped slowly. Victoria came and sat on the arm of the chair. He put his arm round her waist.

'Now you can start house hunting, dear. Find a nice one on the edge of town. They're building some executive homes near Solihull. Let's go and have a look.'

'I don't know, Alex. It will be a pity to leave here after all these years, and we have everything we need here. Not many places round here have two bathrooms. We've spent a lot of money getting this place just right. There's your mom to consider too. She's far too old to move now. It would break her heart to move from this district. All her friends are here.'

'Oh no they're not. You've just seen them. They nearly all came to watch me strike the first blow. She's stopped behind to talk to them.'

Just then, there was a knock on the shop door below. Victoria looked through the window.

'It's your mother, Arthur and Carol.'

While Victoria went downstairs to let them in, Karen asked how the business was doing. She took out a cigarette and lit it. The years had been very good to her. She had hardly any lines on her face, her hair had just a few strands of grey, and her eyes were as bright as ever. She still had the figure of a twenty year old. Having several children had made little difference to her. Hers had been a happy marriage. Jeremy idolised her and she looked at him with affection in her eyes. Her stepson was serving in the Royal Air Force - and was already a squadron leader, married with two children - while of her other sons, two were at college and the two youngest were still at boarding school.

'I have plenty of time on my hands now, Alex. All the kids have flown the nest and seem to be doing well. I only wish we lived nearer. I loved it here when we worked together.'

'Well they do say I'm one of the biggest property owners and developers in the city. Of course amongst them there are those that say I buy the property to sell to the council when they redevelop the place. I am supposed to own most of those old houses that we witnessed being demolished today.'

'Do you?' Jeremy asked, a mischievous twinkle in his eye.

'Not likely, Jeremy. I wouldn't have bought them for tuppence each. It was the best day's work in my life. Like Mom, I won't say I won't miss it. Some of those people are the salt of the earth.'

At that moment Arthur and Carol came into the room with Alex's mother.

'Sit down, Arthur. Pour yourself a brandy.'

He shook hands with Jeremy and kissed Karen. Carol had put on a little weight, not fat by any means. A better description would have been cuddly but over the years, with Victoria's tuition, she had learned to apply her makeup with great skill. Arthur looked round the room.

'Where's Polly?'

'She doesn't stay very long. She has her own flat. We do get a bit worried about her. After her boyfriend died - he never got over working on that Burma railway as a Jap prisoner - she more or less became a recluse. She manages this shop all day but hardly speaks unless it's necessary. Mind you, she's very good with the customers. I bought her a TV to watch when she goes home but she hardly uses it. She attends the Girl Guides two nights a week and the Red Cross one night. The girls at the Guides love her.'

Alex passed Karen one of his new catalogues. She flipped through it.

'Bit different from that first one you had printed, Alex. Must have cost something!'

'Well, it's worth it. I have about two hundred agents now, some in Coventry and Wolverhampton, right down as far as Banbury. I have three girls in the office, two storemen, two more girls packing, and three van drivers.'

'Yes I know. That Charlie who comes to the factory is a cheeky bugger, always trying to date the girls at the factory, isn't he, Jeremy?'

'Yes. One of the girls smacked his face the other day. I don't know what he said to her.'

'If he gets too saucy, let me know. I will give him the sack.'

Jeremy laughed. 'Forget it. Knowing some of the girls in my shop, they all like it and can give back as good as they get. I heard that a dozen of the girls caught hold of him one day and pulled his trousers off. Then covered his John Thomas in wet clay! They wouldn't give him his trousers back, so the foreman lent him one of his old overalls to wear home.'

They all laughed, Arthur imagining what the man must have looked like with seven pounds of clay slapped between his legs.

# Chapter Twenty-Six

Like Alex's, Arthur's business kept growing. The wedding dress hire and sale expanded rapidly. Carol was now in partnership with Victoria, and many of their designs got reviews in the local paper and, on occasions, in the national press and magazines. A small shop next to theirs had become vacant, so Alex bought it and let them have it at a low rent. With the extra space available, they branched out into hiring out glass, chinaware, cutlery, and table linen, renting the remaining part of the shop to a photographer. With Arthur already hiring out wedding cars and these additions, they could now supply everything required for the blushing bride's special day. Arthur and Alex had also stripped out the old chapel, refurbishing it to a high standard, and this was hired out for all types of special occasions including birthdays, engagements, anniversaries and weddings. The front had been torn down and replaced with a new, illuminated one, making it more reminiscent of a Las Vegas casino than an old chapel. Some of the older people in the neighbourhood, who had sentimental memories of the old chapel, tried to object but as it was no longer a place of worship they were overruled. It became very popular for all kinds of functions, and twice a week it was used as a bingo hall.

'I don't know what they will get up to next, Victoria. They are both so full of money making ideas, sometimes I think they must have a guardian angel looking down on them,' said Karen after visiting the new shops and chapel.

Victoria quietly answered, 'Yes', her mind returning to that day he had taken her to the cemetery to see her mother's headstone for the first time. She knew her mother was watching over her and Alex, as well as Arthur who'd taken on Horace's son and treated him as his own, making sure all the while that he remembered his real father with respect.

He now lived in a large house in the better part of the city but the large photograph of Horace still had pride of place, hung above the marble fireplace in the lounge. He never allowed Horace junior to forget his father, so it came as no surprise when he joined the Navy, though not as a boy with an altered birth certificate this time. Arthur and Carol had insisted he should go to college first so he could get a commission in the Navy. He had done well so far. Using his own initiative, he rose to the rank of lieutenant commander and had good prospects for the future. He was also married with two children, and when he came on leave he would tell them, 'I was a very lucky boy, kids. When I was your age, I had two fathers, only my real father had been killed in the war.'

He'd put an affectionate arm round Arthur's shoulders. 'He's my father too but don't listen to him too much. It was him, Uncle Alex and your real father who got up to all the old tricks like sneaking in the railway yards and nicking the coal that fell off the trains, and swimming in the river with no clothes on and getting a police sergeant almost drowned!'

'Better get that gin bottle down, Carol, and that tonic water. Horace is starting me off again on the old days.'

They were always pleased to see them and the children. When they were first married, his wife, Pandora, was inclined to be a bit of a snob but after a few visits to Arthur and Carol's, along with the company of Victoria and Alex, her snobbery soon vanished and she came to look forward to their visits as much as he did. When he got his first command, they all went down to Portsmouth to look over it.

'Your cabin is very small, Horace,' his mother said, when she looked into the cubby hole. With the four of them there, they could hardly move.

'Well, Mother, it is only a small minesweeper. It's not one of the Queens, you know.'

Back on shore, they stood on the quayside and watched him skilfully leave the dock and safely negotiate the narrow harbour entrance.

'I am very proud of him, Arthur, and you too, always thinking of his welfare. I think this is all down to you. I could never have done it on my own. I would have liked another child but what is to be will be. I have got you, darling. The both of you are the most important men in my life. I know his father would have been very proud of him, and if he is watching he will be very proud of both of you.'

She put her arms round his neck, and standing on tiptoe, kissed him. At that moment, a destroyer was passing and sounded its siren with a toot toot, the ship's crew lining the decks as was the custom when a ship left her home port. They gave them a rousing cheer and raised their white covered caps. Arthur laughed self consciously and gave Carol another squeeze around her waist, just for the sailors benefit. They stepped back into their silver grey Rolls Royce and left the dockyard.

As they reached the crest of the steep hill, over looking Portsmouth Harbour and the great naval city, Arthur stopped the car and took out a strong pair of binoculars to scan the sea. He was just in time to see the minesweeper rounding the Nab Tower, a point usually used by ships' pilots to take the heavier ships into Portsmouth Harbour or Southampton Docks.

'I bet we're looking at the happiest ship's captain in the British Navy, Carol.'

'And the way you're looking at the ship, I bet you wish you were out there with him. In a few days, he'll be in the warm Mediterranean. Pandora is going out there in a couple of weeks' time.'

'Which way home, Carol? The pretty way or along the main roads?'

'It's such a lovely day, let's take the pretty way and find a nice country lane to stop in. I love the autumn and a walk through the fallen leaves would be nice. Then we could stop at a country pub for a meal.'

'I know just the place. It's the other side of Banbury. There's a canal with a pub by the side. It's a great place, Fenny Compton. Horace, Alex and myself often went fishing there. We got slung out once 'cause we went swimming. The fishermen nearly killed us, or they would have done if they could have caught us.'

They stopped in a lonely lane, carpeted with golden leaves. The lane was lined with horse chestnut trees. Carol walked alone, her hands thrust deep into her topcoat pockets. Arthur picked up a couple of chestnuts, bored a hole through them with his screwdriver, then threaded them with string. He picked up a couple more and gently threw them at Carol's back.

'Challenge you to a conker fight, Carol.'

She returned to the car, laughing as she took the conker off him, but he warned her, 'I used to be a champion at school.'

Like two children in a school playground, they played for ten minutes before Carol sent Arthur's conker flying in a dozen different pieces. The laughter rippled through the silent lane.

They ate dinner by candlelight at a country pub. Dusk was just falling, but for once they weren't the least bit worried about their business and in no hurry to finish their meal. Carol slipped her hand across the white tablecloth.

'Arthur, I don't think I have ever been so happy.'

He lifted her hand, oblivious to the other diners, and kissed it. 'Yes,' he answered. 'The trouble is, it's gone so quick, thirty-two years, it feels more like thirty-two weeks. Where has it all gone, Carol? I have never told you this before but every year when Alex and myself go to the war memorial to lay our wreaths, I always get the feeling Horace is there. I told Alex this one year and he went silent for a few minutes. It almost floored me when he said, 'That's strange, Arthur, I've had that feeling since the first year we came, and I think that Horace is very happy with the way

181

things have turned out.' Just think, I wanted to be a totter, begging old clothes from the nobs and selling them. My life changed the day that woman walked into the chapel, saw those wedding dresses hanging up and wanted to borrow one. I was about to dump them, thinking no one wanted them. I even ripped one up to make into dusters. Never gave a thought about the rationing and shortages. The old lady gave me five pounds to borrow a dress and returned it all washed and ironed. It was then I knew I was onto a good thing. Then you and Vicky started designing and making them, I just couldn't believe my luck.'

'Yes, that Victoria is a lovely lady, in spite of her upbringing she's no snob. We have been in business almost twenty years now and never had an argument. We seem to think alike. Their marriage was certainly made in heaven.'

He realised then he was still holding her hand across the table and squeezed her fingers gently.

'Alex must be a millionaire by now but he never changes, he's still the same old Alex. And Vicky too, her father left her all that money and it's never been touched. Then, when her mother died, she had claim to that large house but said her sister could have it. She knew how much her sister loved the place. Her sister sent her twenty thousand. They've worked hard, both of them, and deserve every penny, although Alex must be one of the luckiest men alive. I bet if he stepped into a piece of dog's mess, when he wiped his boot he'd find a fiver stuck to it!'

She burst out laughing, causing the other diners in the crowded room to turn and look at her.

Arthur's elder brother worked for him as a manager of his storeroom, banqueting and bingo hall. He was also an expert at throwing out any unruly people as he'd practised weightlifting and body building during his time in the Army, and also for a while afterwards. When he'd left the Army, after completing ten years' service, his size had stood him in good stead for the job. One look at his physique was usually sufficient to quieten even the rowdiest of elements.

They called in at Alex's on the way home. He had moved into his new home on the outskirts of Birmingham. He poured out the drinks but Arthur refused his whisky and soda.

'No thanks, Alex, I'm driving. Just give me a tonic water.'

Alex took them on a tour round the house. His mother had her own small flat in a part of the house. She was pleased to see them and insisted they sit down and talk about old times. Because her eyes weren't as good as they used to be, Alex had bought her the widest screen television he could find.

'How is your mother these days, Arthur? I haven't seen her for months. I must go and pay her a visit before I go away. Alex is making me go to Spain for the winter.' She sat up straight in her chair. 'I wonder, Arthur, would your mother like to come with me? I shall be all on my own over there with no one to chat to. I will miss the old telly. Would you ask her if she'll come?'

Arthur looked at Alex behind his mother's back. Alex nodded.

'What a great idea, Mom. I'm sure she would love to.'

'Yes. Now that the old man is dead I'm sure she will jump at the chance. Mind you, she is a bloody telly addict. I keep telling her she will get square eyes but she's got better eyesight than me.'

'I will get them fixed up in a decent hotel in the morning but we were thinking of getting a villa out there. I mean none of us are getting any younger these days. If we get a fair sized one, then we can use it for decent holidays. Tell you what we'll do, Arthur. We'll take Mom over by car, use one of your Rolls if you like, have a shufti round for a decent villa, get them fixed up in a hotel, then, in a few weeks time, take Victoria and Carol over to see what they think about it.'

'Well, it won't be till after Christmas, it's coming up to our busiest time now. We have over forty weddings on our books, isn't that so, Carol?'

Carol nodded her head.

'So we'll make it the first week into the new year.'

Everything was arranged and within three months, Arthur and Alex were driving their respective mothers across France, over the Pyrenees and into Spain. It was bitterly cold over the mountains but it was what the locals called mild, so they had very little trouble with snow, and as Alex's mother was a true back seat driver, they took it pretty slow. They were delighted with the hotel. It was the first time either of their mothers had experienced such a luxurious place and, being out of season, the waiters and chambermaids fawned over them. Alex took the waiters and chambermaids to one side and gave each one a twenty pound note.

'Now look after the old ladies and there will be a lot more for you when I pick them up early March or April. You will find both ladies easy to get along with but if either of them gives me a bad report, there will be no further tips.'

The waiters bowed and scraped. One man spoke very good English.

'No, senor, we are very quiet out of the season. I will see that your parents are very happy with us. We have few guests, perhaps forty or fifty and the hotel holds up to four hundred. No, senor, they will be well looked after.'

183

Arthur gave the waiters a parting sarcastic shot, 'And don't let the Germans have all the deck chairs round the swimming pool.'

For the next two days, they scoured the coast as far as Gibraltar but eventually came back to one of the first villas they had inspected, just a few minutes from the hotel. It was new, with four bedrooms, three bathrooms, a large patio and a swimming pool. The agent was wringing his hands, certain he had a client. They had told him they would look around first, before coming to a decision. Now they had returned and he could see his commission flashing before his eyes like an electronic poker machine. Would the three bars come up with the jackpot? They hadn't argued about the price.

'Right, get all the papers ready for the morning. I will get things moving.'

'But, senor, the morning, it's impossible. It may take two weeks. Everything must be done legally.'

'I certainly hope it will be done legally.' He wrote out a cheque for five thousand pounds and gave him his business card. 'Get the papers ready and bring them to England. I will get my lawyers to look over the deeds and then I'll give you a cheque in full settlement. Good day, senor.'

They spent the last night with their mothers, having a special dinner with champagne laid on.

'Now, you two, look after yourselves. Don't go sunbathing topless on the beach, leave the toy boys alone, and don't bring us home a pair of new daddies. What do you say, Arthur?'

'Definitely not.'

On their return, they showed Carol and Victoria the pictures they had taken of the villa. Both of them were delighted and Carol was shocked into silence when Victoria insisted that she pay for the villa and Alex, for once, raised no objections. It was the only time Alex allowed her to spend any money on her home or herself since the day they married. Her clothes and little luxuries were all paid for her. There was nothing she wanted that Alex wouldn't buy. At times she found it exasperating, watching her own money accumulate in the bank. So much so, she lost interest and her bank statements remained unopened. Her accountant kept them and he was just as surprised when he learnt that Alex had allowed her to buy the villa.

It turned out to be a cold winter, one of the coldest since the war. Alex bought Victoria a new Jaguar and spent another fortune looking for a number plate VIC 1. It was standing on the drive of their home on Christmas morning.

The night before, he did the usual shopping for her and drove up to the open fronted fruit and veg shop - the very same one they had visited as kids. Over the years, it hadn't changed a bit. Alex doubted if it had had a coat of paint in the last fifty years. The staff were still dressed much the same in dirty brown gowns and gloves cut off at the fingers. But the staff had changed. There were now three young, giggly girls. One had a cigarette perpetually dangling from the corner of her mouth, whilst the other two were more interested in their forthcoming dates that night and could hardly wait for eight o'clock when they could put up the shutters. Not like when Alex was a boy. Then they could expect to still be open at 11 pm.

Some of the goods on sale had changed. There were strange fruits that had been flown in by cargo planes from the tropics, now only a matter of hours away - Israeli melons as sweet as syrup, mangoes, lychees, avocados and different coloured peppers.

The manager spotted Alex's car as it pulled up at the kerb. He ran out to meet it and touched his forehead.

'Already for you, Mr Edwards.'

Three boys appeared, one coloured boy and two blonde lads. They couldn't have been more than thirteen.

'Smashing car, mate. Can it do over a hundred?'

'Never tried it, son, seventy's my limit. I think it's capable of one hundred and twenty though. Been carol singing, lads?'

'Yea,' said the coloured lad, still chewing his gum, distorting his face like an old cow chewing the cud.

'Any good?'

'Not bad. Got about five quid tonight. Done better last night though. The punters are fed up with carol singers. Mind you, we do all right.'

He lifted up a small tape recorder and switched it on. It began playing 'O Come All Ye Faithful.'

'We give them a couple of verses of that and another tune. They don't see the tape recorder so when we knock on the door the punters ask us who's playing the organ in the background. We tell them the bloke that plays it has just gone home!'

Alex laughed and said to the manager, 'Wasn't like that when we were kids. We sang our guts out for a few coppers.' He turned to the group of boys. 'Give them a fiver's worth of fruit, Jim. Have a nice Christmas, lads.'

'Thanks, mister.'

They watched as Alex got into his car then turned to the manager, 'Who's that, mate?'

'Councillor Edwards. You'll never meet a nicer guy. Born in that street.' He pointed to the new blocks of flats. 'Of course, it wasn't flats then, just back to back houses. Tough life but he came up from nothing. Now he owns property all over the city. Him and his mate are financing a big development in Spain. Their mothers live over there. They think the world of them. They asked him to be Lord Mayor but he says he's quite happy on the Housing Committee, and he won't be satisfied till every slum house in the city is knocked down. Pity we don't have more like him on the council.'

The car turned the corner. The shop manager stood there watching the lights fade.